LOVE SLAVE

by

TERRY WAKELIN

CHIMERA

Love Slave published by
Chimera Publishing Ltd
PO Box 152
Waterlooville
Hants
PO8 9FS

Printed and bound in Great Britain by
Cox & Wyman, Reading.

LOVE SLAVE

Terry Wakelin

Charlotte took a sharp intake of breath, yet made no effort to pull away from his touch. Desperately, she wanted to avoid further punishment. Soon the man's hands were between her thighs, fingers jabbing roughly up inside her. She squirmed, as much from the feel of the man's dirty, uncut fingernails as from any sexual sensation.

The man was sweating now and grinned at her with evil intent. He pointed at the floor and grunted unintelligibly, obviously meaning her to lie down. Shaking with fear, she obeyed. Roughly kicking her legs apart he fumbled with his robe to expose a stubby penis before kneeling between her splayed thighs…

September, 1587
Valletta, on the island of Malta

Close-hauled against a capricious south-westerly breeze, the little English galleon *Triumph* slipped gently under the lee of the buttressed, grey-granite walled fortress guarding the entrance to Malta's Grand Harbour.

On the tiny quarterdeck, a tall, well-dressed man drew closer to the girl standing at his side. 'Well, there it is, Charlotte,' said Sir James Brandon. 'Valletta at last!'

Clutching tightly at her uncle's arm, eighteen-year-old Lady Charlotte Brandon hardly heard the strident calls of the sea birds wheeling and diving overhead. The young girl's strong features, flawless peaches-and-cream complexion and full-bodied figure, the whole crowned gloriously by a tumbling mass of shoulder-length golden-blonde hair, made her a vision so striking that an observer might have been forgiven had he mistaken her for one of the mythical Celtic goddesses of old. Green eyes wide with amazement, she gazed almost in awe at the bustling sight which presented itself.

Even Portsmouth and Cadiz did not compare with this!

What looked like a hundred or more ships jostled for space in the sheltered anchorage. Nationalities were myriad: Neapolitan, Venetian, Portuguese, French; ships of all classes and flags were anchored each side of the channel, while graceful Eastern galleys, feluccas, Arab dhows and even a great two-masted Spanish war galley lay side by side along the bustling dock. From all quarters, barges and small craft were scuttling busily to and fro, loading and unloading, ferrying passengers or crewmen ashore, or back out to vessels preparing to leave. The scent of spices and other exotic smells, most of which she didn't recognise, drifted in on the salt-laden air.

Her uncle, still a handsome man in his fifties, though his

thinning hair, originally the same striking gold-blond as his niece's, was now shot through with grey, pointed towards the city. 'There, Charlotte – up there beyond the castle? See? The building with the white dome. Sheikh Omar's villa.'

Almost overwhelmed by the intense bustle and strangeness of it all, the girl looked to where he pointed, her eyes finally focusing on the white-domed building overlooking the bay. 'Oh, it's so big, uncle. Much bigger than I thought it would be,' she said breathlessly. 'All for just one man to live in?'

Sir James chuckled. 'Well, not quite, darling. A lot of other people live there with him. Sheikh Omar is a very important man, one of the few Moors who has the ear and favour of the island's Grand Master. There are servants, guards, slaves and all the people who go to make up his personal retinue.' He grinned. 'And then, of course, there's his harem. No one knows just exactly how many wives and concubines he has, but it's probably fifty or more.'

'Oh, uncle, it's – it's all so marvellous, isn't it? Aren't you glad to be back?' Breathing deeply of the exotic aromas, the excited girl squeezed the man's arm as she turned her attention to the city proper; the high battlements and walls grey, towers and domes a mixture of glittering white and gold in the afternoon sun.

Sir James Brandon shot a quizzical glance at his niece as she stood looking out over the sun-dappled water. Charlotte caught the look and smiled mischievously. That morning she had donned her favourite silk gown, purchased the previous year in the face of stiff opposition from Sir James because of its low-cut and revealing bodice. She sighed; it was almost indecent, she would grant him that. The lust-filled looks she had been getting from the English sailors – looks which, if she were honest, had both pleased and excited her – confirmed it. The silken material clung to her waist like a second skin and her breasts, which had grown considerably over the last year, looked as if they might spill out of the containing material at any moment. She glanced across at her uncle, but his attention seemed to be focused away from her. Momentarily she wondered at the direction of his thoughts. Was he, too, thinking of her father, who had died here before she was born?

The story had been fairly typical of the times. Henry Brandon had been the black sheep sibling of Sir James. His wildness, unpaid gambling debts, fistfights and duels, many the result of illicit dalliances with married ladies, had made him less than popular with his otherwise respectable family. Finally despairing of the young man's future, they had packed him off to Malta to enter the employ of his older brother, then heading what was ostensibly an English trading mission in the Mediterranean.

It was the turning point in the young rake's life. Having married the eighteen-year-old daughter of a fairly well-off merchant before leaving England – an arrangement entered into more as an attempt to placate a family outraged by his indiscretions than anything else – he soon grew to have a real regard for the girl, feelings which grew even stronger when, after a few months, she became pregnant.

The family had been both amazed and pleased at the change reported in their wild and wayward son, while his young bride had also been more than content. Henry's considerate usage of her struck a genuinely receptive chord in her heart. After all, what more could any girl want than the protection and regard of such a dashing young cavalier, who treated her almost as if she were a precious flower?

Then – tragedy! Always a vigorous and active man, Henry had been killed in a freak riding accident, news of which had sent his pregnant widow into premature labour. Charlotte's birth had been long and difficult and Henry's wife never really recovered. Two months after the birth she, too, had followed her husband to the grave.

And so it was that Charlotte's childhood had been spent at Hawkridge, the Brandon family's large estate on the edge of the Essex moors. Sir James himself had rarely been there and, though her grandparents had taken some interest in her, she had mostly been raised by a series of nurses and nannies.

The *Triumph* headed down the narrow channel between the anchored vessels and Sir James addressed his niece seriously. 'Ah – Charlotte, I'd appreciate it if you'd change that dress before we go ashore.'

Charlotte looked at him as if surprised. 'Why, what's wrong with it, uncle?'

'Come, come, Charlotte, you know exactly what's wrong with it,' he began. She smiled at him sweetly and he reddened even more. 'It's one thing to run around half-dressed at Hawkridge, or even here on board, but,' he stared meaningfully at the straining bodice of the dress, 'quite obviously you're not a child any more. I'm just surprised it's taken me so long to realise it.'

Charlotte gave him her most dazzling smile – just like her father's – and he softened at once. No matter what she did, he could never be out of temper with her for long. 'Please, darling, remember what I told you about this part of the world,' he chided. 'Out here ladies do not dress so – so provocatively.'

Charlotte smiled mischievously at her uncle's discomfiture, then surrendered gracefully. 'You're right, of course, uncle. It isn't suitable. Don't worry, I'll change before we go ashore.'

There was a shout from the bow. They were approaching the anchorage.

Ten minutes or so later, almost as the last rope was being coiled, there was a call from one of the *Triumph's* lookouts. 'Small boat approaching, m'lord. The Great Grand Fandango hisself, looks like!'

Joining her uncle at the ship's rail, Charlotte watched curiously as the little boat made its way alongside. The warm wind stirred the scarlet robe of the single passenger sitting so majestically in the bows; a tall black man who, somewhat theatrically she thought, was wearing a tall, snowy-white turban topped with a scarlet plume. He stood up as the small boat approached and, even as they touched, swung himself up and over the side of the ship, showing an agility surprising for such a big man.

'Lord James, welcome back,' said the visitor in almost perfect English, totally ignoring Charlotte and bowing deeply as he spoke. 'Sheikh Omar sends his greetings.'

Charlotte's look of ire at being so ignored was transparently obvious. 'Thank you, Suleiman,' replied Sir James easily. 'It is good to be back.' He took his niece's arm in a firm grasp as if warning her to behave herself, and began the introductions. 'This is my niece, the Lady Charlotte, whom you last saw as just a baby. Charlotte, my dear, this is Suleiman, Sheikh Omar's steward.' Frowning a little at the look of petulance on Charlotte's face, he continued, 'Suleiman has the most amazing command of languages. English is not the least of his accomplishments.'

The black man's eyes flickered without expression over Charlotte's low-cut bodice; then he bowed deeply and courteously again. Charlotte's displeasure dissipated a little and she even managed a tiny smile in return.

'Welcome, my lady,' said Suleiman courteously. 'I hope your stay here shall be a pleasant one.' Turning back to Sir James, he went on eagerly, 'News of your coming has preceded you, my lord.' He grinned broadly, showing white even teeth. 'May I ask, what cargo is it you carry?'

The Englishman shrugged his shoulders carelessly. 'I thought that, this time, grain might be welcome. What do you think? Is there a demand?'

Suleiman chuckled. 'Truly my lord is a magician. Always he smells out where there is a profit. For over a month now there have been shortages. Meantime the price has trebled. Even now there are a dozen or more fat merchants waiting on the quayside.'

Sir James smiled. 'I leave it to you to deal with them. It has been a long trip and I am impatient to see friend Omar again.' He turned to Charlotte. 'Gather up your possibles, darling. We'll be away shortly.' He turned to Suleiman. 'About ten minutes or so. Will that be all right?'

The huge black man bowed again. 'Of course, my lord. Take all the time you require.'

As usual, Sir James had underestimated the time it would take his niece to get ready, and it was half an hour or so before they were finally ensconced safely in the little boat and heading for shore. Charlotte had taken her uncle's advice about covering up quite literally. Swathed completely in one of his old cloaks, with a fold of the material pinned over the lower part of her face, there was virtually nothing to be seen of her.

Once ashore, brushing aside the urgently gesticulating merchants, Suleiman led them to a curtained litter attended by six black slaves waiting on the cobbles. The Englishman glanced enquiringly at the turbaned steward.

'Apologies, my lord,' said Suleiman, a little uncomfortably. 'Sheikh Omar suggests you take the litter. There has been some recent unrest in the city.'

James looked faintly surprised. 'Well now,' he murmured, as if to no one in particular, 'and I had thought to be a friend to all. Still, if Omar thinks it prudent, then ride we shall.' Suiting action to the words, he offered a hand to his niece and helped her inside.

With a grateful smile, Suleiman drew the drapes. 'We go straight to the villa, my lord,' he said. 'Sheikh Omar awaits you there.'

The slaves took up their burden and made their way along the quay to the gate that led into the city proper. Quickly adjusting to the jerking, swaying motion of the litter, Charlotte peeped out from behind the drapes, amazed at the number and variety of open-fronted shops and stalls lining the busy, twisting streets.

It was warm and, beneath the all-enveloping cloak, the English girl was sweating freely, quite amazed that the six slaves seemed to be able to carry such a heavy burden so easily, and at such a pace. After ten minutes or so they turned off through a large spike-gated archway into a delightfully shaded courtyard. The litter was set down carefully, and Suleiman came to help them out. She looked around as she stepped to the ground. The courtyard itself was spacious and, in the centre, surrounded by a green lawn in which rose beds had been carefully planted, stood a softly tinkling fountain, the source of the water the open mouth of a carved stone dolphin on whose back rode the beautiful figures of a naked girl and boy engaged in obvious sexual congress. Charlotte looked at the statue and reddened. The two figures were anatomically perfect in every way, the boy's erect penis shown clearly parting the lips of the girl's vagina.

Still blushing, she glanced at the wide marble steps leading up to the magnificently decorated doorway which seemed to be the main entrance to the white-domed villa, noting the heavily armed guards standing at each side of the door. Evidently Sheikh Omar took no chances with uninvited callers.

Her uncle took her arm and, with Suleiman ushering them up the steps, they entered the villa. In the cool of the entrance hall they were met by turbaned retainers in silk robes who, bowing and scraping as if the sheikh's visitors were royalty, first took their cloaks, then led them into a large reception room. Sir James breathed a visible sigh of relief when he saw that, following his advice, Charlotte had changed her dress to one which showed considerably less of her figure.

Not knowing quite what to expect, Charlotte looked to the raised dais where, like a prince, a distinguished looking, grey-bearded Arab reclined on soft cushions surrounded by half a dozen women, all heavily veiled and clothed in rich silken robes.

The sheikh got to his feet as they entered. 'James, my brother,' he smiled, 'too long have you been absent from my house.'

'Omar, brother,' replied Sir James Brandon easily. 'My heart leaps to see you once more.'

Though this was the first time she had heard Arabic spoken by anyone except her uncle, Charlotte found that, thanks to his tutelage, she was easily able to understand what was being said.

The stately old Arab smiled at Charlotte. 'And this delightful creature…?'

'This, of course, is Charlotte, my niece,' said Sir James, taking her by the hand to lead her forward.

'So,' said the sheikh, 'the little baby I once bounced on my knee has come home at last.'

Charlotte bowed her head and curtsied, a gesture of respect that brought an indulgent beam of approval from the old Arab. 'My uncle has told me much about you, excellency,' she replied haltingly in Arabic, childishly pleased when she saw one eyebrow lift in faint surprise. 'I was very young when my uncle took me away, and do not remember you clearly, but it pleases me very much to at last be able to pay my respects to his most valued friend.'

Sheikh Omar smiled, obviously pleased by the somewhat flowery phrases which had taken Charlotte so much time to rehearse. 'So, the niece of my old friend has learned to speak the language of the Prophet. May Allah bless his name. I salute you and bid you welcome, daughter. Your loveliness graces my house. Please, both of you, come sit at my side and take refreshment.'

Following her uncle's example, Charlotte made her way to the cushioned dais where, within moments, a large and heavily ornamented silver tray appeared, upon which were loaded various sweetmeats and all the paraphernalia required for making that sweet mint beverage which the Arab calls 'tea'.

Helping herself to one of the strange-looking sweetmeats, Charlotte glanced curiously at the veiled women, noticing that although many were of a darkish hue, several seemed to have skins almost as white as her own. Where did they come from? she wondered. Were some European? Were they wives, or just concubines? These and a hundred other thoughts slipped through her mind as she studied the gorgeous silken robes, the filmy veils and the dark, kohl-lined eyes which stared back at her with as much curiosity as her own.

'Well now, daughter,' said the sheikh seriously, 'first, we must see to your needs.' He snapped his fingers at one of the veiled females, who immediately rose from her place to prostrate herself at his feet. 'This is Meylissah,' he said. 'She will be your body slave.' He smiled down paternally at the prostrate girl and, to Charlotte's great surprise, addressed her in English. 'Unveil yourself, Meylissah. This is now your mistress. You will obey her as you would me.'

The English girl was shocked. Were all the women here slaves? And this particular girl? Omar had spoken to her in English! Surely it was not possible that an English girl could be held such?

The girl moved obediently to kneel in front of Charlotte. Gracefully, eyes lowered submissively, she removed her hooded head-dress and veil. Charlotte's eyes widened in surprise. The girl was almost as light-skinned as herself, though her hair was dark. She looked to be no more than seventeen or eighteen, and was quite beautiful. The lovely high-cheekboned features might have graced a social gathering anywhere.

'I shall be your most obedient slave, mistress,' the young girl said in softly accented, though perfectly understandable English. 'Command me and I will obey.'

The princely old Arab chuckled at the bemused look on

Charlotte's face. 'For sometime Suleiman has been instructing her in English,' he told her. 'Already she understands much and I had thought she might be of some use to your uncle as a translator. Now I see it is Allah's will that she serve you instead.' He turned to Sir James. 'The girl has the gift of tongues; a thing many of her people have. Apart from English and Arabic, she also speaks French and Spanish, and is also quite fluent in Greek and Italian.'

'But I have no need of a body slave,' Charlotte began to protest.

The sheikh was obviously going to brook no argument. 'You must take her then to please me,' he said firmly. 'She is young like you, and speaks your language well. Maybe she will stop you getting bored while your uncle and I see to our business.'

Charlotte looked helplessly towards her uncle. Sir James merely smiled and inclined his head. He knew his old friend very well. The richest and most powerful merchant in Valletta was used to getting his own way. It was no good arguing with him.

'She is lovely. Where did you find her?' Sir James asked in a whispered aside.

'She was taken in the raid on El Marsa last year. My friend Bashir financed it and had her on his string.' Sheikh Omar answered. 'Like the fool he is, though, Bashir did not recognise the girl's true worth and allowed her on the block with the rest of the slaves. My agent saw her there and purchased her for me.' He turned back to Charlotte, addressing her directly. 'If she displeases you, daughter, send her to Suleiman. He is expert with the whip and will not disfigure her. Suleiman is eunuch, of course,' he added quickly, seeing Charlotte's frown. 'She will be quite safe with him in that way.'

Charlotte caught her breath at the casual statement. The thought of anyone using a whip on such a beautiful young girl chilled her to the marrow. Of course she knew that, here in the east, slaves were often treated quite harshly by their owners. She knew, also, about eunuchs and what was done to make them so. Her uncle had been quite explicit, thinking it best that she be prepared for such things. 'Th-thank you, my lord,' she stammered. 'I am sure the girl will be most... suitable.'

The kneeling girl took hold of her new mistress' hand and brought it to her lips. 'Command me and I shall obey, my lady,' she whispered fiercely. 'I promise mistress shall have no need of the whip.'

'Now then, daughter,' interjected the sheikh, 'I expect both of you are tired from your trip.' He looked at her indulgently. 'Go you now with Meylissah. She will show you to your quarters.'

Charlotte rose to her feet a little reluctantly, realising she'd been rather summarily, even if politely, dismissed. She glanced towards her uncle and received a reassuring nod as the two men began to talk quietly together. 'So what is going on, Omar?' she heard him ask quietly. 'Suleiman tells me the English are none too popular in Valletta just now.'

'Bad things have happened, my friend,' she heard the sheikh reply before she passed out of earshot. 'It seems your El Draque's depredations in the New World have also reached new heights. A dozen or more settlements and towns sacked, many ships sunk and much treasure taken. King Philip, it is said, is beside himself with rage and plans invasion of your country. Malta's Knights, of course, will support Philip. So you see – this is perhaps not the best time for you to be visiting us here.'

Favoured One

That the tall blonde girl on the balcony was exceptionally beautiful would have been obvious to the most casual of observers.

Clad in a thin, almost transparent sleeping robe, she gazed as if entranced across the rosy, dawn-lit roofs and spires of the old city to the jumbled mass of masts and rigging of the many ships moored in Grand Harbour, turning her head briefly when another girl, clad almost as lightly in a silken *sifsari*, joined her on the balcony. With a grace born of long practice, the newcomer, a slimmer, dark-haired girl of about the same age, dropped to her knees and bowed respectfully. The status of each was thus established. The first girl was free; the second a slave.

The slave girl, unveiled and just as clearly naked under her own diaphanous garment, was also quite lovely. Not so tall, perhaps, nor as generously curved as her mistress, but still quite breathtaking in her own way.

Lady Charlotte Brandon yawned and stretched, the rising sun outlining the full-bosomed curves under the gossamer robe. 'Well then, Meylissah,' she said somewhat breathlessly in English, 'late again? I've been up for simply ages.'

The slave girl replied in the same language. 'I beg forgiveness, my lady. Other duties have kept me from your side.' The voice was low and pleasant; her English very good, though clearly it was not her native tongue. Nervously she looked around. 'Mistress should not stand on the balcony so,' she admonished gently. 'Maybe someone will see.'

Charlotte glanced carelessly at the darkened windows of the other apartments. 'There is no one to see, Meylissah. Everyone is asleep.' She smiled. 'And the air is so cool and refreshing out here.'

Meylissah remained uneasy. 'Please, my lady.'

Realisation dawned and Charlotte was suddenly contrite. Of course the girl was right. Walking around practically naked inside the apartment was one thing; outside on the balcony quite another. Familiar with the strict discipline

16

maintained in the household, she knew that, should anyone from the neighbouring apartments catch sight of her so blatantly exposed, it would be the slave who would bear the brunt of her host's anger for not better looking after his guest. Unbidden, her gaze strayed down to the heavy whipping frame from which miscreants were hung naked to receive punishment. In Sheikh Omar's household, punishments inflicted on errant slaves were administered summarily and ruthlessly. Only yesterday she had watched horrified as Suleiman administered a sound whipping to a girl caught stealing extra food from the kitchen. She shivered at the memory of the slave girl's screams and pleas for mercy as the whip striped the soft flesh of her back and buttocks. She pulled her sleeping robe closer. 'You are right, of course, Meylissah,' she said apologetically. 'Come, let us go in.'

Inside, Charlotte stretched out thankfully on soft cushions and dabbed at a trickle of perspiration already running in the valley between her breasts. She breathed deeply, trying to draw some air into her lungs. Here in the apartment, even with the doors and windows open, it seemed so hot and humid; nothing like the clean fresh air of the Essex countryside. Loosening her robe, she lay back with a murmur of contentment as pleasant memories of the long temperate summers she had enjoyed as a girl flooded into her mind. With a sigh she remembered bathing *sans* clothes at the secluded lake the previous summer, secretly thrilling at the thought that perhaps one or other of the village boys might actually catch sight of her unclothed body.

Remembering the cooler air of the balcony with some regret, she sighed as Meylissah padded sinuously across the chamber to where the breakfast tray, loaded as usual with a variety of dishes, sat on a small side table. 'Oh, Meylissah, I shall get fat,' she protested cheerfully at the sight of the laden tray. 'You feed me far too well.'

'Truly Allah blesses mistress with much beauty,' said

17

Meylissah, her frankly envious glance directed at the other's fuller figure. She indicated the many dishes on the tray. 'Eat just a little from each, and – *inshallah* – stay the same.'

Charlotte smiled a little to herself. *Inshallah* – as Allah wills – was a sentiment much in evidence among the slave girls and concubines in Sheikh Omar ibn Saiid's household; a sentiment which no doubt helped them towards an unquestioning acceptance of their lot. To the true believer, everything was *maktub* – written.

How very different everything was here. The language, customs, even the morality. Their host was a slaver – a trade regarded as quite respectable here in the east – supplying girls and young men to many of Valletta's brothels as well as to the ruling Knights, to whom he also passed information gleaned from his many other business interests, principally in Ottoman-controlled Egypt and North Africa.

Charlotte looked at Meylissah's lithe figure and sighed again, conceding with a wry smile that certain parts of her own anatomy were certainly a lot more generous than seemed usual here. Certainly none of the women she'd seen was as tall or big-bosomed as she.

Taking the girl's advice, she helped herself to no more than a mouthful from each dish, eating with her fingers as was the custom, rinsing them in a bowl of scented water between each course. Tasting a tiny portion of delicious honey cake, she mumbled, 'Would you like some, Meylissah?'

'Oh no... not fitting, mistress. Meylissah eat later.'

Suitably reproved, Charlotte placed the dish to one side and allowed herself to sink deeper into the softness of the cushions while Meylissah sank submissively to her knees beside the couch. 'Massage now, mistress?' asked the slave girl softly, bright eyes and a sudden huskiness in her voice belying her innocent expression.

'Mmm... thank you,' replied Charlotte, stretching luxuriously as she allowed her robe to slip from her shoulders. This was certainly the life. Despite her first misgivings about owning a slave, the past weeks being looked after by Meylissah had been most pleasant. The girl had been able to impart much about the eastern way of life to her mistress and, just as importantly to the English girl, enabled her to pick up more and more of the strange Arabic tongue she had determined to learn.

And of course there had been the other things; things only a girl steeped in the Sapphic traditions of the harem might know, and be pleased to demonstrate to her at first bemused, yet decidedly interested mistress.

Charlotte had known from puberty, in pure biological terms, what it was that men did with the women they desired, and that babies were the common result of such liaisons. She knew, also, there were certain things one might do to make sure that this did not happen. In that respect her uncle had been at pains to make sure her education had been most complete. Indeed, she had eagerly looked forward to the day when she, too, might sample the pleasures of a physical relationship. Reality, unfortunately, had meant disappointment to her growing libido and, despite entering boldly into a number of *affaires d'amour* with various lads of her own age, all had remained unconsummated and her passions unquenched.

With Meylissah, however, things had proved to be decidedly different.

The slave girl shrugged off her *sifsari* and, unstoppering a small vial, tipped a little of the contents into the palm of one hand. Then, as Charlotte turned over on to her stomach, she began to rub the sweet-smelling oil gently into her shoulders.

Charlotte gave an appreciative sigh, realising with a sudden startling insight just how desirable such a girl as Meylissah might be to a man. Trained from an early age to please whoever owned her in every possible way, the beautiful slave would be a priceless possession. She shivered as another thought entered her mind. What must it be like to be owned, body and soul: to have no will of one's own; for one's body to be totally and utterly subject to the will of a master or mistress? Then, as the oily fingers delved deeper, the thought was driven from her mind. Sighing with pleasure, Charlotte widened her thighs as Meylissah began to rub the sweet-smelling substance deep into the flesh around and between the soft buttocks, one sly finger sliding down to insert itself gently into the shaded, puckered little entrance.

'You like?' whispered Meylissah, probing yet deeper as another finger found the entrance to Charlotte's sex channel and slipped gently inside.

Charlotte was lost to the powerful sensations building inside her. 'Mmm… yes… oh yes,' she sighed. 'Don't stop… *please.*'

Meylissah smiled and slapped her gently on the bottom. 'Please to turn over now, mistress,' she ordered.

Eagerly, Charlotte turned over on to her back, closing her eyes as the knowing, oily hands began to massage her upper body, now paying particular attention to her breasts.

'Ooh,' she breathed, her legs spreading of their own accord as a gentle hand slipped down first to her stomach and then beyond to the downy blonde muff at the juncture of her thighs, one finger gently parting the puffy lower lips to seek out and tease the already stiff little nub of flesh sheltering under its protective hood. Then Meylissah reached up to take each erecting nipple between thumb and forefinger. Charlotte stifled a groan. How easily the girl aroused her! Briefly she wondered what her uncle would say if he ever discovered what was going on. Yet how could a pleasure so sweet, so all-consuming, possibly be wrong?

Meylissah bent her head to lap sensuously between her mistress' spread thighs, her darting tongue flickering knowingly between the already wet lips, thumbs and forefingers alternately rolling and squeezing the stiffening nubs of flesh.

'Nnnng… mmm… ooh,' murmured Charlotte as the sharp little teeth nibbled gently and, alternately, a warm wet tongue licked maddeningly at her most secret place. She squared her shoulders, lifting her breasts as her nipples were mercilessly stretched and squeezed. 'Don't stop, Meylissah… please, don't stop.'

Breathing heavily herself now, Meylissah lifted shining lips from between her mistress' thighs. She smiled and squeezed a little more. 'Harder, mistress? Like this?'

'Yes – *yes*. Harder… do it harder. I love it… you know I love it!'

Dutifully, the knowing fingers squeezed and tugged ever more forcefully at Charlotte's nipple flesh while, at the same time, the lascivious tongue returned to its earlier work.

Charlotte's hips were moving wildly now, thrusting her pelvis upwards so that the cunning lips and tongue might more easily invade her body, her breath coming in short gasps as she approached inexorable orgasm. Arms and legs spread wide as if in sacrifice, she abandoned herself to the sweet torture, moaning deep in the back of her throat as the fingers pinched and pulled at her swollen teats, while all the time Meylissah's lapping tongue drove her on and upwards towards ecstasy.

She gave a small groan of disappointment as the pinching fingers left her breasts momentarily, then Meylissah had shifted around so that they were in the classic *soixante-neuf* position and both mouth and fingers resumed their tasks.

Charlotte lifted her lips eagerly towards the smooth, hairless pudenda hovering just over her face, allowing her own tongue to slip inside the fleshy folds and imitate what the other was doing to her. Licking gently around Meylissah's trembling clitoris, she knew with a sense of immense gratification that she was filling her partner with as much pleasure as she was experiencing herself.

To Charlotte, this was the best part of the simultaneous

loving, each knowing exactly what sensations the other was feeling as she moved steadily towards climax. She reached up to the bobbing breasts above her and began caressing the erect nipples in turn. Of course it couldn't last for long and, within minutes, they came at the same time, the writhing Charlotte suddenly convulsing into a shattering series of orgasms which, as Meylissah tried desperately to continue her oral ministrations between the thrashing legs, threatened either to suffocate her or at the very least throw them both from the couch.

Gradually the paroxysms lessened and Meylissah was at last able lift her head from between her mistress' thighs.

The exhausted Charlotte motioned weakly with one hand, the other patting the cushions at her side. 'Here,' she gasped, 'come lay with me for a while.'

Compliantly, Meylissah did as she was bid, laying her own breathless, sweat-sheened nakedness alongside that of the other girl. 'Mistress enjoy?' she asked softly. 'Relaxed now?'

As if in answer, Charlotte kissed her long and hard. 'Oh, yes, you little minx,' she breathed. 'You know exactly how to relax me.'

For long minutes, while they regained their breath, the two girls remained still, Charlotte's fingers toying gently with the other's breasts and erect nipples while Meylissah slipped two fingers back into her mistress' dripping sex. Charlotte felt warm and fulfilled, knowing that the other girl had experienced a climax equally as shattering as her own. She sighed with contentment, feeling the warmth of the slave girl's body against her own and the fingers moving gently inside her. She thought back to her encounters with that succession of disappointing young men, mentally comparing their clumsy and inept fumblings with those she had just experienced, and gave an inward snort of disgust. No wonder Meylissah preferred girl-to-girl sex.

Or did she? The sudden, startling thought slipped

22

treacherously into her mind as she remembered the way Meylissah had flirted with one of the guards who had escorted them to the marketplace just the other day. This was a trained slave girl, disciplined to serve whoever owned her in any way, shape or form. Could it be a sham? Did the girl really enjoy making such sweet love to her? She shivered, suddenly cold. 'Tell me, Meylissah,' she asked sharply, 'do you have a lover here? A man, I mean. Perhaps one of Sheikh Omar's guards?'

Meylissah shifted uneasily and averted her gaze. 'Oh, no, mistress,' she whispered.

Charlotte's heart pounded. Quite obviously the girl was lying. Annoyed now, she decided to press the point. 'Don't lie to me, Meylissah! Who is it? That good-looking young fellow who escorted us to the souk? I saw how he looked at you – and you at him.'

'Oh, no, mistress. I cannot make love with guard. Is not permitted for me.' Meylissah dropped her gaze as she fumbled for the right words. 'I am… *gösde*, mistress.'

Charlotte did not know the term. 'I'm sorry, Meylissah. I don't understand. What is *gösde*?'

Embarrassed, Meylissah sought to retreat, surrendering only when the other insisted. 'Is harem word, mistress,' she whispered hesitantly. 'Means "favoured one".'

Charlotte thought she understood. 'Oh, I see. Who is it that favours you? Sheikh Omar?'

Meylissah shifted uneasily, knowing she must answer now her mistress had asked the direct question. 'Lord James, mistress,' she whispered. 'Often does he take his pleasure with me.'

Charlotte suddenly felt as if someone had kicked her in the stomach. Visions of her uncle and the young slave girl together began to whirl crazily in her mind and she thrust Meylissah unceremoniously from her side.

Meylissah fell to the floor, her wretchedness growing visibly as she recognised the shock and distress on her

23

mistress' face, though she could have little idea how she might have offended. She struggled back to her knees beside the couch and bowed her head respectfully. 'A slave begs forgiveness, mistress,' she whispered, the ritual phrase sounding hollow to Charlotte's horrified ears.

Charlotte forced herself to be calm, managing enough control to speak rationally as shocked understanding swept over her. 'I see,' she said bitterly, pangs of anger and, strangely, something akin to jealousy sweeping through her. 'So this is why you are sometimes so late coming to me in the mornings – because my uncle has not finished "taking pleasure" with you?'

Meylissah looked up nervously and nodded, acknowledging the truth.

Charlotte was devastated. Inside her head a voice was telling her to be calm and not to do or say anything she might later regret. One part of her wanted to scream and rage at the girl. Didn't she realise how wrong it was? Her uncle was old enough to be the girl's father. Yet, even as she asked herself the question, she recognised its hypocrisy. Wasn't she herself equally guilty? How could she blame the slave girl? Meylissah obviously had no choice in the matter.

Almost as if reading her mind, Meylissah said softly. 'I am but a slave, mistress,' she whispered, 'yet I am content. I find great honour in serving my lord.'

Charlotte turned on her stomach, trying desperately to calm herself. It was not the girl's fault, she thought. Poor, pliable little Meylissah; born to serve men's – or women's – lusts. It was all perfectly natural to her.

She tried to picture her uncle and Meylissah together, wondering how he could take pleasure with a girl of her own age. Indeed, until that moment, Charlotte had not thought overmuch about her uncle's physical needs, cherishing the perhaps girlish notion that the love he'd had for her dead aunt still sustained him. Now all her romantic illusions were shattered. And yet, could she really blame him? To her

Uncle James, now in his late fifties, Meylissah must have seemed the stuff of dreams: a beautiful, ever-welcoming sexual partner, trained never to answer back and to see the use of her body as the legitimate right of her owner. The very thought that, with the merest gesture, he could command the fullest and most intimate use of that lithe and beautiful body must have been a temptation almost impossible for him to resist.

Charlotte could see Meylissah was working herself into a lather of panic about the whole business, and wondered whether the slave girl had been instructed by her uncle not to talk to Charlotte about it.

'A slave begs forgiveness, mistress,' Meylissah's whispered ritual phrase once more broke the silence.

Charlotte at last managed to pull herself together enough to smile down at the anxious girl, albeit a little tremulously, realising suddenly that, for some reason, her limbs were trembling. 'It's all right, Meylissah,' she answered huskily. 'It's not your fault. It's just that with my uncle being so much older, I had not thought he would take a slave girl to his bed. That's all.'

The worried Meylissah let out her breath explosively. 'Lord James not have slave girls in England, mistress?' she asked softly.

Charlotte shivered again, coming to the inescapable conclusion that, in reality, she knew little or nothing about her uncle's relationships with women. 'Things are different in our country, Meylissah.' She sighed. 'In England a man has but one wife. There are no concubines or slave girls or harems. My uncle's wife – my aunt – died some years ago and I had not thought him to seek a woman's company since then.'

Meylissah shrugged her shoulders and managed a smile of her own. 'Is not good for such a man to be so long without a woman, mistress. Lord James is a great man, a considerate man. He treats me well. I am honoured to serve him.' She blushed prettily. 'He has great need of me, mistress.'

Charlotte shivered again, suddenly cold as she tried to adjust to the fact that the man she thought she knew so well was sleeping with a girl she had come to regard as her closest friend. A thought struck like a hammer blow and she looked wide-eyed at Meylissah. 'Does – does my uncle know what we do together?' she asked.

Meylissah had the grace to look away. 'Yes, mistress,' she whispered. 'It was he who instructed me to give mistress pleasure.'

Charlotte sat up, open-mouthed, unable to believe what her uncle had ordered the girl to do. 'You mean...?'

Meylissah hung her head. 'Mistress is angry?' she asked in a timid voice.

Charlotte breathed deeply, the shock still seeping into her mind. Yet in truth should she be so surprised? Her uncle had spent so much time here in the east, where such things would probably be considered quite normal. She looked with a little more compassion at the still frightened, kneeling slave girl. 'Tell me the truth,' she said gently. 'Do you like making love with me – or is this, also, just a slave's duty?'

Meylissah looked up with wide open eyes, as if to ask how her mistress could even think such a thing. 'Oh, mistress,' she whispered, a tear forming in the corner of her eye. 'Surely you know. As my lord has great need of me, so, too, have I great need of you.'

Charlotte took a deep breath. It was wanted she wanted to hear, certainly. But what if the girl was lying? Then she thought back to the beautiful passion they had just experienced together and her doubts vanished.

Right at that moment Charlotte realised she was shivering violently. She tried to shift her position on the cushions but her limbs, shaking and strangely leaden, refused to respond. Bile rose in her throat a second time and she felt as if she were about to be sick.

Meylissah was peering at her worriedly. 'Mistress not

well?' she enquired.

'I... I don't know. I feel a little sick – and suddenly I am very cold.' A bout of dizziness shook her and the room began to spin. 'Something is wrong. Call my uncle, quickly!' she managed to whisper before her senses finally left her.

A Passage is Arranged

The day was warm and not a little breathless, the smells and vapours of Valletta's maritime heritage hanging heavy on the early evening air. On the shaded afterdeck of the great oared ship moored alongside the dock, a perspiring Charlotte held a perfumed handkerchief to her nose in the lingering heat, watching with some curiosity as a gang of sweating sailors, guarded by a full troop of heavily armed soldiers, loaded seven heavily sealed trunks aboard. Vaguely she wondered at the contents and why they demanded such a guard.

The ship, of course, was not just any vessel. This was *the* ship: the sixty-oared, three-masted, one hundred and seventy-foot galleass *San Cristobal*, the pride of King Philip of Spain's Mediterranean fleet, so perhaps such precautions were normal.

The dockyard was busy and there was much to occupy the English girl's attention as she stood on the gently swaying deck, only subconsciously aware of the timber complaining and groaning all around her. The bout of fever which had confined her to her bed for so many weeks no longer afflicted her and it was a pleasure to be up and about again.

All along the wharf, moored close together, ships and boats were being loaded or unloaded. From a galley a few yards or so down the dock a line of female captives, no doubt taken in a raid on one of the Moslem convoys, were at that moment stumbling down the gangway. Strangely, as one might have expected, there were no screams, no wails from the wretched girls chained neck to neck in what the slavers called 'coffle'. Silently, one after the other, they followed their captors with heads bowed, numbed perhaps by the extent of the catastrophe which had befallen them.

Charlotte no longer questioned the morality of such things. She had been in this part of the world long enough to recognise that Christians preyed on Moslems – Moslems on Christians. That was how it was, and perhaps the way it had always been.

There were sixty or so girls in this particular coffle, all young and comely; most were clad in the vestiges of their original clothing, now just rags. Some, those perhaps who had borne the brunt of their captors' attentions during the voyage, had no coverings at all. Charlotte knew what would happen to them. All slaves were taken first to the *bagnos*, the stinking human warehouses situated behind the walls of the grim fortress which overlooked the entrance to the harbour. This was where they would receive instruction in obedience and the duties of a slave before being sold in one or the other of the island's slave markets. One or two might be lucky enough to attract a ransom, if their relatives were rich enough – or cared enough – to pay, but most would simply be sold to the highest bidder.

The smell from the slaving galley was sickening and Charlotte pressed the perfumed scrap of silk closer to her nose. Quite obviously there were few or no sanitary arrangements for prisoners on such a ship.

Dockyard workers and sailors crowded noisily around the chained girls as their feet touched dry land for the first time in weeks, rough hands tearing at the brief rags which were all that clothed most of them. Charlotte breathed deeply at the sight, her attention caught by one particularly lovely girl who walked with her head up, ignoring the jabbing fingers and hands reaching under the tattered remnants of her clothing. She looked proud and unashamed, almost as if she were untouched by her humiliation, and Charlotte felt a sudden sympathy for her. How must it feel, she wondered, to be a slave, beautiful and desirable as was this girl, yet totally at the mercy of fierce men and their basest instincts? Though she could not have said why, the thought was strangely stirring.

Another commotion along the wharf drew Charlotte's attention momentarily to where two approaching men were surrounded by a mob of ragged children, all clamouring noisily for alms and each trying to outdo the other in their quest for a copper coin or two. One of the men, a tall, handsome, broad-shouldered fellow in his late twenties, was richly dressed in the Moorish fashion. The other, obviously servant or guard to the first, was a hugely muscled, bare-chested black man dressed in spotlessly white eastern-style baggy pantaloons tucked into soft leather boots. Slung carelessly across his naked shoulders, unsheathed, hung a gleaming, curiously curved sword. Plainly, thought Charlotte, this was not a man to be trifled with.

Today it seemed the urchins were to be fortunate. The richly dressed young man laughed and threw them a handful of silver coins, then passed on his way as the ragged children scrambled and fought for their reward. Charlotte looked at him curiously as he drew near the gangway. Though not quite so tall as the big Negro, he was almost as broad across the shoulders. She studied his features covertly, pondering his ancestry. His dark face and clothing were certainly of the east, yet to her mind the strong-jawed features might well have had their origins in a legacy that was more Greek than Arab.

She also wondered a little at his profession. Soldier of fortune? Merchant prince? His rich robes seemed to deny the first, yet he had little of the look of a merchant about him. To begin with, he was definitely not fat and, in Charlotte's experience, fatness was almost a condition of such employment.

Ignoring the armed soldiers and sweating sailors, the young man nodded amiably at the guard. From where she stood, Charlotte could clearly hear what was said.

'I am sorry to trouble you, friend, but I seek passage to Valencia. Is your captain aboard?' The young man's Spanish was excellent, just a slight hint of an accent betraying the fact that it was not his native tongue.

The sailor's demeanour was immediately deferential. Charlotte understood why. Fare-paying passengers were few and far between and the richness of the man's garments more than hinted at his ability to pay. Half of all passenger fares went straight into the captain's pocket and no sailor would care to risk his displeasure by turning one such away – even a Moor.

'Yes, sir!' replied the sailor, saluting smartly. 'Captain Diaz's cabin is on the afterdeck.' He pointed up to where Charlotte stood. 'The small deck, excellency – up there.'

The dark-faced man nodded and glanced sideways at his companion. 'Wait here, Zamil,' he ordered. 'I shall not be long.' He climbed aboard, then made his way along the raised centre-deck between the rows of sun-blackened figures slumped across the great sweeps. These were the oarsmen: wretched, whip-scarred slaves drawn from the ranks of criminals, prisoners of war, heretics and other so-called 'enemies' of the state. One or two dirty bearded faces looked up momentarily as the man passed, but for the most part the rowers remained slumped where they were.

As the stranger approached Charlotte noticed one stubborn, stray lock of black hair straggling out from under the *kuffiaya*, or hooded part of his robe, a lock which partially covered a pale scar running a good three inches down his temple. Now just where he had obtained that? she wondered, her curiosity increasing still further as she noticed the startling blueness of his eyes.

The uniformed figure of the ship's captain appeared in the

doorway of the stern cabin just as the visitor reached the deck and Charlotte turned away, feigning disinterest. Nevertheless, she listened closely to what was being said.

'My compliments, *señor*,' said the young man pleasantly, holding out his hand. 'My name is Salim bin Rahdi. My friend Bashir suggested I see you. I wish to book passage to Valencia for myself and my servant.'

The captain took the outstretched hand soberly, his eyes taking in the richness and cut of his visitor's apparel in one quick glance. He knew of Bashir, of course. Who had not heard of the second richest merchant in Valletta?

'Moor?' he asked gruffly.

Salim smiled affably and nodded his head. 'Yes, captain... though like you, I am a good subject of Spain, which has long been my family's home.'

Captain Diaz eyed the man shrewdly. 'We sail on tomorrow's dawn tide,' he said gruffly. 'Can you be aboard by then?'

Salim nodded. 'Easily. My baggage is small and easily packed.'

'Just yourself and your servant? No women? No harem or anything?'

The Moor grinned. 'No, captain, no women. Just myself and Zamil.'

Obviously relieved, the captain made a gesture towards the open cabin door. 'Very well, then,' he said. 'Let us go inside. There we can discuss the matter of the passage fee in private.'

In the large ornately decorated stern cabin of the ship, the two men faced each other across the captain's desk. With a smile, Salim bin Rahdi brought out a hefty little leather bag, which he tossed carelessly on to the desk. 'I trust this will be sufficient, sir?'

The Spaniard's dark eyes lit up as he picked up and weighed the little bag of gold coins. Quite obviously it contained considerably more than the usual amount of passage-money. Instantly his manner became more gracious. 'You are most generous,' he remarked, reaching for a bottle and two glasses. 'Will you take a glass?'

Salim shook his head. 'It is very kind of you,' he smiled, 'but, like most of my countrymen, I'm afraid I have no head for wine.' He grinned apologetically. 'Even one glass makes my head swim. Please forgive me.'

Disappointed, the captain set down the bottle. It would be extremely rude of him to take a glass if his guest would not. He sighed, reaching for his quill. 'Very well. In that case, I will just write you a receipt for your gold.'

The young man shook his head again. 'A receipt is hardly necessary between gentlemen.' With another friendly smile he turned to leave. 'I am very grateful that you allow us to travel with you.'

The captain's hand closed over the gold and swept it into his pocket. 'A great pleasure, your excellency. But please be aboard by first light. We sail on the tide. I will give instructions for a cabin to be prepared. What about your servant? Do you wish him quartered with the crew, or will you keep him with you?'

The young man smiled. 'Zamil will sleep in my cabin. I am used to having him close.'

The captain sniffed. The peculiar sexual habits of the Moors were well known. This one was probably no different.

'Just one other thing,' continued Salim. 'The lovely lady outside? She is a passenger also?'

The captain's face clouded. 'Ah, yes, of course, the English milady. She also travels with us to Valencia.' He raised his hands in the age-old gesture of helplessness. 'You understand that it was not my wish to have such on board as a passenger – but in this instance I had no choice. The lady's uncle is a man of great influence.'

Salim looked interested. 'Really, captain? An English

milady? Her uncle a man of great influence... and you do not like her?'

The captain flushed. 'You know what I mean,' he rejoined. 'It is not a question of like or dislike. It is just that... well, in my experience unescorted women passengers have no place aboard ship. They are unlucky; and they cause trouble amongst the crew.'

'Yes, I have heard this,' replied Salim easily. 'Still, if we are to be shipmates...' His expression was curious. 'Unescorted, you say? An English milady who travels alone? Surely this is not usual?'

Captain Diaz grunted and shrugged his shoulders. 'Well, she has her *duenna* – her companion, of course. A slave called Meylissah or some such heathenish name.' The captain coughed, then continued. 'The circumstances are a little exceptional. The lady herself is niece to Sir James Brandon.'

Salim lifted an eyebrow. 'The English special envoy?'

The Spaniard nodded. 'The same. Lady Charlotte was ill of a fever when Sir James was called urgently back to England on some diplomatic business or other and he was forced to leave her here under the protection of his friend, the Sheikh Omar ibn Saiid. Now that she is recovered, she goes to join him.' He stood up and held out a hand. Clearly, he did not wish to enlarge on the conversation. 'Now sir, I wish you a pleasant voyage. Please be aboard before first light.'

The young man smiled, white teeth gleaming in the dark face as he took the outstretched hand. 'Thank you again, captain. Until tomorrow, then.'

'Until tomorrow,' echoed the captain.

Of the blonde Lady Charlotte there was no sign as Salim bin Rahdi came out of the cabin, but as he made his way back along the centre deck towards the gangway, one of the sun-blackened figures at the oars hissed at him, 'Remember me, cap'n?'

33

Stopping abruptly, the Moor looked up as if interested in the complicated rigging of the big ship. Almost imperceptibly, he shook his head.

A whisper drifted up again. 'No matter... I know you, cap'n. Saw you in Algiers two years ago with that old devil Dragut.' The man's eyes gleamed. 'Knew you the minute I saw you talkin' to that Dago captain on the aft deck. Hawkins, Matthew Hawkins is my name; cap'n of the *Bonaventure* out of Bizerte, taken these eight months past by a Dago squadron off the Azores.' He gestured towards the oarsman on his right. 'This here's my master gunner, John Frith.'

'Privateers?' asked Salim softly.

The man nodded. 'Two ships; my *Bonaventure* and Fletcher's *Corso*. You remember Mad Jack?'

The Moor nodded.

'Well, the *Corso* managed to show the Dagos a clean pair o' heels, while we was rammed and boarded. They took most of us alive, 'cept for a dozen or so – and I reckon they were the lucky ones. Forty-nine souls wounded or took prisoner; forty-eight men and a wench. The wounded they just heaved overboard with their hands and feet tied.'

Salim looked down squarely for a moment, his expression hardening at the sight of the whip marks crisscrossing the sun-blackened flesh. 'A wench, you say?' he asked softly.

The galley slave nodded again. 'A young French bawd I picked up from a Somali slaver just before we sailed. She was sent here with us. They got her in the forward cable tier – for use of the officers.'

Salim looked up as if to gaze at the ship's rigging. 'The rest of your crew?' he whispered. 'How many left?'

'Just the two of us here.' The galley slave coughed weakly. 'Thirty of us made it into Valencia as captives. Twenty they burned in the main square within the month. *Auto da fe*, they called it. Said we was heretics. The rest they sentenced to the galleys. Four of us – John here, myself,

Jacob Longthorpe, my first mate, and Richard Proctor – found ourselves together on this hell ship. Richard and Jacob ha' both been weakening fast these past weeks.' He indicated the two conspicuously vacant places on the oar with a grim look. 'This morning, just before first light, the Dagos weighted 'em down and tossed 'em over the side.' He coughed again and wiped his mouth with a grimy hand. 'Jacob was still alive, I think. Good job the little Frenchy didn't see that. She had a soft spot for him.'

'I am sorry for your bad fortune, friend,' whispered Salim. 'But don't give up hope just yet.'

Hawkins tried to smile. 'Too late for us, I think, cap'n. But please – do what you can for the little Frenchy. Bawd she might be, but she don't deserve what those devils ha' been doing to her.'

The Moor's expression was carefully neutral as he turned and made his way down the gangway to the dock. The sailor on guard saluted smartly.

'Everything all right, excellency?'

'Yes, thank you. We sail with you tomorrow.' He indicated the big Nubian. 'Zamil will bring my luggage later. Will you see it is placed in our cabin?' He brought a gold piece from under his robe and held it out.

The sailor's eyes lit up. 'Of course, excellency. Just leave it to me.'

Salim clapped him on the shoulder. 'Thank you, friend,' he said. 'Until tomorrow then.'

Rejoining Zamil, Salim walked away, his smile quickly fading as he passed the black-painted, rakish-looking slaver tied up in the next berth. Although she had been unloaded earlier in the day, the disagreeable stench still drifted like a miasma from her open ports and hatches.

A little further along both he and the black man stood aside to allow two men and a female to pass by. One of the men, a fat disagreeable-looking fellow, was richly dressed; the other – smaller, dark and swarthy – was obviously a servant. Of the female, veiled and dressed in a voluminous all-concealing Arab *ha'ik*, there was little to be seen, though her dark eyes, mysterious above the veil, looked at them with some interest as they passed by. She was taking quick, very small steps and, from beneath the long cotton garment came the chink of chain and the sound of a small bell.

Salim bin Rahdi smiled. It was an old slaver's trick. Underneath the *ha'ik* the girl would be chained and belled. Just enough chain at the ankles so she could walk but not run, and belled so she might easily be found even on the darkest of nights. He looked boldly at the swathed female and the suddenly startled, kohl-lined eyes widened at his temerity.

The fat man intercepted the glance and a look of anger clouded his face, although it was very carefully not directed at the men.

'Come, slut!' he growled, reaching out to grab the girl viciously by the shoulder. 'Must I leash you every time a man passes by? I shall punish you later. Hurry now! We have business to attend to.'

A Girl is Kissed

For three days the *San Cristobal* sailed seemingly alone on an empty sea, a favourable wind driving her steadily on towards Marsala on the eastern tip of Sicily. From there she would set course for the safer, Spanish-patrolled Straits of Bonafacio, that narrow strip of water separating the island of Corsica from its more southerly cousin, Sardinia.

Once past Marsala, however, the capricious wind fell off, greatly slowing the ship's passage, so that the unfortunate wretches on the oars were forced to labour long and hard under the ever-present lash of the unrelenting Spanish oarmaster. Salim bin Rahdi spoke no more to the galley slave, though an observant onlooker might have noticed his expression darkening each time his gaze fell on the sweating, straining wretches who, urged cruelly on by the constant crack of the whip across naked backs, struggled to heave mightily on the giant sweeps.

Charlotte and Meylissah continued to make love as and when they wished in the privacy of the cabin, and the English girl could not remember being happier. Twice each morning and in the afternoon, they would take the air on the canopied aft poop-deck, as did the Moor, Salim bin Rahdi, and his Nubian. Sometimes the fat Spanish merchant and his swathed and veiled slave girl would join them for a time, though conversation seemed to be limited to a nod of the head and a brief word of greeting.

It was on the third morning that Meylissah went down with a fever. It seemed to be not as severe as her mistress' had been, but even so Charlotte was worried and reluctant to leave her alone. Only after repeated assurances from the slave girl that she really was all right was Charlotte finally persuaded to leave the stuffiness of the cabin for a turn on deck.

She made several circuits of the small vessel, listening with half an ear to the slap of canvas and the groan of the rigging, very much aware of the rolling deck under her feet and the tang of sea air in her nostrils; a clean smell which helped somewhat to offset the reek of salt-encrusted timbers and the unwashed bodies of the sailors. She was standing at the ship's rail, senses alive as she watched the gentle swell of the grey-blue sea, when she suddenly became aware that she was not alone.

Turning her head, she saw Salim bin Rahdi staring at her from the stern rail; a stare which sent the most curious icy sensation all the way down her spine. For a moment she met his eyes – eyes of the most startling blue in the dark face – then, seeking to evade the uncomfortable scrutiny, she turned back to look out over the vast expanse of sea.

He made no sound as he crossed the deck and yet, seconds later, she somehow sensed he was standing directly behind her. Charlotte was not normally nervous, but at that moment she tensed in every muscle of her body. Mouth dry, she spun around.

'What is it? What do you want?' she asked in English, then cursed her stupidity. He would not understand, unless her tone of voice managed to convey the meaning of her words.

Salim smiled and lifted his hands expressively, his eyes appearing to scan her every feature. 'Forgive me, my lady... I did not mean to frighten you,' he replied softly in Spanish.

Charlotte shifted a little nervously. Up close, like this, the man was quite intimidating. Hesitantly she groped for the right words. 'I am not frightened, *señor*... I was thinking of other things. My companion is ill,' she managed finally.

The Moor frowned. 'Meylissah? Nothing serious, I hope.'

'I don't know. A touch of fever. I had it recently myself.'

'I have some knowledge of fevers and medicines. Would you like me to take a look at her?'

Charlotte considered for a moment. 'Thank you,' she replied, 'if her condition worsens that would be most kind of you. But for the moment she is sleeping peacefully and I have no mind to disturb her.'

'Very well. But if her condition does give cause for concern, please let me know.'

For the rest of that morning, and again in the afternoon, Salim bin Rahdi accompanied her as she took her exercise, proving himself to be the most congenial of companions, though she remained very nervous of him. True, she thought him attractive in his eastern, somewhat exotic way, and the chance to increase her limited knowledge of the language of the Moors was something she found difficult to resist. Obviously rich and well-travelled, he had that self-confident and commanding manner which went hand in hand with the possession of great wealth and power. Beneath the handsome face and polite veneer, however, Charlotte could sense a ruthlessness that frightened her. A dangerous man, her every instinct warned her; a man she might do well to avoid. And yet, while she might never have admitted it, even to herself, it was precisely these qualities – as much as the man's natural magnetism and dark good looks – which attracted her. He was, in short, unlike any man she had ever known.

The unfriendly winds continued and it was three days more before the expected shout came from the main masthead.

'Deck there! Land ho!' A momentary pause, then, 'And sail ho!'

Buffeted by the breeze, the warning shout drifted faintly down from the galleass' topmast. On the shaded afterdeck the immaculately turned-out lieutenant was immediately alert.

'Where away, sail?' he shouted.

Back came the shout, 'A point off the port bow, sir!'

Hurriedly, the lieutenant moved to the rail to lift his telescope.

Boots clattered on the companionway steps behind him and the captain puffed his way on deck, dragging at his jacket and pushing his hat in place as he tried to maintain some semblance of dignity.

'What is it, lieutenant?' he asked.

The young man saluted smartly. 'The Straits are in sight, sir – and there are some small vessels off our port bow. Heading our way, looks like.'

'Can you make them out?' asked the captain worriedly.

His subordinate shook his head and handed over the telescope. 'No, sir. Too far away. Small though; black sails... Fishermen out from one of the coastal villages, most likely.'

The captain lifted the glass himself. 'Hmm,' he murmured. 'Maybe... maybe not.'

The young officer suppressed a smile. Captain Diaz had a reputation for being cautious. Of course the galleass might well be considered a tempting target by the Moslem corsairs who made regular raids from the north coast of Africa, but this was a long way north for such a raid, and the Straits were regularly patrolled by Spanish and Neapolitan warships. He gave a mental shrug. It really didn't matter. In addition to her powerful ram, the *San Cristobal* bristled with cannon: ten on the forecastle, four at the stern and thirty-two smaller swivel guns broadside – sixteen each side – mounted on the gun platform above the rowing benches. In a fight she would be more than a match for the best of them. Any pirate – Moslem or otherwise – foolish enough to come within range would be swiftly blown out of the water.

'Another half an hour or so of daylight, sir,' he commented. 'The sun will be down before we're close enough to see who they are.'

Captain Diaz ignored the remark. 'Come about and ease the oars,' he ordered. 'We'll let the wind take her for a while, then turn back on our original course after dark.'

The lieutenant knew better than to protest. He gave the order and the great galleass heeled over, digging her bows into the swell as the wind finally got the chance to belly the sails, which filled with a crack and much dragging of the rigging.

Charlotte was about to go on deck for some much needed air when she heard the lookout's shout. She picked up her cloak, pausing for a moment to look at the still figure lying on the other bunk.

'Are you awake, Meylissah?' she whispered softly. There was no reply, just the soft, ragged sound of breathing. 'Meylissah,' she whispered again, 'are you asleep?' Again, there was no response. Quietly, she tiptoed to the bunk and placed a hand on the sleeping girl's forehead. It was still hot and dry. She frowned, thinking that if the fever grew any worse she would ask Salim bin Rahdi to take a look at her. He had impressed her with his knowledge and confidence; he would know what to do.

Meylissah moved restlessly in her sleep. Not wishing to wake the slave girl, Charlotte stepped back, pulling the cloak around her bare shoulders as she turned for the door.

Stepping out on to the deck, she smiled inwardly as she saw Diego, the young lieutenant, turn towards her eagerly. From the first the young man had made no secret of his admiration for her and, if she was honest, she rather enjoyed the attention.

Captain Diaz ignored her as usual, his eye remaining firmly pressed to the telescope.

'What is it, captain?' she asked in Spanish, bracing herself quite naturally against the roll of the deck.

The older man indicated the black dots which were the unknown vessels, so indistinct now against the rays of the setting sun that she had to strain her eyes to see them. 'The Straits of Bonafacio and some small boats, my lady,' he replied dourly. 'Fishermen most likely, out from the coast, but we are taking no chances. We'll change course for a while, just in case, and turn back after dark.' He closed the telescope with a snap, then, setting his chin against the wind, moved away to stand by the helmsman.

Charlotte leaned on the side rail, cloak flapping in the wind as she drank in the clean air, so refreshing after the stuffiness of the cabin.

The lieutenant braced himself wide-legged on the swaying deck, his admiring gaze tinged with more than a little lust. With an effort he forced his voice to be calm, looking longingly at the creamy upper slopes of his companion's proudly jutting breasts, half-revealed by the fashionably low-cut gown under the wind-blown cloak. Casting a glance at the captain and seeing he was again busy with the telescope, he moved closer, holding his breath as, seemingly innocently, the English girl stretched, the cloak streaming back in the breeze to reveal the bountiful mounds almost threatening to burst from their confinement.

As if unaware of the effect she was having, Charlotte breathed deeply of the clean air, then relaxed and smiled impishly at the young officer. 'How will this change of course affect our passage, Diego? Will there be much delay?'

Diego took a deep breath. 'Oh, no, we can easily make up the time,' he replied, eyes still drawn irresistibly to the glorious globes which, almost every night since first seeing her, he'd caressed in his dreams. 'A few fishing boats will not delay us for long.'

If his companion noticed the direction of the young man's gaze, she made no mention of it, but merely leaned closer to him. 'I'm so glad,' she said. 'I am a little worried about Meylissah. The sooner I can get her to a doctor, the better.'

'She is no better then?' asked the young officer, moving even closer as the lightly perfumed smell of his lovely companion became more evident.

Charlotte turned to face him with a smile, her breasts brushing against his arm. 'A little,' she replied. 'But the fever still clings, I fear.'

'Lieutenant!' The captain's shout abruptly took the young man's attention and he jumped.

'Coming, sir!'

Charlotte smiled secretly as Diego hurried away. She enjoyed flirting with the young officer, and could not deny that he was quite handsome in his own boyish way.

As she inwardly acknowledged her attraction to the ship's lieutenant, a movement at the after-companionway hatch caught her eye, and she looked round just as Salim bin Rahdi came on deck followed by his towering black servant. Seeing her, the Moor spoke quietly to his companion, who nodded and turned away. Salim himself, smiling in his usual friendly fashion, walked to where Charlotte leaned against the ship's rail.

'Ah, Lady Charlotte,' he said in his usual immaculate Spanish. 'I heard the lookout's shout and the ship has turned. Has something happened?'

Charlotte's attention was immediately diverted from the retreating Diego. 'Nothing very important, I fear,' she replied a little breathlessly, her mind suddenly and inexplicably taken with the thought of a possible *liaison d'amour* with this powerful and extremely enigmatic man. She tried to picture the body under the flowing robe. Was his shaft bigger than those of the boys she had known? At once she berated herself. Dear God, what was she thinking of? Her uncle would have had a fit if he could read her thoughts at that moment.

Blushing hotly, she turned away and pointed towards the distant coastline. 'Some small boats on the horizon, that's all. The captain wished not to take any chances, and has changed course for a while.'

The Moor frowned. 'Small boats, you say?' He held up a hand to shade his eyes from the dying rays of the sun. 'And what did your lieutenant make of them?'

Covertly, Charlotte studied the features turned to her in profile, fighting a sudden, inexplicable temptation to tidy the one stray lock of black hair curling stubbornly over the forehead. Then, embarrassed and not a little irritated with herself that she should even think such things, she sought to cut short the conversation. 'For your information, Diego is not *my* lieutenant,' she said acidly.

Salim smiled at her tone, his steel-blue eyes examining her candidly. 'Ah, yes... Diego. For a moment I had forgotten his name,' he replied.

Charlotte blushed. Who did the man think he was? 'Diego thought they were probably fishing boats,' she replied shortly.

The Moor's expression remained mild. 'Well – he was probably right,' he replied. 'Still, the captain is wise to be careful. These are dangerous waters.'

43

Still annoyed, Charlotte made as if to walk away and he turned towards her. Quite without thinking she turned her face upwards and, for a tiny moment, their faces were but inches apart. She breathed deeply. He smelt clean, with just a hint of dried cinnamon on his skin. Then, as if it were the most natural thing in the world, he leaned forward to take her in his arms and, to her utter disbelief, kissed her. In that moment her knees turned to jelly and she was helpless in his grasp. Then, in spite of herself, she was kissing him back while his hands made free with her body. From beneath his robe the unmistakable feel of a semi-erect penis, plainly much larger than any she had known, nudged its length powerfully between her helplessly parting thighs. She felt the strength of the muscular arms confining her and recognised the primal knowledge that this man could almost certainly subdue her with one hand if he so wished. That thought, coupled with the unrelenting pressure of the hardened shaft against her lower body, sent an incredible thrill up her spine. Her nipples stiffened against the material of her gown and, with a shock, she realised she was in a state of high sexual arousal. This was no boy who held her – this was a man! And in that moment she was no longer the English aristocrat, Lady Charlotte Brandon, but just a female, responding to one of the oldest and strongest instincts known to her gender.

Shouted orders and the slap of calloused bare feet on the deck brought her quickly back to reality. Frantically she tore herself from the young Moor's close embrace. Blushing crimson, she did what she had always been taught was the correct response in such a situation. She slapped him hard across the face.

As soon as she had she regretted the action. For a moment she was even tempted to apologise, but it was too late. For one heart-stopping second, as she looked into the glittering blue eyes, she thought he might even strike her back. Instead, he just bowed slightly and turned away. Moments later she heard the angry clatter of his boots on the companionway steps as he went below.

Charlotte was mortified. Red with shame and embarrassment she glanced to where Diego and Captain Diaz still stood, deep in conversation. Obviously they had seen nothing of the incident and she breathed a sigh of relief. At least her show of unladylike behaviour would not become public knowledge.

At the captain's dinner table that evening, Charlotte sat quietly and listened to the men's conversation. The Málagan slaver was in good form, smiling a lot and monopolising much of the talk, though he addressed little of it to Charlotte. The big table was set at one end of the large cabin under the large windows which stood open to the warm evening breeze. The captain and three of his officers, one of whom was Diego, were seated in a row on one side, the three passengers – herself, the fat Málagan whom the captain had previously introduced as Señor Valdez, and Salim bin Rahdi – on the other. Behind the Moor, as if on guard, stood the big Nubian, Zamil. The rest of the cabin had been cleared to leave a large open space in the centre. Idly, she wondered why.

Señor Valdez was talking to Salim. 'So, you travel to Valencia also, *señor*? The captain tells me your father is a merchant. In what does he trade?'

Salim bin Rahdi smiled at the blunt question. 'Oh, many things,' he replied easily. 'Spices, oils, precious metals.'

'Slaves?' enquired Señor Valdez bluntly.

Salim shrugged casually. 'Sometimes,' he admitted.

The captain addressed the Málagan. 'Forgive me, *señor*, but are not slaves the major part of your own business?'

Valdez laughed shortly. 'Yes, indeed! And, I must confess, the most profitable.' He waved an airy hand. 'I supply oarsmen for the king's ships and many beautiful girls for all the best brothels in Spain.'

There was an abrupt silence and Charlotte's face reddened.

Unperturbed, the slaver continued: 'However, I am sure all this talk is boring Lady Charlotte.' He leered across at her. 'With the captain's permission, I have arranged a little entertainment for us.' He turned to Captain Diaz. '*¿Con permiso…?*'

His host nodded and Valdez clapped his hands sharply. From the curtained doorway to the inner cabin a veiled, dark-haired girl ran to the centre of the room, her oiled body glistening in the yellow lamplight. Scandalised, Charlotte tut-tutted to herself. But for her veil and a shimmering length of semi-transparent silk caught at neck and waist by gold chains, the dancer was practically naked. Gold slave bracelets graced her wrists and ankles; both, interestingly, were fitted with rows of little bells, all tinkling softly as she moved. A swarthy man, Valdez's servant, followed her, carrying a small drum in the crook of his arm.

'This is my Egyptian, Leila,' announced Valdez, proudly. 'She will dance for us.'

There was a murmur of appreciation from the men as, hands fluttering as if to cover herself, Leila dropped to her knees and placed her head to the floor at the drummer's feet. Charlotte could see the slave girl was around the same age as herself. The drummer snapped his fingers and immediately the girl raised her head, continuing to kneel submissively as he ripped the silk coverings from her body.

Charlotte blushed. As eastern custom dictated, the girl's body hair had been completely removed. A glint of gold at the dancer's breasts caught Charlotte's eye and she bent her head for a closer look. What in God's name have they done to her? was her horrified thought as she saw that the flesh of both the girl's nipples had been pierced and set with heavy gold rings, each ring supporting a tiny golden bell.

The drummer snapped his fingers again and the girl widened her thighs in response. Charlotte gasped with

46

renewed horror. There, snapped shut through holes punched in the dancer's outer labia, clearly visible below the smooth and hairless pudenda, hung a golden padlock from which dangled the last bell.

Charlotte's composure – that of an aristocrat trained almost from birth not to betray her feelings – almost wavered at the barbaric sight. She fought the wave of revulsion and outrage which flashed through her as the final snap of the drummer's fingers sent Leila to her stomach, flattening herself to the floor at the man's feet.

Curious despite her shock, Charlotte noticed the man was carrying a length of chain about six feet long. This he dropped to the floor at the dancer's side before settling the small tom-tom more comfortably in the crook of his arm. A preparatory rap on the instrument brought Leila back to her knees and Charlotte gazed, fascinated, at the naked, oiled body glistening so seductively in the soft lamplight.

How beautiful she is, thought Charlotte a little enviously, anger fading as she subconsciously compared her own more voluptuous curves to the depilated, lissom young figure kneeling in the centre of the cabin.

There was a hush from the men as, at a further signal from Valdez, the drummer began to beat out a rhythm on his instrument and slowly, very slowly, Leila began her dance. Bells tinkling, the drum ordering her movements, she knelt to retrieve the chain from the floor, lifting it high above her head before placing it around her neck, the two ends reaching down her oiled body, coiling on the deck at her knees. Sharper beats urged her once more to her feet, taking the chain with her. Hips swaying sensuously to the beat of the drum, she slowly turned, wrapping the links tightly around herself.

Charlotte breathed deeply, keenly aware of her own damp arousal beneath the folds of her heavy dress. The message was clear; this was the dance of the slave girl surrendering to her master. Meylissah had told her about it. She looked round the circle of onlookers, seeing that each was as enraptured as the next.

Now, it seemed, the dance could begin in earnest. Slowly, as ordered by the drum, the girl unwound the chain from her body. As the unwinding was completed, the audience saw her eyes widen in feigned surprise, holding the chain at arm's length as if seeing it for the first time. Then, tenderly, she brought it close and embraced it.

Cleverly, as she danced to the drum's commands, Leila wrought erotic impressions with the chain, first winding it around her waist, then her gold-tipped breasts, and even passing it between her legs. Charlotte blushed at this, even as the drum rapped sharply, three times, sending the naked dancer to her belly. There, still under the drum's command, she continued her gyrations, first on her stomach and then, as ordered, even more sensuously on her back. Eyes fixed as if pleading on the instrument, she attempted to rise, but the drum denied her, pinning her to the floor like a beautiful impaled butterfly. Moments later it allowed her to half-rise, then drove her down again to her belly. Rising once more as the drum commanded, she continued to move helplessly to the insistent beat. She was sweating freely, senses patently inflamed, her sexuality bold and challenging almost as she displayed herself freely to the watching men. Down to her knees, then up again, chain drawn tight between her legs as she moved to the primitive rhythm, it seemed she must soon orgasm helplessly, and several of the watchers, young Diego among them, cried out in pleasure as she seemed to control her needs just in time.

Leila now moved to where Valdez sat at the table, swaying seductively before him with legs splayed wide as he took a small key from his pocket and, reaching forward, unlocked and removed the golden padlock.

It was time for the tempo – and the purpose of the dance – to change.

A short series of raps from the drum brought the dancer up

short, before slower, more sensuous beats dismissed her to the pleasure of the audience. Turning, chain tight again between her legs, she made her way gradually around the table, boldly parading her oiled nakedness for each man in turn.

Charlotte suddenly realised what was about to happen. She snatched a look at Diego, who was obviously caught up in the sensual moment. Then she glanced at the dark-faced Salim bin Rahdi, colouring in confusion when she saw him scrutinising her seriously in return. Behind him she could see Zamil's lust-filled gaze fixed on the naked dancing girl. Obviously the big Nubian was amongst those profoundly affected by the erotic spectacle.

Distantly, she heard Valdez laugh as Leila went to her knees in front of one of the officers. Quite clearly he was about to be the first to sample her charms. Charlotte was suddenly hot with her own awakened sexuality. She felt the moistness between her legs increasing and pressed her thighs together, desperately trying to control her breathing as she imagined how it must feel to be so commanded to the service of men. Her eyes met Salim's and once more her breath caught in her throat at the look on his face. He was studying her thoughtfully, a faint smile curving the handsome mouth. She looked away, face bright red. He knew! He knew what she was thinking – what feelings were running through her body. Suddenly it was all too much and she knew she had to flee the cabin. Jumping to her feet and mumbling some kind of an apology she stumbled from her chair and out of the oppressive, lust-filled atmosphere. Diego frowned and made as if to follow, but Valdez held out a hand to stop him.

'Let her go, young man,' he chuckled. 'Lady Charlotte is a little embarrassed by our entertainment and she will not thank you for your attention. For now, it is better to leave her alone.'

Salim bin Rahdi also smiled at Charlotte's confused

retreat. Then, as the sweating Leila spread herself in front of the chosen man, he turned back to the spectacle.

Meylissah was still asleep when Charlotte re-entered the cabin, though her breathing seemed much easier and her fever appeared to have broken. Face down on her own bunk, Charlotte dimly heard the applause and excited shouts of the men, then a little later the cheers and shouts of, 'To me... to me,' as the slave girl, at Valdez's whim, began intimately to entertain each in turn. Burying her face in the pillow so as not to wake Meylissah, Charlotte sobbed her anguish as the noise went on and on and she pictured what was happening in the cabin above. How could they, she thought bitterly and then, as the unthinkable crystallised in her mind, how could *he*?

She tossed and turned for a long time, unable to sleep. The *San Cristobal*, once her helm was turned for the coast again, began to pitch and roll in quite a disturbing manner as the strong Mediterranean swell, driven by the gusting north-easterly, once more made itself felt.

She eventually drifted into a fitful sleep full of troubled dreams; dreams of soft, pierced flesh, steel-blue eyes, strong hands roaming over her nakedness and strong lips crushing her own. In one such dream she saw herself in a darkened chamber – and manacled! She did not realise this until, in the dream, she tried to move. She was naked and the irons were tight about her wrists and ankles, holding her fast to a grim stone altar in an outstretched X position. Struggling for memory she lifted her head, looked around her dimly-lit prison and screamed. All around were other girls, all beautiful, all as naked as she and chained in some way.

Men were there, too – many men, using the helpless girls in disgusting, perverted, almost unthinkable ways. Mouths, bottoms, breasts, vaginas... nothing, it seemed, was sacrosanct. Yet the chained girls seemed to welcome their usage.

One particular man – a very large dark-faced man she was sure she had seen before, yet who for some reason she did not quite recognise – entered the chamber and approached where she lay. She moaned in shame as he looked down at her splayed nakedness, excited despite her humiliation, her loins already oiling themselves at the thought of what was to come.

'Be silent,' warned the intruder. 'Make no noise.' Swiftly he mounted the altar and pressed himself between her parted legs. She shivered with excitement, her wrists and ankles jerking spasmodically against the metal bonds which held them as she realised he was already hugely erect. 'Shh!' the man warned again, his hands on her breasts, kneading and massaging, fingers pulling at her suddenly hard nipples, his solid length nudging inexorably at her love portal.

Then he had slipped easily inside her, filling her with the solid length of himself as he moved steadily and determinedly towards his, and her own, gratification. Writhing under him, she felt as if her lower half was filled with a great moving pillar of flesh pistoning in fast friction almost to bursting point. The man – still she could not fathom his identity – paused for a moment and then drew back, relieving her a little of the feeling of fullness, before surging right back into her again, even more fiercely than before. He reached between their joined bodies and Charlotte felt his fingers pulling apart the lips of her sex to expose and caress the erect nub of flesh that was her clitoris. It was enough. She lifted her hips in rapturous response, head flung back, mouth gasping as the full force of orgasm burst suddenly upon her.

She awoke to find herself on her own bunk, covers flung aside in disarray, her dress pulled up to her waist. She was slick with sweat, fingers still moving between her spread thighs as the throbbing violence of her orgasm began to wane. From where had her imagination called forth such frighteningly arousing images? In sudden panic, Charlotte looked to where Meylissah lay on the other bunk, deeply relieved to see the girl was still sleeping peacefully and had obviously noticed nothing. Still shaking, she removed her clothes and climbed into her night-dress.

Attack

In the little cable tier where she had been held prisoner in the months since her capture, a naked girl lay with wrists and ankles secured tightly to the corners of a filthy bunk as the *San Cristobal's* first mate took violent possession of her helpless body.

It was a common enough occurrence. Since her capture she had been used in one fashion or another almost every day by a succession of Spanish officers. This particular brute, though, liked to tie her down, seeming to gain even more pleasure by having her completely helpless as he took her.

The mate's hands descended once again to maul and squeeze her swollen, discoloured breasts and the girl gave another half-stifled squeal of pain through the wadded, sour-tasting cloth stuffed deep into her mouth as the thin cords noosed tightly around the base of each cut into the soft flesh. Then he was climaxing and, belly heaving, the girl struggled desperately to match his frantic thrusts.

'Fail to please me, bitch,' the mate had warned her, squeezing her tortured globes till she thought she might faint from the pain, 'and I'll cut these off!' She'd believed him. The devil was capable of anything.

It was at that moment the door opened to admit a tall, bare-chested figure. From where he lay between the girl's legs the Spaniard looked up in alarm and tried to withdraw. Too late! Quick as a striking snake the figure lunged with a sword and the first mate collapsed limply on top of his terrified victim.

With a look of disgust the swordsman heaved the corpse from the spread-eagled girl and allowed it to slide off in an untidy heap to land on its back, a viscous trail of semen escaping from the still erect penis to collect in a little pool on his stomach. Frightened, the girl lifted her head to stare up at her rescuer.

The intruder placed a finger to his lips and, drawing his dagger, gently cut the cords around her breasts. 'Remain as you are,' he whispered. 'Soon the ship will be taken and then I will come back to release you. Do you understand?'

Wide-eyed, the girl nodded her comprehension.

'Good. Do so and no harm will come to you.' The door closed quietly behind him and the girl allowed herself to slump back on the bunk. Breathing heavily, she stared into the open yet lifeless eyes of the sadistic brute who would never again abuse her.

At the helm of the *San Cristobal*, in that dark cold blackness which precedes the dawn, the sailor on watch was expecting the ship's mate on his inspection. Lounging at the tiller, he was thinking somewhat wistfully of the girl he'd left behind in Valletta and wondering with a stab of jealousy whose bed she shared tonight. Lord, she'd been a looker! He remembered the smell of her; the sweaty feel of her nakedness as they'd lain together that last night. Would she still be waiting when he returned?

The sound of a measured tread brought the helmsman upright as he made out a tall but indistinct figure approaching. The bastard was late this morning; he'd probably been having fun with the French whore they kept for their amusement. At that moment the wind took the mainsail, cracking it like a gunshot. Startled, the helmsman looked upwards, only for the shadowy shape to leap forward, striking down expertly with the club-like instrument he carried in his right hand. It was a terrible blow. Caught squarely on the temple, the helmsman pitched lifeless to the deck.

Swiftly and silently the figure made fast the tiller and then, just as quietly, lit a lantern and hoisted it slowly to the masthead and back down again. Seven or eight times he did the same thing, until he caught an answering flash of light far out in the blackness. Leaving the lantern burning at the top of the mast, he faded back into the darkness as silently as he had come. Pilotless now, the galleass sailed on into the night with no sound, apart from the wind and the creak and rattle of the spars and blocks, to be heard. At intervals around the deck lay the prone and silent figures of the ship's watch.

Minutes later, oars muffled, sails furled, two black-painted Arab galleys slipped out of the darkness like ghosts. Cautiously at first, then with increasing confidence when no alarm was raised, a stream of ragged, well-armed men swarmed aboard.

It was all over very quickly. The Spanish, waking bleary-eyed in their bunks, were no match for the attackers. Those who resisted were killed, the rest quickly herded into the ship's hold where they were stripped and chained.

Surprise was complete: not a cannon fired; not an arrow loosed. Having subdued all resistance the jubilant pirates ran to loot the ship.

Down in her cabin Charlotte was jolted awake by the cheers and sounds of running feet on the deck above. Frightened, she scrambled from her bed to fumble frantically in the darkness for her clothes. She was still fumbling when the cabin door, which she had bolted from the inside, was dealt a blow from the passageway beyond. At a second assault the sagging door burst inwards with a crash. There, framed in the light from the passage, blood still dripping from the double-headed axe held carelessly in one hand, stood a darkly bearded giant of a man in gore-stained robes.

The English girl was terror-stricken. What was happening? Was this yet another nightmare? Surely she must waken soon...

The corsair stepped into the cabin, his fingers closing on her shoulder, and she jerked away frantically, tearing her nightgown from throat to waist as she did so. Desperately, as her assailant's other hand fastened on her waist, she kicked and pummelled until he lost patience and struck her a casual flat-handed blow which laid her, dazed and barely conscious, across the bunk.

It was at this point that, from the cot in the corner, a female whirlwind launched herself on to the assailant's back, striking down wildly with the razor-sharp dagger she kept always under her pillow.

'Run, mistress! Run!' gasped Meylissah.

Taken by surprise the huge corsair gave a cry of pain as the blade penetrated his neck and lodged there. White with anger he reached back with one hand, fingers closing around Meylissah's throat to pluck her from her perch. As her face twisted with pain he held her out at arm's length, then threw her across the cabin like a rag-doll. Meylissah screamed as she flew through the air, the sound cutting off abruptly as her head hit the wall with an ominous thump.

Charlotte responded to the sight as though crazed. Fingers crooked like talons, she went straight for the giant's eyes. Fortunately for him his reflexes were quick enough to save his sight, though in leaping clear he did manage to lose his footing, pitching over backwards with a crash.

Reason returned to Charlotte and she tried to make her escape, but she was not quick enough. Even as she stepped over the fallen corsair his fingers closed on her ankle and, with a savage growl, he jerked her down beside him, tearing off the remainder of her nightgown in the process. Holding her with one hand he climbed to his feet and reached back to pull the dagger from his neck. Effortlessly he propelled her to the little bunk and, still dazed, she did nothing to resist as he turned her on to her stomach and bent her over with her face in the covers.

Charlotte groaned and tried to move, but a meaty hand in the small of her back ensured she stayed exactly as she was. Suddenly something fleshy and hard began to force itself between her legs and she realised what was about to happen. Frantically she wriggled to one side and kicked out as hard as she could, catching her attacker square in the groin as he fought to hold her still.

Paralysed for a moment or two by pain, the giant released his grip on Charlotte and straightened up, both hands cupping his injured groin as the breath flew from his body. Charlotte squirmed away, but found her path of escape still partially blocked by the sheer bulk of her would-be rapist.

She tried to slide past the groaning man, and did not even see the blow that slammed her to the deck, senses whirling, stomach heaving. Her attacker, infuriated by Charlotte's resistance, had completely lost control. Picking up the dagger he bent over his fallen victim and, taking her by the hair, jerked up her head so her throat was exposed. Stunned and helpless, Charlotte felt the sharp steel, still bloody from the man's wound, lodge itself in the soft skin under her jaw. She looked into his pain-filled eyes and saw only death waiting there. Fatalistically lifting her throat to the blade, she braced herself for the agonising slash that would end her life.

It never happened. Even as her attacker's arm flexed there came a shout from the shattered doorway.

'Stop!'

Startled, both Charlotte and the intruder looked up. Standing in the doorway stood a bare-chested Salim bin Rahdi, the muscles in his huge shoulders rippling as he lifted the scimitar held carelessly in one hand. 'Stop, I say!' This time there was an edge to the voice that cut like a knife.

Snarling, Charlotte's assailant came to his feet in one fluid movement, dragging her with him by the hair. She gasped for breath as her scalp was almost ripped from her head. Menacingly, he moved the dagger blade closer towards her throat. 'She is mine!' growled the giant, defiantly. 'I kill her or let her live as I decide. It is corsair law.'

Salim smiled lazily and then, so smoothly that Charlotte hardly saw it happen, the razor-sharp point of the scimitar was at the giant's throat. Charlotte gasped. The movement had been so quick, so deadly; not at all the action of a merchant.

'Very well, Jahwar of the Berbers,' he said quietly. 'Now you are mine, to kill or not, as I decide. This, too, is corsair law. So – do we come to an understanding or do I send you to Allah's mercy?'

Charlotte understood only a portion of the conversation, but her rescuer's meaning was clear. If she died, her assailant was promised a similar fate.

The bearded giant's face showed indecision if not fear. It seemed he, too, had been impressed by the speed of the other's attack. For a moment he stood quite still, obviously coming to the realisation that he would be a dead man in seconds if the other so desired. The scimitar jabbed again, this time bringing a spot of blood to the skin.

'Make up your mind, girl-killer!'

Jahwar appeared to make up his mind quickly. Carefully, so there could be no mistaking his intent, he turned the blade of the dagger away and offered the weapon, hilt first, to his antagonist.

Salim stretched out his hand, took it and tucked it in his belt. Abruptly, he withdrew the scimitar. 'Go now, foolish one,' he said easily, looking without humour on the man who, but a moment before, he might so easily have killed. 'No, leave the axe.' Jahwar had stooped to pick the fearsome weapon from the floor. 'You may retrieve it later.'

Silently, the giant Berber crossed to the shattered doorway, then turned to face Salim. His face was white with suppressed anger. 'So be it,' he hissed. 'For the moment the *nasrani* slut is yours. Do with her as you wish, but do not think that Jahwar of the Axe will forget!'

Then he was gone.

Although much of the Arabic exchange had gone over her head, Charlotte was in no doubt that she owed her life to the handsome young Moor. Suddenly her knees felt like jelly and she sensed they might not support her for very much longer.

'Thank you, Salim,' she faltered, crimson with embarrassment now they were alone and he was able to study her nakedness with such undisguised interest.

'Your life is now mine, Charlotte,' he said softly. 'Quickly, now, do you accept my leash?'

She gaped at him, her words coming as a disbelieving whisper. 'Leash...?'

'Yes, leash. Mine,' he indicated the upper deck, from where she could hear the whoops of the jubilant pirates, 'or theirs. Which do you prefer?'

She looked into the steel-blue eyes and shuddered, sudden understanding flooding into her mind. 'You are one of them?' she whispered.

'Yes.'

Still she did not want to believe.

'Well?' he demanded.

There was no help for it. Bitterly, she faced him. 'My clothes... I need to get dressed.'

'Clothes will not be necessary,' he said quietly.

She stared at him in dismay. Surely he didn't expect her to remain as she was. 'But...' she faltered.

'No time to argue,' he growled. 'Turn around, quickly.'

Trembling, Charlotte did as he ordered, making no protest as he quickly fastened her wrists together with cord. 'Please,' she whispered, face crimson with embarrassment, 'allow me to cover myself.'

There was a scream from overhead, followed by a heavy splash as what could only have been a body hit the water.

58

From his belt, Salim bin Rahdi produced a strip of braided leather. 'Be silent,' he snapped.

Breathlessly, she stood helpless as he slipped the leash over her head. With a sense of horror she looked up into the bronzed face of her captor and tried to come to terms with what was happening. She was naked and tied – and totally at his mercy. She looked desperately to where the crumpled figure lay by the bulkhead. 'Please,' she begged, 'Meylissah, my maid... is she dead?'

Dropping the leash, Salim strode across the cabin to the prone figure and gently turned her over, pressing his fingers to the maid's neck to search for a pulse. Meylissah gave a little groan and stirred under his hand.

'She lives,' he said simply.

Charlotte's eyes filled with tears of relief as, still dazed, Meylissah struggled to her feet and submitted first to being stripped, then tied and leashed. A sharp tug on her leash brought the English girl back to awful reality.

'Come,' ordered her captor.

She looked up at him desperately. 'No... please,' she choked, as the leash tightened on her throat. 'Do not take us like this, please, I beg you!'

Salim was unmoved. 'Come,' he repeated flatly.

She looked into his eyes and recognised there a strong resolve. He was not to be swayed. Shivering with cold and fear, both she and Meylissah followed numbly as he led them out through the shattered doorway and into the corridor beyond.

On deck, the fighting was over. Naked and bound, a small group of Spanish officers was grouped together in the middle of the deck. Charlotte looked around in horror. Already triumphant corsairs were throwing dead and wounded alike over the side, while others ran to loot the ship and release the galley slaves. With a sick feeling she saw the bodies of the young lieutenant, Diego, and Valdez the slaver being heaved into the sea. Of Captain Diaz there was no sign and her heart sank even further at the thought that he had probably already been disposed of in similar fashion.

Charlotte looked up and her heart thumped in her chest. On the canopied afterdeck, not a hand's breadth away from where, only yesterday, she had imagined herself insulted by a kiss, stood a terrifying, mailed and helmeted figure. Behind him stood the huge figure of Zamil and, kneeling beside him naked and tied as she was, the sloe-eyed Egyptian dancer, Leila, golden padlock with its little bell still hanging between her parted thighs.

The corsairs were chanting, stamping their feet in time as they shouted a name. Charlotte shivered, her heart cold as ice. The armoured figure was ageing now, the great red beard flecked with grey; but still there was no mistaking his identity. Throughout the Mediterranean his name was anathema to Christians.

'Dragut! Dragut Bey! Dragut! Dragut Bey! Dragut!'

The shouts filled Charlotte's ears like the bells of doom. Dragut Bey, the legendary corsair lord: he of the red beard; scourge of western shipping and master of a dozen ships. Redbeard the bloodthirsty, whose Christian prisoners filled the slave markets of the Barbary Coast; whose black-painted galley he called *Jihad*, which freely translated from the Arabic, meant *Holy War*.

Another jerk on the leash urged the two girls forward and the corsairs began to chant a different name. 'Khalif! Khalif!'

Salim lifted an acknowledging hand and the English girl trembled with increased horror. She was beginning to understand just what had happened to her. No wonder the Moor had not seemed like any merchant she had ever known. She knew him now. Or rather, knew *of* him. Not as the merchant, Salim bin Rahdi, but as Khalif Barbar, more commonly known as 'the barbarian' to his Spanish and Neapolitan enemies. No one knew his real name, but it was rumoured he had once been a galley slave of the Spanish.

She trembled anew. Khalif Barbar had almost as grim a reputation as Dragut Bey himself.

As they approached, Dragut Bey turned to the Moor with a wolfish smile. 'So, Khalif, once again we triumph,' he rumbled. His eyes flickered over the two naked girls. 'And what have we here? Two more beauties! I see your eye for slave flesh has not let you down.' He laughed, indicating the kneeling figure at his side. 'And, as you can see, Zamil too has made a capture.'

The Moor smiled. 'Yes, my lord, so I see.' He held out the two leashes. 'This one is an English milady,' he said carelessly, indicating Charlotte. 'She should bring a fair price on the block. The other was her body slave.'

Dragut accepted the leash and examined Charlotte with an expert eye. 'An English milady, you say,' he murmured, running a none-too-gentle hand across her breasts and down over her rump. He thrust his fingers intimately between her legs, then chuckled and glanced sideways at the younger man. 'A juicy slut,' he pronounced.

Charlotte almost died of shame. It was true. In spite of her terror she could feel her juices running.

The old corsair snapped his fingers, still shiny from her secretions. 'Kneel!' he ordered, indicating that both girls should place themselves alongside the other captive.

Charlotte felt a sudden surge of anger and, for a moment, almost considered disobeying him. Then a sharp tug on the leash changed her mind and, with a little sob, she followed Meylissah's example and dropped to her knees.

'Dragut! Khalif! Dragut! Khalif!' The chants went on and on until the old pirate lifted a hand for silence.

The noise subsided and one half-naked warrior stepped forward to salute with bloodied sword.

'The prize is ours, my lords,' he shouted. 'What orders? Will you give us the female slaves for our pleasure?'

The corsair chief grinned as if contemplating the thought and Charlotte shivered with fear. Although the dialect they used was different to Meylissah's, she understood much of what was being said. Was this to be her fate? At the mercy of this crew of cut-throats; taken over and over again until they tired of her? And then what? Killed in any one of a dozen slow and agonising ways for their amusement, the fact that she was English and an aristocrat adding even more spice to their game?

Dragut smiled wolfishly, displaying discoloured teeth. He shook his head, almost regretfully. 'No... I think not, Saiid,' he said. 'They are but common sluts and for them to be used by so many lusty brethren would probably be fatal for them. Far better to fetch both alive to the marketplace.' He grinned slyly. 'This is, after all, a profit-making venture.' He glanced down at the captives. 'And dead sluts bring no one a profit.'

Charlotte bridled at once. She had understood enough of the exchange to know what Dragut had called her. She raised her head defiantly, her eyes flashing. 'I am not a slut!' she declared. 'My name is Lady Charlotte Brandon. My uncle is Sir James Brandon, a powerful man who will pay much for my release.'

Dragut regarded the kneeling girl with some interest. 'So,' he marvelled, 'you speak our language.' He gave a sardonic bow. 'I beg your pardon, my lady. Obviously a mistake has been made.'

Hope surged in Charlotte's breast at the pirate's words – a hope stifled almost as soon as it was born.

'Of course, it would not be proper to treat such a lady as yourself as a common slut,' he said. He grinned and turned to the crew. 'Run out a plank,' he shouted. 'We have made a mistake. This *nasrani*, who I took to be slave flesh, is in reality a great lady in her own country. Therefore, as we have sworn to take no prisoners, only slaves, she must die as a real lady would wish.'

Dragut stepped back and instantly, as his men cheered, Charlotte was hauled to her feet by a grinning Zamil.

Tugging on her leash until she thought she might choke, he dragged her to where a group of villainous-looking corsairs were already lashing a plank of wood to the side of the ship. She looked back in terror at Salim bin Rahdi for help, but could discern no sign of pity or concern in the dark, expressionless face.

Thrust up on to the swaying plank, Charlotte almost lost control of her bowels as, looking down into the blue water, she saw the unmistakable shapes of half-a-dozen or so great sharks tearing at those bodies which were still floating.

'Blindfold her,' ordered a grinning Dragut, and she moaned in terror as a dirty rag was tied tightly around her eyes, cutting off her vision.

A sharp pain in her buttocks as a sword point jabbed at her flesh made her jump and, to a great cheer from the corsairs, she took one unsteady pace along the plank. It wavered and bent under her feet and she could sense the water and the terrible predators it contained beneath her. She cried out in terror. Whatever else fate held for her, she could not face that. 'No!' she screamed. 'Please, don't kill me! I am not a lady. I am a slut – a whore! Please... please... don't kill me!'

Rough hands hauled her from the plank and removed the blindfold. She was forced to her knees again and, blinking her tear-filled eyes, Charlotte looked up numbly at a frowning Dragut.

'So, now you are a slut,' said the old corsair, 'and content to be treated so?'

Charlotte moaned with shame and hung her head.

'Answer, girl,' repeated the pirate. 'Are you lady – or slut?'

There was no help for it. Charlotte was completely defeated. 'Just a – a slut,' she finally managed to whisper.

Dragut was satisfied. He turned to Zamil with a grin. 'Take them below and secure them well,' he ordered. He held up a warning hand. 'And for the moment, make sure they remain untouched.'

The huge black man nodded. 'Come,' he ordered tersely, taking up the three leashes.

'No!' gasped Charlotte, as the braided noose once more tightened on her throat and threatened to cut off her wind. In her extremity she looked towards the man she had known as Salim for help. 'Please, I beg you, tell them! My uncle will gladly pay any ransom you ask.'

The Moor's face remained expressionless and Charlotte caught her breath as Zamil bent over her. The Nubian's skin was slick with sweat and his muscles rippled as he picked her up in his arms. Effortlessly he lifted her and stepped forward to the deck rail. Charlotte looked down in trepidation. The main deck was at least eight or ten feet below.

'Ho!' shouted Zamil to the men below, then casually opened his arms as the man directly underneath looked up. Charlotte gave a piercing scream as she fell. The surprised pirate almost managed to catch her, though he was not alert enough to prevent himself being knocked to the deck amid howls of laughter from his comrades.

'Fool, Zamil,' gasped the man, struggling out from underneath the winded Charlotte. 'You might have killed me.'

There was another howl of laughter from the watching corsairs, and Zamil grinned hugely. 'Forgive me, Saiid,' he chuckled, turning to pick up the gold-nippled Leila and hold her, too, out from the rail. 'Here… this one is not quite so heavy, I think.'

This time the pirate was ready and managed to catch his human prize without any trouble. Still grinning, Zamil repeated his action with a trembling and white-faced Meylissah, then swung down to reclaim his charges.

Encouraging them with sharp swats to their backsides, he swiftly herded the three girls below decks. There, he threw open the door to a tiny windowless cabin and thrust them inside. 'Kneel,' he growled.

Charlotte, looking in despair at the room's occupants, hardly heard him. On the floor was the body of a man, a Spanish officer by the look of him. On the bunk, securely tethered by her outstretched arms and legs, lay another young dark-haired female, gagged with a wadded cloth. The girl was naked and, as she looked closer, Charlotte's flesh crawled to see her bruised and discoloured breasts, along with other marks of abuse that some devil had inflicted on the soft flesh.

'Kneel,' Zamil repeated.

Shocked to the core and sick at heart at what she perceived to be her betrayal by Salim bin Rahdi, otherwise known as Khalif, Charlotte remained on her feet even as Leila and Meylissah fell submissively to their knees. Bound and vulnerable as she was, she nonetheless tried to speak with some dignity. 'Please,' she said, trying desperately to recall the Arabic words, 'I am not a slave. My uncle will reward you well if you return me to him. Release me, I beg you.'

Casually, Zamil cuffed her round the head, the blow setting her head spinning. 'Learn to obey,' he commanded. He pointed to the floor at his feet. 'Kneel.'

Tears welling from her eyes, still Charlotte persisted. 'Please, Zamil,' she begged, 'I am not a slave. You know this. Your master knows this. Much gold will be paid for my release. Do not treat me so, I beg.'

Zamil's eyes narrowed and he reached out to take a murderous-looking, three-thonged whip from its hook on the wall.

'You have already admitted to being a slut and a whore, *nasrani*,' he growled. 'I have told you to obey. Do you wish to be taught?'

The meaning was clear, yet still Charlotte's ravaged modesty would not allow her to retreat.

'Please…' she whispered, this time in her own language.

'I am not a slut or a whore... do not treat me so.'

'Very well, foolish one.' Taking hold of one soft shoulder, he forced her easily to her knees, then jerked her wrists sharply upwards to press her nose firmly to the dirty deck. Charlotte gasped in terror as her rounded bottom and the backs of her thighs were presented as a perfect target. Then she screamed, shoulders almost threatening to break under the strain as once, twice, three times the whip fell. The pain was almost unbelievable. Charlotte couldn't even scream; the shock had taken her breath away so completely.

Utterly vanquished, she writhed at the Nubian's feet. 'Oh, God have mercy,' was all she could gasp.

Still Zamil had not finished with her. Reaching down he took her by the hair and pulled her back to her knees, roughly kicking them apart as she fought for breath. 'A slave kneels thus!' he grunted.

Charlotte was shaking uncontrollably, nine crimson swathes of fire lining the creamy flesh of her bottom. Never had she felt such atrocious pain. Zamil examined her candidly, initial anger cooling a little as he regarded his shuddering but now acquiescent captive. He turned to replace the whip on its hook and then looked back sternly.

'Silence now,' he ordered. 'Remain as you are until I return.'

The door banged shut and Charlotte, bottom on fire where the lash had struck, looked at her companions in misery and began to sob aloud.

Leila's reaction was not entirely sympathetic. 'Stop that,' she whispered fiercely. 'Did you not hear? We are commanded to be silent... and I fear the lash, even if you do not.'

'Please, mistress,' urged Meylissah. 'You must be silent now or we shall all be whipped.'

The words penetrated Charlotte's brain and, desperately, she tried to stifle her sobs. The thought of being whipped again was unthinkable. Another assault with that fearsome weapon would surely kill her. She looked at the sprawled body of the Spanish sailor and shuddered, managing to gain control of herself only with a mighty effort, though her shoulders continued to shake silently.

Leila regarded her impassively, shifting slightly on her haunches to make herself more comfortable. The glint of gold caught Charlotte's eye and she shuddered at the sight of the heavy rings set in the tender flesh. What sort of world was this, she thought, where men might do such barbaric things to helpless women?

Feeling more alone than she had ever felt in her life, Lady Charlotte Brandon – now a naked, tethered slave – knelt on the dusty floor of the cabin, her silent tears continuing to fall as the awful reality of what had happened began to sink in.

Retribution

Like two sleek sharks cradling a cumbersome whale, the corsair galleys *Jihad* and *Persephone* lay warped either side of the captured galleass. The *San Cristobal* was wallowing, first to one side and then the other; a stiffish offshore breeze along the Mediterranean swell doing nothing to steady her as she lay with sails furled and oars banked.

Around half the surviving Spanish were already chained to the rowing benches of the galleass, replacing those unfortunates who had been the previous occupants. Others were prisoner at the oars of the two galleys. At Khalif Barbar's direct order, the two surviving Englishmen had already been released from their chains and were even now being cared for in a cabin below.

Angry growls came from the corsairs as one poor whip-scarred wretch was laid gently on the deck. For him, rescue had come too late. Starved and beaten until he was not much more than a blood-encrusted skeleton, he had died, still chained to his oar, almost at the moment of liberation.

Chained hand and foot, one small group of carefully selected Spanish prisoners remained huddled together in a forlorn group by the mainmast, corsairs and freed slaves alike circling them threateningly. Questions were asked, fingers pointed accusingly, and the *San Cristobal's* brutish oar-master was dragged from the little group to be kicked, punched and spat upon.

There was a chilling, vengeful shout from one of the freed slaves, a gaunt figure with an unsheathed scimitar in his hand. 'He is mine. I claim the right!'

Amid hoots and jeers, the oar-master, struggling and pleading for mercy, was dragged from the little group of prisoners and frog-marched to the same plank that had been the instrument of Charlotte's surrender. The victim, foreseeing his fate, threw himself to his knees in front of the slave, tears running on his cheeks as he begged desperately for his life.

It was useless.

With an impatient growl, the former occupant of the rowing bench hauled the man to his feet and forced him up on to the plank. For a moment the man stood absolutely still, terror-stricken at the sight of the menacing black fins cruising the bloodstained water around the ship. Then the scimitar jabbed sharply between his buttocks, forcing him, blubbering and pleading, to shuffle awkwardly out on to the swaying little platform. Desperately, the man turned to face his tormentor, his entreating words silenced by the sight of the razor-sharp blade jabbing at him. Reluctantly, step by hesitant step, urged on by the relentless blade, the wretch backed away along the crazily dancing plank. He was near the end now, teetering desperately as it bent further and further under his weight.

With a despairing shout he leaped backwards, away from the slashing blade, to vanish with a huge splash beneath the surface of the waves. A mighty cheer went up from the corsairs as, moments later, his head broke the surface, mouth gaping wide as he dragged great gulps of air into his straining lungs, kicking out desperately with his chained legs to stare up entreatingly at the shouting, cheering faces grinning savagely down at him.

For long minutes the Spaniard trod water under the gaze of the jeering corsairs, striving desperately to keep himself afloat as the encircling black fins came closer and closer to their meal. It was a hopeless task. Finally, even as the last desperate strength left the struggling body, two of the patrolling sharks attacked at the same time, tearing savagely into their screaming victim before he vanished forever beneath the red-stained water.

It was the beginning of what might have become a massacre. Kicking and struggling, another man was dragged from the group and hoisted up on to the plank. Having seen and heard the fate of his companion the Spaniard babbled crazily, pleading for mercy as the pirates crowded around.

In the galleass' great stern cabin, surrounded by seven great boxes filled with gold and silver ingots, Dragut Bey, admiral of corsairs, ignored the cacophony of howls as he sat with Khalif.

The younger man looked up as the noise intensified. 'Perhaps it would be better to take a hand,' he said. 'It would be folly to lose too many.'

Dragut sighed and held out his cup. Swiftly and expertly one of the naked girls kneeling at his side refilled it with sweet cordial from a large, gracefully spouted pot. Around her neck hung a braided leather leash, marking her as recently captured. The old corsair frowned at his companion. 'Yes, all right, go. Save as many as you can.' He frowned again as another wailing cry came from above. 'We shall need them to pull on the oars.'

Up on deck, the former slave had taken hold of his pleading victim's genitals with one hand, dagger raised in the other.

At that moment Khalif, followed by Zamil, appeared on deck.

'Stop!' shouted the Moor. 'I want no more killing.'

The would-be executioner, bloodlust unquenched, turned angrily. '*Who* says stop?' he snarled. 'For too long have I laboured under the whips of these vermin.' His voice rose with anger and frustration. 'Now I kill them!'

Khalif approached him calmly. He spoke in his normal tone yet, in the hush that had followed his appearance, his voice carried to every man on the deck.

'Killing these men serves no purpose,' he said reasonably. He stared evenly at the former slave. 'Believe me, I know how you feel, but it is not always possible to do all that we want, even when it seems justice might be served.' He gestured towards the rest of the cowering Spanish. 'These dogs will be needed at the oars if we are to fetch our prize safely to port. Also, much gold will they bring when we stand them on the auction block.' He was standing very close to the recently freed slave now, his voice lowered almost conversationally. 'The Turkish Sultan pays well for galley slaves. Believe me, chained to his oars, they will suffer much before they die.'

Still defiant, still angry, the slave was not so easily convinced. 'And who are you to deny me vengeance?' he snarled. He turned and spat at the prisoners. 'It was I, not you, who pulled on the oar. It was *my* family, not yours, who were butchered by these swine.' His face twisted in anguish as he remembered. 'My father and mother tortured; my wife and child both violated in front of my eyes!' He lifted the dagger threateningly, his voice rising as his fury mounted. 'How can you know how I feel? Every night since I have slept with their screams ringing in my ears.' He lifted the dagger further. 'I care nothing for the Turkish Sultan, nor you! I say they die, now!'

In an explosion of movement so fast that many of those watching could hardly credit it, Khalif slipped under the threatening blade, his right fist connecting solidly with the man's chin. The former slave went limp and Khalif caught him before he fell, easing him gently to the deck.

Facing the watching corsairs, Khalif spoke calmly. 'He disobeyed, yet I shall not kill him.' He indicated the cowering prisoners. 'All these vermin together are not worth his life. I know how he feels...' He held up his hands so the scars on his own wrists could be clearly seen. 'I, too, as many here know, once served on the rowing benches of the Spanish.'

For a moment there was absolute silence, then a swelling murmur of agreement from the onlookers. Khalif beckoned and Zamil stepped forward, muscles rippling in his huge frame. 'See to this man's needs,' ordered Khalif, indicating the man he had felled. 'Tend him well. We have need of such men.' He indicated the shaking, bleeding Spaniard still mounted on the plank. 'Tend to this man also, and secure the rest below. Hurry now. Soon we must be on our way.'

Earlier, Zamil had returned to the cell where Charlotte and the other girls were held, along with Khalif's shipmaster, Issa. Zamil had released the girl on the bunk while Issa dragged out the dead Spaniard. Zamil made a sharp gesture with his hand and clicked his fingers. Both Leila and Meylissah, knowing what was expected, immediately bent forward to place their foreheads slavishly to the floor. The girl who had been so abused by the *San Cristobal's* first mate also slid gingerly from the bunk to follow suit.

Charlotte, as yet untutored in such matters, remained on her knees with her terrified gaze fixed on the giant figure of the Nubian. She was trembling violently, the nine burning scarlet weals across her bottom a constant reminder that she dare not arouse her captors' anger again.

Zamil frowned and indicated the humiliating posture adopted by the other girls. 'A slave kneels thus when a master enters,' he said sternly. 'Learn quickly, or—' he

71

pointed to where the slave-whip hung on the wall.

Although not fully understanding the words, Charlotte knew enough Arabic to immediately comprehend the man's meaning. The gesture towards the whip could not be misinterpreted. And yet, despite her very natural fear of the punishing instrument, Charlotte was still not quite able to quell a rising feeling of anger that such an ignorant barbarian should hold power over her: anger at the perfidious Salim bin Rahdi, better known as Khalif Barbar, whose treachery had brought her to such a predicament, and anger at herself as she remembered the attraction she had once felt for he who she now perceived as her betrayer. Still, she must not argue or show defiance. Embarrassed and humiliated as she was, she was determined to give these men no more reason to punish her with the terrible whip. And so she obeyed. As gracefully as she could, trembling and fighting to suppress her feelings of repugnance, she too bent forward to press her nose to the grimy deck.

For long moments, while the men made rude and intimate observations regarding the naked bodies of the girls, all three remained as they were, Charlotte sensing rather than seeing Issa and Zamil moving around behind them as if to view them from all angles. Charlotte reddened once more as she realised just how much might now be seen of her most intimate parts.

'Rise.'

As if in a dream Charlotte heard the casual command and tried to obey. She promptly overbalanced, finding out immediately that, without practice, it is extremely difficult to arise from the ritual obeisance position with hands tied behind one's back. Leila and Meylissah accomplished it gracefully, the girl from the bunk rather more awkwardly, while Charlotte only managed to sprawl forward clumsily on her belly.

Zamil was entirely unsympathetic. With an impatient growl he tangled his fingers in her tumbled hair, callously ignoring his victim's scream of pain as he hauled her back to her knees.

Charlotte's eyes were full of tears, her scalp feeling as if it had come free of her skull. Desperately, she tried to reason with him again.

'P-please,' she stammered, 'release me now. Your reward will be great. Please, Zamil. You know I am not a slave.'

'So,' marvelled the Nubian, 'you still think yourself not to be a slave?' He snorted. 'Why should you think so? You are chained, are you not? You are naked, are you not? Have you not already admitted that you are a slut – and felt the kiss of the whip for disobedience?'

Charlotte's gaze swung to where the instrument of pain hung on the wall and she shuddered, her buttocks contracting involuntarily.

Zamil grinned. 'To me,' he continued, 'you look to be good slave-flesh; juicy and ripe for the block.' He walked round her, eyeing her with a professional detachment somewhat belied by the unmistakable look of lust in his eyes.

Charlotte squirmed with embarrassment. 'Please, Zamil,' she whispered, 'do not look at me so.'

A thought seemed suddenly to strike the Nubian and he knelt down beside her. 'Are you still virgin, slut?' he asked, reaching between her legs as if to confirm his suspicion.

It was at this last indignity that Charlotte finally lost control. 'Don't... *don't*!' she screamed, almost out of her mind with rage and embarrassment. So incensed was she that, without regard for the consequences, she did the only thing left to her – she bent her head and sank her teeth into the flesh of the man's arm.

With a grunt of pain Zamil prised her teeth loose, then slapped her hard. Head spinning from the force of the blow, she still managed to glare up at him defiantly.

'You – you animal!' she gasped.

He growled and made a motion towards the whip hanging

by its loop on the wall. Meylissah gasped and Charlotte's heart nearly stopped. What had she done? Any more lashes from that terrible instrument would more than likely be the finish of her. Yet still her rebellious spirit would not allow her to retreat, even though she knew what would result from her defiance.

There was silence for a moment, both man and girl locking eyes in a battle of wills. Then Zamil scowled and reached for the whip. 'It seems you have learned nothing, slut,' he hissed. 'Have I not warned you that disobedience brings much pain?'

Charlotte's face blanched.

'For the moment I have not the time to teach you the true meaning of obedience,' the Nubian went on. 'Your chastisement, therefore, will have to wait a short while. In the meantime, you may reflect on your misdeeds – and the punishment to come.' With this he reached out to take her by the hair in one hand while, with the other, he hung the terrible weapon around her neck.

Face white, Charlotte stared up at him, defiance shining in her eyes despite her fear. The leather was cold against her flesh, the three terrible thongs hanging down between her breasts. Still she could not surrender. 'Go to hell!' she whispered.

There was another distinct gasp from Meylissah.

Zamil scowled again. 'I shall return shortly, oh arrogant one, to teach you the error of your ways. And be assured, when I have finished, your pride and arrogance will be gone – and you may wish yourself in hell!' With that parting promise, he turned on his heel and left the cabin.

The tall Tunisian, Issa, looked down at the distraught Charlotte and shook his head. 'I think perhaps you will regret that bite and your words of defiance,' he said nonchalantly. 'Zamil does not forget, nor forgive, very easily.' He turned to Leila and Meylissah. 'Stand up, slaves,' he ordered. 'What are your names?' he asked quietly, untying their wrists.

Both girls gasped with relief as their hands were freed.

'Names?' he barked.

'My – my master called me Leila, lord,' replied the Málagan slaver's dancer, rubbing at the marks on her wrists.

'Meylissah, lord,' replied Meylissah.

The tall corsair reached out with both hands, weighing and testing a breast with each. Releasing Meylissah's, he continued to toy gently with the gold ring transfixing Leila's nipple. She suffered his touch without protest, even to the point of thrusting out her breasts for his touch. Issa smiled in satisfaction. 'Goodly names, slaves. They suit you well.' He jerked a commanding finger. 'Go you now to the great cabin in the stern. Hurry! You shall wait on my lord Dragut and Khalif.'

He had hardly finished speaking before both girls were heading towards the door. He grinned in satisfaction, then flicked a glance at Charlotte and sighed. Still hot with anger, Charlotte's tearstained gaze met the Tunisian's defiantly. With a frown, he touched the whip hanging around her neck. 'Reflect on your misdeeds, *nasrani*,' he said softly. 'Later, Zamil will use this to stripe your white hide from head to toe. Then perhaps you will learn obedience to the will of men.'

He turned to the girl who had been so cruelly tied on the bunk. 'Your name?' he asked.

'Fleur, lord,' she replied.

'Are you obedient?'

'Oh yes, lord.'

'Very well then. Remain as you are.'

The braided leather of the whip was cold against Charlotte's neck as Issa left the cabin, reminding her yet again of what she had become: just a thing regarded as little more than an animal to be bought and sold, or even whipped, at the whim of these terrible men. She had a long while to consider the injustice of her situation. Zamil, evidently, had other duties to perform in preference to the punishment of a rebellious slave.

Even as Charlotte reflected on her position, the girl whose breasts had been so abused whispered a question. '*Qui est vous?*'

Charlotte was frightened. Zamil had forbidden her to talk, yet she felt she must answer.

'Charlotte,' she whispered back.

'*Anglaise?*'

'Yes… I am English.'

'I am French. Name Fleur. My captain call me Frenchy.'

'Your captain?' whispered Charlotte, her appalled gaze fixed on the bruised breasts. 'He did that to you?'

The girl smiled wanly. 'Oh, no. He is Captain Hawkins of English ship *Bonaventure*. Spanish catch him. Now he slave, too… chained to oar.'

Charlotte's gaze travelled over the welted flesh. 'The brutes. How could anyone be so cruel?'

Fleur cupped her breasts tenderly. 'Most not bad,' she whispered, 'just use for pleasure, not want to hurt.' She looked down at the bruises and winced. 'But first mate… he is devil! Want hurt Frenchy all time!'

'First mate? The – the dead man?'

The French girl nodded weakly.

'Who – who killed him? Was it Zamil?'

'Zamil… you mean big black man?'

Charlotte nodded.

'No. It was another… big man with blue eyes.'

Charlotte took another deep breath. Khalif – it must have been he!

Suddenly there was a bloodcurdling scream from the upper deck, followed by the desperate sounds of a man pleading for his life. The pleadings stopped abruptly to howls and cheers from the pirates and Charlotte froze with dread. She looked at Fleur, who was also white-faced with fear. Trembling, Charlotte shrank back against the wall as the wailing began again. The screams, wilder and more terrified this time, were now accompanied by raucous cheers as if from a watching audience. She tried not to think what they might be doing to the poor man.

Minutes – or was it hours? – later, the yelling stopped. She listened intently. A man spoke in a threatening tone and there was another despairing cry. Then the shrieks started again. Another victim, she realised. Mercifully, this time the noise did not go on as long as the others. There was a harsh shout and her heart jumped. It was Khalif's voice, she was sure of it. A man shouted back angrily and she heard a fierce argument going on. Then came the distinct sound of a scuffle and the thump of a body falling to the deck.

Silence.

Then Khalif's voice once, this time obviously giving orders. She strained her ears, but could not make out the words.

The noise of men moving purposefully about shipboard business began: blocks creaked; sails cracked and snapped in the wind. Charlotte tried to shift her position as painful cramps in her thighs and calves threatened to overcome her fear of what might happen to her if she straightened her legs. She listened desperately to the sounds filtering down from the deck and tried to imagine what was happening. How long would it be before the Nubian came for her? And how would she be able to bear further punishment from the terrible whip?

Orders were shouted, spars rattled and canvas flapped. Then she heard the rumble of wood on wood as the oars were run out. Measured footfalls began on the catwalk between the rowers and a deep voice called out the cadence. Charlotte's heart thumped in her chest as the ship's previous belly-churning, wallowing motion changed to a more comfortable sway. They were under way, but to who knew where?

Some time later the sound of a key turning in the lock set Charlotte's nerves jangling. Despite her previous resolve, she found her limbs trembling and for a moment she thought she might faint. Now would come the reckoning. Whatever had possessed her? she thought despairingly. Why could she not have just submitted to his touch? The whipping she had already received had been dreadful, almost unbearable, yet still she had been unable to control her temper. God in Heaven, what punishment would the Nubian inflict upon her now? Shaking, she bent her head to the floor in the humiliating posture Zamil had previously demanded, eyes squeezed tightly closed as she awaited her fate.

Footsteps approached and stopped in front of her.

'You may rise now, Charlotte,' said a familiar voice, and she lifted her head to see Khalif standing there.

Charlotte shook her head hopelessly. 'I am not your enemy, Khalif,' she blurted. 'Why do you treat me like this?'

'Your uncle treats with the Spanish and you travel on Spanish ships at your convenience. This makes you my enemy.' He smiled, eyes feasting on her naked body. 'You are also very beautiful. What do you expect? You are a prize of war, Charlotte.'

Filled with a righteous indignation, Charlotte bridled immediately. Despite her previous terror, she was unable to help herself. This was the man who was the root cause of all that had happened. She hated him. Her voice shook and tears filled her eyes, yet still she tried to convey her contempt. 'I shall not be a prize for you. On deck my courage failed me, but it will not again. I will die before I submit to you or any of your pigs.'

Khalif frowned. 'Zamil thinks you should be whipped,' he said softly. 'Perhaps he is right.'

Charlotte's heart quailed at the thought, yet still she could not retreat. 'And will you whip me yourself, brave captain?' she whispered. 'Whipping a defenceless girl is what I would expect from traitorous scum like you.'

Khalif's smile faded a little at the last insult. Reaching out, he lifted the whip from between Charlotte's breasts and hung it casually back on its hook. 'Are you all right?' he asked, turning to Fleur.

She nodded weakly. '*Oui, m'sieur.*'

'Good. Get back up on your bunk and rest. Someone will come for you later.' Turning back to Charlotte, he continued, 'Traitor, my lady? Traitor?' There was a mocking tone to his voice. 'Scum? Possibly.' He lifted his arms so she could see the scars on his wrists. 'Sworn enemy of those who slaughtered my family and condemned me to the rowing benches? Yes. But traitor? I think not.'

Charlotte did not trust herself to speak further as he lifted her to her feet. Her legs were a little unsteady and she was forced to lean against him for balance.

His gaze took in the tears on her cheeks without comment. Then he took off his cloak and wrapped it around her nakedness. 'Come with me,' he ordered quietly.

Waiting in the great stern cabin, Dragut Bey had listened as the cheering and savage shouts for vengeance from the main deck subsided. He was keenly aware of the high regard in which the corsairs held his second-in-command. If they listened to anyone, aside from himself, of course it would be Khalif.

At that moment he was examining, with some curiosity, one of the two longbows taken in the raid. He had managed with great effort to string the thing, but had then found it almost impossible to draw it back properly. He shook his head in exasperation and threw it angrily into one corner. What was the use of such an awkward weapon? Much better and easier to use were the corsair crossbows.

The old pirate held out his cup and immediately a naked slave girl moved to replenish it. She hardly seemed to aim the spout, yet managed to fill the cup perfectly, spilling not a drop of the precious liquid. Then, eyes lowered submissively, she set down the pot and resumed her kneeling position.

Dragut ignored her as if she were part of the furniture. Hundreds – thousands, in fact – just like her were held captive all across Islam. Indeed, the girl's beauty notwithstanding, there was nothing particularly remarkable about her except that, on closer examination, it might be seen that the pert nipples crowning the girl's breasts so beautifully had at some time been pierced and set with decorative gold rings, a practice certainly not common for a serving slave. Also evident was the fact that the girl's outer labia had been similarly treated and at present bore the weight of a small golden padlock. The girl was, of course, no ordinary slave. This was the fat Málagan's favoured Egyptian, the trained dancing girl and pleasure slave.

The door opened and Khalif entered the cabin.

'That was well done, my friend,' said Dragut cheerfully.

Khalif grunted and sat down. Immediately another girl, similarly naked, moved to kneel at his side. This one, too, was dark-haired and very beautiful, though her nipples and labia bore no rings or padlock. Khalif's gaze fell on the discarded bow and one eyebrow lifted, but he said nothing.

'To business, then,' said Dragut, settling himself more comfortably. 'One or two things have happened since last we met.'

Khalif held out his cup for Meylissah to fill. He seemed not even to notice the girl's action, taking it for granted that she would perform her task perfectly.

'I give thanks,' said Dragut, lifting his own cup to his lips and drinking deeply, 'that I was able to hold station long enough to keep our rendezvous.'

'I too, my friend,' returned Khalif. 'These damned Spanish are no hands at sailing, or time-keeping, for that matter.'

Dragut scratched his groin reflectively. 'It seems a new

80

Bey rules in Tunis, a man called Mulay Aruj. He arrived some months ago with the Sultan's warrant and a strong force of Janissaries.'

Khalif leaned forward. 'Mulay Aruj?' he murmured. 'I have heard of him.'

Dragut, mouth half-full, nodded. 'A devil in human form, from all accounts,' he mumbled. 'Murder and torture go hand in hand under his rule. Tunis groans under the weight of it. By his order, just a month ago, two corsairs were impaled on the city wall for refusing to turn over their cargoes to him.'

Khalif's expression darkened and his brows knitted together in a frown. 'How can this be? Tunis has always been a haven for us.'

'No longer, I'm afraid. Mulay, it seems, is a very successful slaver and, as you know, our Sultan cares little who supplies him with new girlflesh. Now, with a royal warrant in his hand, all corsair ships in Tunis must serve the new Bey or take the consequences. He has his own auction house and sends the pick of female slaves to the royal harem. He also demands and takes a fifth of everything brought into port. All who oppose him are killed.' Dragut turned his head and spat. 'Not a month ago he sent emissaries to me demanding that we, too, join his alliance on pain of death.'

'And how did you respond?'

The old corsair shrugged his shoulders. 'As you might expect. I sent the messengers' heads back in a basket. So be warned. For the present you and I are no longer welcome in Tunis.' His face lightened a little. 'Still, there are plenty of other ports.' He leaned forward and dropped his voice. 'More importantly, I received certain dispatches two days ago. We are summoned to a meeting of the Brotherhood.'

'Do you know why?'

'I am not sure, though it seems probable that it has something to do with this Mulay Aruj and what is going on in Tunis.' He coughed and then went on, almost as an afterthought. 'Oh – and there was something about a big Spanish war fleet gathering.'

'A war fleet?' mused Khalif. 'What does that mean, I wonder?'

'I don't know. We will surely learn more when we get there.' He looked at Khalif seriously. 'The messenger was most clear about the urgency, so I suggest we make all haste. In Algiers we should receive a pretty price for the King of Spain's great galleass and crew.' He reached out absently to fondle one of Leila's gold-tipped breasts and, instinctively, she squared her shoulders and thrust them out, welcoming his touch.

'What about the *San Cristobal's* cannon?' asked Khalif.

'The cannon? Do you want to keep them?' Dragut frowned.

Khalif nodded decisively. 'From what you say about this Mulay Aruj, not to mention a Spanish war fleet, I think we should. Added to those we already have at the fortress, they might serve us well. And if we take them into Algiers, the Dey will surely want them for himself.'

Dragut made up his mind quickly. 'I agree. Perhaps you should take them to the fortress, then follow on as quickly as you can to Algiers. Given the urgency of the dispatches, I think one of us should get there as quickly as possible. It does give us something of a problem, though. Swords and crossbows are all right for close quarters, but the *San Cristobal* without cannon is a ripe plum ready to be picked. What happens if you run into a Spanish patrol?'

Khalif pursed his lips. 'Not likely, but... Yes, you are right. I will keep six of the bigger guns aboard, just in case, and Jahwar can escort us in *Persephone*. Then the Dey shall have them as a gift and not be displeased.'

Dragut nodded slowly.

Khalif held out his cup and Meylissah quickly filled it once more.

'Which brings us to another matter,' said Dragut, now reaching forward to fondle expertly between Leila's conveniently positioned thighs. She writhed silently as the old corsair's fingers penetrated her lower body to investigate the depths of her moist passage, yet still managed somehow not to spill any of the liquid she was pouring.

Khalif looked at the old corsair questioningly.

'Jahwar now bears you a grudge.' Dragut frowned. 'I can understand how you feel, but did you have to take the English milady from him at sword-point? Juicy she may be, but you know how touchy these Berbers are about such things. He will find it difficult to forgive.'

Khalif smiled grimly. 'The idiot was about to cut her throat,' he replied. 'And as you observed earlier, there is no profit in dead slave girls.'

Dragut's fingernail scraped Leila's clitoris and her hips jerked involuntarily. 'You'll sell her then?' he asked mildly.

Khalif's tone was casual. 'Perhaps. Her ransom would certainly be high.'

Dragut sighed. 'Well… she is your captive. You must do as you wish, but watch your back from now on. The Berber is a dangerous man to cross.'

Khalif looked unworried. 'Perhaps. But he is too good a man to lose unless I have to. I will apologise as soon as I can and I'm sure he will see sense. If not…' He shrugged and placed a hand on the hilt of his scimitar.

Dragut laughed and, removing his fingers from the writhing Leila's sexual passage, slapped her hard on the rear. He grinned at her yelp of pain. 'Very well, I leave the matter to you, then.'

Leila rubbed ruefully at her reddened bottom.

'Thine is a nice body, girl,' commented Dragut casually.

'Thank you, master,' she whispered, then gasped as a calloused finger probed none too gently between her bottom cheeks.

Dragut scowled and instantly she froze, proffering herself

even more blatantly. Placated, the pirate lord removed his questing finger. 'Ah, well,' he yawned. 'Time to go.' He got to his feet and gathered his cloak around him. 'It has been a long night, and a busy one… and we both have a long way to journey.'

Khalif, too, stood up and the two men embraced. Together they left the cabin and walked to the ship's side. 'Take care, old friend,' said Khalif as Dragut swung a leg over the rail. 'Do not get caught by the Spanish!'

Dragut chuckled. 'I will see you in Algiers. Meantime, let the Spanish take care. Allah protects me, as he does all true believers.' Just before swinging down to the deck of the Arab galley with an agility that might have done justice to a man half his age, the old corsair turned back to his companion. 'I am curious, my son,' he said in a low voice. 'The English milady… you really do not want her?'

The younger man shrugged his shoulders unconcernedly. 'Perhaps – perhaps not. I have not yet made up my mind,' he replied.

Dragut grunted. 'Well, as you decide. Ransom her, sell her, keep her… it is your choice!' He winked and smiled. 'No need to deny yourself, though. Whatever you decide, it is well known that the Dey is not particularly interested in virgins – if, indeed, she is one.' He gestured back towards the cabin. 'In fact, do as you wish with all of them!' He groaned theatrically, lowering himself over the ship's side. 'Allah knows, I grow too old for such juicy dishes.'

Now it was Khalif's turn to smile. Old or not, Dragut Bey still possessed an unquenchable zest for the pleasures of the flesh – as his seventy-odd concubines and twice as many children testified.

A Girl Finds a Master

In the *San Cristobal's* great stern cabin, wrists confined in iron manacles, Charlotte knelt at Khalif Barbar's side as he reclined on a pile of cushions set against the wall under the cabin windows.

On a low table, to one side, stood a tray containing sweetmeats and the almost mandatory long-spouted jug of mint tea. The large ports stood open and a cool breeze gently caressed her brow.

Yet again she was naked.

Of the three other girls there was no sign. Were they, perhaps, being similarly humiliated by other corsairs? she wondered bitterly, her mind a riot of confused and frightening thoughts. 'Slave', Zamil had called her. Her mind rejected the thought as unthinkable, yet how could she, or the others, resist whatever these men wanted to do to them?

'Please,' she had asked with as much dignity as she could muster when Khalif had taken back his cloak, 'may I have my clothes?'

His reply had been short and uncompromising. 'Clothes are not necessary for a slave.'

She shook her head hopelessly and shivered as he continued to look at her, her mind only now beginning to accept what had previously been unthinkable. She thought back to all that had happened: her close encounter with death at the hands of the giant Berber; being stripped and paraded for all to see; the whipping by Zamil; being forced to kneel as she was. Everything served to underline the undeniable fact that this unfeeling brute was, to all intents and purposes, her master.

Was it only yesterday she had insulted this young man? Now she was naked and totally helpless before him. To her utter shame and embarrassment, she suddenly realised she was sexually aroused. Under Khalif's gaze something was happening: an emotion or feeling until now unconfessed, yet over which she had little or no control, was taking hold of her body. Blushing, she felt the heat in her lower body; a sensation fed and stirred by her tacit acceptance of sexual subjugation at his hands.

He examined her candidly and her breath came faster. Could he know what was happening to her? The feeling was strong and growing; it was something primaeval, something to do with her very femaleness. She could feel the moistening of her loins and was powerless to prevent it. The seconds stretched on and still he continued to gaze. Unconsciously, her breath became shallower and more urgent. Her heart beat ever faster.

Khalif smiled knowingly and Charlotte felt her face and neck turning crimson. He knew entirely the effect he was having on her. How easily had he aroused her, just by looking...

Defensively, she raised her chained hands in front of her breasts. 'Let me go,' she pleaded weakly, blinking back tears of shame. 'Please... you know my uncle will pay you well for my release.'

He said nothing.

'You say the Spaniards murdered your family and made you a galley slave. But I am English – not Spanish. What have I ever done to you?' She shook her head, angry again. 'I will *not* be a slave, to you or to anyone else.' Her voice grew stronger. 'My uncle will have your head for this.'

He considered her grimly and Charlotte's heart thumped in her chest. Had she gone too far? She did not wish to feel the shocking pain of the whip again. What he said next, however, was as shocking as it was unexpected.

'Are you a virgin, Charlotte?'

Her mouth fell open at the obscene intimacy of the question.

'Answer,' he pressed.

She looked away, cheeks flaming, and refused to answer.

'Shall I call Zamil?' he asked casually.

Her head jerked around and she trembled at the thought of that terrible instrument of pain, knowing she would do absolutely anything to avoid it.

'Answer me,' he ordered. 'Are you a virgin?'

She closed her eyes. Humiliating as it would be, she had no choice but to answer him. 'Yes,' she whispered wretchedly.

He nodded. 'I thought so.'

Suddenly she was gasping. Without warning he had reached out to touch her. Exploring, caressing, squeezing, hands delving between her thighs to take incredible liberties with her body. She could not stop him. Her girlish muscles were as nothing in the face of his powerful male strength. Under his touch her hips widened and moved of their own volition, the suddenly slick touch of her telling its own story.

She moaned in shame as he took the hand away.

He held up his fingers, still wet with her juices. 'You see, milady or no, you are still a female like other females.' He smiled. 'A slave to men and your own appetites.'

She shook her head weakly.

'Come closer,' he commanded.

She did not move.

'Perhaps Zamil can convince you to obey,' he said softly.

Her heart thumped, yet somewhere deep inside, still not recognised fully for what it was, that other treacherous feeling once more began to take root. She trembled. Was there not a part of her that wanted – no, needed – to surrender to this man? Was it merely the memory of Zamil's whip that prompted her, or was it something else; something in her own psyche? Not that this beast would be averse to the sight of her writhing under the lash. Oh, how vile he was! How could he do this to her?

Nervously, she drew closer to him. She could almost smell her own arousal.

He indicated the tray on the small table at his side. 'Can you serve?'

Trembling visibly, she nevertheless managed a comprehensible reply. 'I think so.'

'You think so – what?'

For the tiniest moment she was puzzled, then understanding dawned. By her own words she was now to acknowledge his mastery of her.

He repeated the question. 'You think so *what*, slave?'

There was no escape. The swine! How she wished she had the strength to withstand him. Had God but granted her one wish, Khalif would have been struck dead by a thunderbolt at that very moment. Yet despite her anger the heat in her loins mocked her silently. And if she disobeyed, what then? Another whipping? The very thought chilled her blood.

'I think so... master.' The words were like bile in her mouth.

He smiled. 'Serve, then,' he ordered, holding out his cup.

Angrily, she reached for the long-spouted jug of mint tea and poured into the proffered vessel. To his surprise she did so perfectly, handling the awkward artefact as if she had been doing it all her life.

'You have poured before,' he observed calmly.

Despite her embarrassment, Charlotte managed to regain a little poise. Whatever he did to her, however much he humiliated her, it could be no worse than Zamil's terrible whip. Even so, her dented pride demanded that she not be too obsequious. She lifted her hands to display the iron manacles.

'Not with my hands chained,' she replied bitterly.

He frowned a little at her tone.

'My maid, Meylissah, taught me,' she continued, somewhat hastily. 'Your jug is no more difficult than hers.'

He sighed and waited.

She knew what he wanted and knew she could not resist. Shamefaced, still she felt her treacherous body oiling itself.

She shivered, not just from fear.

'Master,' she finally whispered.

Nonchalantly, he took a small key from within his robe and, bending forward, unlocked and removed the manacles from her wrists.

Charlotte rubbed her wrists in relief, then looked up in surprise as Khalif abruptly changed the subject. 'This Meylissah... you and she are close?'

'Yes,' she whispered.

Khalif scowled and once again her heart missed a beat.

'Master,' she repeated.

'She has served you a long time?'

'Not long. She was a gift from Sheikh Omar, my uncle's friend in Valletta, yet she is as my sister.' She blushed inwardly even as she spoke. She did think a lot of Meylissah, it was true – but not as a sister!

This time he did not comment on her omission and, in that second, she was tempted to bargain with him.

'Please,' she whispered, 'do not make me a slave, I beg you. Ransom me, please. You have said I am beautiful. I will do anything... anything you want.' Her heart was thumping and once more she felt the moistness beginning to pool between her legs.

Khalif's voice became firm again, dashing her hopes and expectations to the floor with a few well-chosen words. 'Do not try to bargain with me, Charlotte. Your offer means nothing. You are my captive now – my slave. I can do with you exactly as I wish... and believe me, I shall.'

She opened her mouth as if to argue, and he held up a hand to silence her.

'Do you understand?' he asked grimly.

Charlotte's heart sank. What was the use of arguing or trying to bargain with this man? For the present she was just what he proclaimed her to be: a slave. 'Yes, I understand,' she whispered bitterly, defeat showing at last on her face.

Once more he waited pointedly for her to complete the

sentence.

'Master,' she whispered. She held her breath as he reached for her breasts, palms brushing gently across her nipples, which were already fully erect. Then she breathed out noisily as one hand swept down to her stomach and beyond. Frightened again, she grasped his wrist with both hands in an attempt to stop a further advance.

'Don't… please…' she begged.

The wrathful look on his face was enough to still her protests and she relaxed her grip. Slowly, reluctantly, she widened her thighs to allow him easier access. Not satisfied with this, he removed his sash and took her arms behind her back, swiftly binding her wrists together. Then he began to caress her again, sliding two fingers deep into her already moist tunnel, thumb dextrously teasing her rapidly stiffening clitoris.

'Oh, oh…' she panted, her body already beginning to move of its own accord under his knowing touch.

Confidently, Khalif continued to delve as he wished, Charlotte's thighs widening even more as, giving up the unequal struggle, she abandoned herself to his caresses.

'Oh, God… please, oh please,' she moaned, leaning back, body thrust out, knuckles white, hands clenching and unclenching spasmodically behind her back as his fingers brought her pleasures and feelings more powerful and erotic than any she had known, even with Meylissah. She was totally helpless, her defences in tatters. He had complete control of her, bringing her closer and closer to the orgasm she fought against, yet sought so desperately. Mouth open, breathing heavily, her eyes stared wildly and the sweat began to shine on her body.

Three times, cleverly, he brought her to the brink, each time pulling back to stop just short of the sexual fulfilment she so desperately craved.

Then he took his hands away and leaned back to shed his robes. Shaking as if with the palsy, she looked at him, fascinated, as he undressed. The sight of his powerful body mesmerised her and she gasped at the erect evidence of his desire for her, seeing in her mind's eye her own soft nakedness spread open for his conquest. He was so big, how could she possibly accommodate him? Yet she knew she wanted to, more than anything. She breathed deeply, suddenly dizzy with the strength of her desire for this man who now literally held her very life in his hands.

'Come here, slave,' he growled, holding out his arms and lying back on the cushions.

Heart thumping alarmingly in her chest, she trembled as she lowered herself into his encircling arms. He pulled her close and she felt the hardness of his body against her own. He kissed her and she shook uncontrollably. Despite her natural apprehension at what was about to happen, she was unable to protest. His kiss became more demanding, forcing a response from her. His tongue entered her mouth to fight a duel with hers, the very intimacy of the act serving to inflame her even more. She moaned huskily as he began to caress her, thighs already moist with escaping juices. His hands moved to her breasts and her nipples hardened in natural response. His fingers closed on them roughly and she was immediately lost. Lifting her breasts to his touch she surrendered completely, kissing him back with rising passion.

She jerked, panic-stricken for a moment, as his erection brushed her thigh. He kissed her gently and her qualms dissolved as quickly as her passions rose. She needed to feel him inside her. After everything he had done, her body would not be denied; she was as much a slave to her own passions as she was to him. Truly, at that moment, he was her master and, though she could barely admit it, she loved it.

Squeezing her sensitive nipples as she writhed under him, he kissed her over and over. She thrusting her breasts upwards to welcome the sweet torture. Once more his tongue sought the inside of her mouth as hers, in turn, sought his. Then, taking his time, he gradually manoeuvred her so that she lay on her back, and he partly on top of her. She took his weight easily and, unasked, opened her legs wide so he could lie between them. Again his manhood brushed the entrance to her virgin channel. The thick staff parted the lips of her sex and she moaned. The sound encouraged him. It was not a frightened sound, but one of rising pleasure and passion.

Kissing her savagely he reached down between them to part the fleshy lips and thrust himself inside. Gradually, a little at a time, he slid into her until at length he was three-quarters encased in her tight but welcoming channel.

He reached between their joined bodies once more to caress her clitoris. She looked up at him wide-eyed, breathless as he moved sharply and decisively to impale her completely with one powerful lunge. Ignoring the sudden pain, completely lost to the sensations gripping her body and mind, Charlotte sought to bring him even further inside her. Crying out with passion she moved in time with him, instinctively bringing her legs up and round to make a saddle on which he could ride.

Mouths locked together in a kiss, they moved on together towards climax. Charlotte gasped wildly, surrendering utterly to his maleness as he continued to lift her to heights of eroticism she had not known could exist.

The feeling was far too intense to last long. Crying out her need, bucking and twisting under him, Charlotte felt her orgasm burst upon her; her frantic movements sending him, too, over the edge.

Slowly then, eyes wide in wonder and delight, she came down from her peak, relaxing unconsciously as he continued to move within her. Gently he kissed her again, her lips parting readily under the pressure of his tongue.

He pulled back, rising on his elbows to look down at her. Tearfully she gazed up at him, then lifted her lips for a further kiss. He obliged, then pulled her close, cradling her possessively against his chest. She laid her head on his shoulder with a sigh, wriggling as close as she could. Head buried on his shoulder, she murmured something.

'What?' he growled.

She looked up at him, eyes heavy-lidded from spent passion. 'I didn't know…' she whispered. 'I had no idea…' She struggled for the right words to express her feelings.

He smiled. 'Go to sleep now,' he ordered. 'It has been a long day and I wish to rest.'

Until he mentioned sleep, Charlotte had not realised how tired she was. As was Khalif. Almost within moments of her laying her head on his shoulder, they were both asleep.

The next she knew she was being wakened by Khalif's gentle caresses. Seeing the lustful look on his face she immediately turned on to her back, widening her thighs in invitation. He smiled and shook his head, lifting her so she sat astride him, hands still tied behind her back. Slowly and carefully, making sure of her pleasure, he took her again. This time he was very thorough, taking his time and guiding her to several climaxes. And, once more, as her sexual appetite took control, Charlotte surrendered herself completely.

Later, lying in his arms with her head on his shoulder, she slept again. She did not stir, not even when he left her embrace to go on deck.

Several hours later Charlotte awoke to the appetising smell of spicy food as both Leila and Meylissah entered, accompanied by a grinning lad of about sixteen. Leila was carrying a tray containing several delicious looking dishes. Both girls were still unclothed, and Charlotte could see that the little golden padlock no longer swung between Leila's thighs.

'This is Achmed,' Meylissah said softly with a respectful nod in the direction of the boy. 'By the Rais' command, he

93

is now our keeper and we must obey him in all things.' Turning her head so that the boy could not see, she made a silent grimace with her mouth. 'He has the power to punish if we disobey,' she whispered softly.

'Rais?' asked Charlotte.

'Means "lord",' interjected Leila. 'Rais is Lord Khalif. You understand?'

Eyes wide, Charlotte nodded, noting with trepidation the silver-handled whip tucked into the sash holding up the youth's ragged pantaloons. She found it difficult to speak. Submitting to the likes of Zamil was one thing, but to be at the mercy of a mere boy was the final indignity.

Meylissah smiled gently, helping Charlotte to sit up so she could untie the sash still confining her hands. 'Rais Khalif take pleasure with mistress last night?' she asked softly.

There was no point in denying it. Red-faced, Charlotte nodded, feeling the lingering, somewhat bruised sensation inside her sex channel and the clinging stickiness at the juncture of her thighs.

Leila moved forward, pouring a cup of dark liquid from a small jug as she did so. 'Drink now,' she instructed, offering the cup to the somewhat bemused Charlotte. 'Maybe make safe from baby.'

Charlotte, who until that moment had not given the matter a moment's thought, felt her heart lurch at the thought that she might already be carrying Khalif's child. She raised the cup to her lips and took a mouthful. The liquid tasted quite pleasant, though a trifle bitter.

'Make me safe?' she whispered. 'What is it?'

Leila looked serious. 'This "cup of roots". Girl drink, most time no have baby.'

Meylissah smiled and a bemused Charlotte shook her head. She had never heard of such a thing. Still, if the other girls believed it, it could do no harm to do as Leila suggested.

Leila still hadn't finished. 'Lay back now; show how

make safe more.'

Nonplussed at the other's matter-of-fact tone and still more than a little embarrassed at her lack of clothing, Charlotte nevertheless made no demur. Leila picked up what appeared to be a small sponge from the tray and, dipping it liberally into what remained of the dark liquid in the cup, pressed it to the blonde triangle of hair at the base of the English girl's belly.

'Open legs,' she ordered.

The watching Achmed's grin widened as, blushing a deep red, Charlotte obeyed, stifling a gasp as Leila pushed and prodded the soaking wet sponge right up inside her body.

'Lift legs now.'

Too stupefied to disobey, Charlotte lifted her legs until her knees were pressing against her breasts. Leila gave a satisfied grunt and continued to push and probe, wadding the soaking sponge deep inside the somewhat astonished girl's sexual passage.

'Is good,' grunted Leila. 'Now when Rais take pleasure, no baby comes.'

Achmed, still grinning widely, said something in a rapid Arabic dialect that Charlotte did not understand. Questioningly, she looked at Meylissah.

The Circassian looked a little uncomfortable. 'He say you make good slave, mistress. Bring much when sold.'

Charlotte let her legs drop, the colour of her face and neck betraying her lingering embarrassment at being so displayed to the watching youth.

Leila displayed no such emotion. Sitting back on her heels she helped herself to a triangle of pastry, indicating the tray with a 'you, too' gesture to Charlotte. After a moment's hesitation, mouth watering at the appetising smell, Charlotte lifted one of the triangles to her mouth and bit into the middle part as had her companion. Trying to ignore the watching lad, she tasted it. The filling, some kind of spiced ground meat, was absolutely delicious and she suddenly realised how hungry she was. Forgetting her embarrassment, she managed a shaky smile.

'This is splendid. What is it?'

'Call "brik",' mumbled Leila, mouth still half-full of her own pastry.

It was a start of sorts and from this beginning the three girls began to talk while they ate, hesitantly at first, then more freely as tensions eased. Achmed, losing interest now Charlotte's private parts were no longer so blatantly exhibited, left the cabin to pursue his other duties.

Once the ice was broken, Leila proved to be a mine of information. Most interestingly, she told Charlotte that while Redbeard journeyed to Algiers Khalif and the rest of the corsairs would first take the *San Cristobal* to a fortress somewhere in order to offload the gold and some of the ship's cannon before sailing to a rendezvous with the old corsair, when they would sell the ship and the slaves.

'How is it you know all this?' she asked.

'I listen to the Lord Dragut and the Rais,' replied Leila.

'And what about Rais Khalif?' asked Charlotte softly, a blossoming pinkness in her cheeks somewhat betraying her inner feelings. 'Who is he really? Where does he come from?'

Leila was immediately forthcoming. 'Rais is *bedu* – son of sheikh. Parents and sister killed by *nasrani* slavers when Rais just a boy. He sold as slave to very bad man. One time Rais kill bad master and escape. He join corsairs. Now adopted son of the Lord Dragut Bey.'

'*Nasrani* slavers, Leila? Where from? Were they Spanish?'

'Not know.' She managed to blush prettily. 'Zamil tell me of this when he take pleasure with me last night. He say Rais' sister cut face of slaver chief who mount her on stake as punishment.'

'Mount her? You mean impale her?'

Leila nodded gravely. 'Yes. Kill very slowly. Rais forced

to watch.'

Charlotte breathed hard, shocked into sudden appalled understanding by Leila's casual description of the girl's fate. Little wonder indeed that the enigmatic corsair hated the Spanish, if the men who had done this terrible thing to his family were of that race.

She was curious about Leila. How did the girl come to speak English so well? Meylissah, of course, had been taught by Suleiman. But surely this was not common practice. 'How is it you speak my language, Leila?' she asked. 'Have you met English people before?'

Leila frowned. 'Some… not much. Master travel plenty; many times command Leila serve sailormen. Serve French, Spanish and Portuguese, sometime English sailormen, too. Earn much silver for master; learn speak many tongues.' She smiled proudly.

Charlotte was horrified. The girl's meaning was perfectly clear. Leila's previous master had obviously not only been a slave merchant but also a whoremaster, renting out his girl's sexual services to any who would pay.

Seeing Charlotte's disquiet, Leila sought to explain. 'Leila not mind to serve sailormen,' she explained softly. 'Sailormen kind to slave girl. No hurt; give plenty sweetmeats. Plenty sailormen want buy Leila – take back to ship. Offer much gold, but master not sell.'

Charlotte's feelings showed plainly on her face and Meylissah hastened to explain further. Leila was a slave by her own admission, but from what she said she had always been well fed, most of the time clothed more than adequately, and had hardly ever suffered from lack of a place to sleep. Mostly she had been cared for and looked after like the valuable piece of property she was. So what if it was part of her duties to service a master and those others who, from time to time, he might decree? Women had served men like this since the dawn of time. Did the peasant's wife in Egypt or the Bedouin's chattel in the desert

97

live as well? No, of course not. In fact, in Meylissah's considered opinion, there were many worse things than being a slave. Women served men and, however you dressed the matter up, no man was really very much better, or worse, than the next. So why not make the best of it? It was certainly better than starving in the slums.

Charlotte sighed. It was no use arguing. Quite obviously the values which had been instilled in her since birth had no place here. 'This fortress, where is it?' she asked.

Leila shook her head. 'Not sure,' she replied. 'Island maybe… not far.'

Charlotte's expression betrayed her uneasiness. 'What else, Meylissah? Are we to be sold in Algiers, or will they keep us for themselves?'

Meylissah shook her head. 'Perhaps Leila and Meylissah sold. Not mistress,' she replied. 'Mistress maybe just held for ransom, then set free.'

'Oh, no. My uncle will surely ransom you as well… and Leila, too, if I ask.' Both girls looked pleased at the prospect and, over the next half hour or so, prompted from time to time by Charlotte, they recounted most of what they could remember from the men's conversation.

Some things remained vague, but Meylissah was certain about Dragut Bey's reference to an important meeting with the Dey of Algiers and the fact that Khalif was to follow him there after delivering the gold to this fortress, wherever that was. And it was not until Algiers that the ship, and the slaves, were to be sold.

Jahwar Takes Revenge

Any hopes Khalif might have had of a speedy passage across the Gulf were quickly dashed. Within the hour the fickle wind had backed so that even with sails close-hauled and the struggling galley-slaves whipped to maximum effort, the *San Cristobal* was able to make little headway. For two whole days the weather remained hostile and even Jahwar in the escorting *Persephone* struggled to maintain station.

Throughout this time Khalif kept his new slave close, using her whenever and however he wished. Mostly she enjoyed the usage, though there were times when, almost as if he was angry with her for some undefined reason, he took her so savagely and quickly that she was left painfully unfulfilled. Even this rough treatment still held pleasure for her. The sight of his features in the full flow of passion never failed to stir her, and the thought that it was she who provoked this apparently all-consuming desire was a ready balm for her bruised flesh.

Though she was permitted clothing during periods of exercise with the other girls on the deck, in private Khalif kept her naked most of the time; a state of affairs which, had she been asked, she would have admitted she did not really mind. It was not cold and clothes merely constituted a hindrance to his frequent demands on her body; demands which, were she honest, delighted her as much as they did him.

She did not tell him about Leila's uterine sponge which, for all this time, remained lodged deep in her body. Her feelings were confused. On the one hand it would obviously be better for her not to conceive – and yet, if it did happen, would she in truth be so unhappy about it? She was unable to deny she was already deeply in love with the man. Did he love her in return? She was not sure, yet there were indications that he cared. He was so possessive, so fiercely protective of her and, much of the time, so gentle and caring she could hardly believe he did not. And now, padlocked around her neck by his own hand, was a silver collar. She was strangely proud of this; even more so when Leila translated the script engraved at each side of the hinge, which read 'the slave of Khalif'. How could she not take it to be a declaration of his feelings for her?

Then, as she lay in his arms after a particularly exhausting bout of lovemaking, her fantasies were brutally destroyed. 'May I speak, master?' she whispered softly.

He nodded.

'What will happen when we reach Algiers?'

He frowned. 'What do you know about Algiers?' he asked sharply.

'Leila told me,' she replied in a small voice. 'She overheard your conversation with Dragut.'

He looked at her silently, his expression unreadable. For a moment she thought he was about to declare his love, then his measured reply crushed her girlish romantic hopes as savagely as if he had ground her heart under his boot. 'What will happen is what always happens,' he said slowly. 'The slaves, the ship and the cargo will be disposed of and the money divided amongst the crew, each according to his proper share.'

She flinched visibly, as if he had struck her. White-faced, she looked deep into his eyes as if searching for some inner truth which might belie what she was sure he was about to say. She could see no sign of compassion in his expression. Nevertheless, she forced herself to ask the question.

'I am a slave?'

He nodded.

'Am I also to be – disposed of?'

He looked at her angrily. 'Of all the ridiculous questions. Yes, you are to be disposed of.'

That day the weather worsened and, for many hours, Charlotte, together with Leila and the French girl, Fleur, was confined in the large stern cabin while Khalif took personal charge of the running of the ship. Meylissah was employed in the ship's galley, preparing food for the crew.

Charlotte was inconsolable, shattered by the undeniable

fact that Khalif intended to sell her despite all she had hoped. Inwardly, she berated herself for her stupidity. Of course a man like him, a corsair chief, would have his pick of beautiful slave girls; in fact, if truth be told, he probably had a whole harem of them somewhere.

Both Leila and Fleur understood their companion's distress perfectly; Leila especially. Leila had tried to tell Charlotte how lucky she had been to have her first experience with a man who had obviously been quite considerate of her inexperience, even to the point of allowing her pleasure during the act, and that many other girls, herself included, had suffered at the hands of selfish, brutal men. She had told the story of her own defloration, by the evil-smelling brothel-keeper who purchased her from her desperate parents. The painful memory still haunted her dreams. Afterwards it had been he who, grinning, had first tied her down and then, while she screamed and begged for mercy, callously pierced the tender flesh of her labia and nipples with a red-hot saddler's needle in order to fit the golden rings and padlock. Despite the fact Leila still bore those rings, Charlotte remained unconvinced that she had been more fortunate than others.

By late evening the wind began to abate and, once more able to make headway, the ship's movement took on a more comfortable motion.

The sound of the cabin door opening sent all three girls to their knees. Charlotte, desperately hoping it was Khalif come to claim her again, perhaps to tell her that he had changed his mind and that he loved her and would not sell her, was bitterly disappointed when she saw it was the young lad, Achmed, who stood in the doorway.

'Come, Leila. Zamil summons you.'

The dancer's smile lit up her face and, with a sudden flash of understanding, Charlotte realised Leila was more than happy to serve the big Nubian.

Achmed smiled at the French girl. 'And you, Fleur, there

101

is a certain English captain who seems very anxious to see you.'

Fleur's face lit up. 'Captain – my captain?' she squealed.

Achmed smiled and nodded. Turning again, he reached down to pat Charlotte gently on the head, much as one would pat a kitten or a pet dog. 'Sleep now,' he said softly. 'Maybe someone comes for you later.'

Charlotte awoke to the noise of the door opening and her heart leapt. Khalif! He had come for her! Perhaps he had changed his mind, and would now tell her that he intended to keep her for himself. Still half-asleep, she pushed back the covers.

Then a familiar, hate-filled voice made itself heard over the thumping of her heart. 'So, *nasrani*!' it whispered. 'Once again we meet, and this time there is no one to interfere.'

Terror-stricken, Charlotte looked up into the twisted, shadowy features of Jahwar, who had come so close to taking her life. She shrank back as the big hands reached down for her. 'No!' she gasped. 'Please, no!'

'Come, slave,' growled the huge Berber, 'it is time to leave.' He drew a long-bladed knife from his robe and pressed it to her throat. 'One sound – any tricks – and I send you straight to Allah. Understand?'

Charlotte groaned as, tangling his fingers in her hair, Jahwar dragged her to her feet. Where was he taking her? Where was Khalif? Where was Achmed? These and a hundred other questions ran through her brain as the tall corsair lifted her to her feet and opened the cabin door. The answer to one question lay outside on the deck. Achmed, a pool of blood at the side of his head, lay still in a crumpled heap; unconscious or dead, she couldn't tell.

Swiftly and silently Jahwar pushed her forward, past the inert body of another corsair, who was obviously one of the deck guards. She looked back at the ship's tiller. Another body lay there. At the other end of the ship a light gleamed from the foredeck cabin and, behind the half-open door, Charlotte could hear the buzz of conversation. She hesitated for a moment, thinking she might scream, then Jahwar's blade pricked at her throat, urging her forward. It was no use; if she tried to raise the alarm she would be dead in seconds. At the ship's side she looked down and, as her eyes became more accustomed to the darkness, she saw a corsair galley drawn tight alongside.

'Quickly,' hissed the Berber, thrusting a stout rope into her hands. 'Over the side. Your companion is already my prisoner. No tricks now, or you both die.'

With a shiver Charlotte took hold of the rope. The Berber meant every word; she could see it engraved on his dark, implacable face. Momentarily she wondered who he meant by 'companion': was it Meylissah, Fleur or Leila? Obediently she swung her legs over the side and slithered down the rope, straight into the arms of a waiting corsair.

With a satisfied grunt Jahwar followed. Whispered orders were given, ropes cast loose and, using the oars as poles, they pushed away from the *San Cristobal's* side. Commanding her tersely to be quiet, Jahwar shoved Charlotte to her knees and took the tiller, softly calling out the beat as the sweeps bit into the waves. Charlotte knelt on the planked deck of the galley, shivering in the cold night air. Her heart sank as the dark bulk of the ship faded into the night.

Jahwar jerked a thumb at Charlotte. 'Hang this slut from the prow with the other one,' he ordered.

Charlotte suppressed a scream as she was jerked to her feet and frog-marched forward to where Meylissah, as naked as herself, was hung by her hands and feet out over the water. Swiftly, two corsairs tied Charlotte's arms and legs together behind the carved post, then turned her so she, too, hung helplessly out over the water, back bent like a bow, side by side with her former body slave. The ropes at her wrists and ankles were cruelly tight and it was not long before pins and needles, then cramps, began to torment her limbs.

Hours passed and still the girls hung there, until eventually Charlotte drifted into a trance-like state where time seemed to stand still and the pain in her limbs was but a distant memory. Then, as the moon came out from behind the scurrying clouds, the sound of a furious commotion and men shouting filtered slowly into her consciousness. Painfully, she lifted her head and saw they were sailing on a parallel course to the *San Cristobal*, no more than forty yards or so away. Furious figures crowded the rail of the great galleass and the yawning muzzles of cannon became clear.

Straining her head around, Charlotte's heart leapt as she made out the unmistakable figure of Khalif on the afterdeck of the galleass.

Jahwar's triumphant shout came from behind. 'Look to the prow, Khalif Barbar! As you once took a slave from me, I now take two from you.' The Berber laughed harshly and tapped the brass-bound box upon which he sat. 'Also, I claim our rightful share of the gold.'

There was a moment's silence from the *San Cristobal*, then Khalif's shout carried clearly from the surging galleass. 'Why have you done this, Jahwar? What is it you want?'

'I have what I want, Khalif!' replied Jahwar. 'The gold and the slaves are mine by corsair law. I but claim my rights.'

Khalif's shout came again, more placatory in tone this time. 'Very well, but there was no need to steal; you and I both know there would have been a fair division of spoils in due time.' There was a moment's hesitation, then he added, 'The slaves, however, are another matter; a matter between us two. Come now, we have been comrades for a long time. Must we fight over something so trivial? Yet I admit both are valuable to me. Name your price.'

Charlotte's heart jumped at his words. She was valuable to

him! He admitted it! But was it too late? She felt the galley swing and, twisting her head, saw that they were fast turning away from the galleass.

Jahwar's voice was triumphant as they pulled away. 'No, Khalif, I will not sell either to you – at any price. Look upon them for the last time!'

Charlotte's mind was racing. Khalif wanted her back! Perhaps he had some feeling for her after all, despite what he had said about selling her. The galley continued to swing away and Charlotte was forced to strain as she tried desperately to keep the galleass, and Khalif, in sight for as long as possible. Her mind was screaming for him to somehow rescue her from this nightmare. Yet she was forced to recognise the truth, which was that there was very little he could do at the present moment. Jahwar's galley, *Persephone*, was very much faster and much more manoeuvrable than the larger, more cumbersome *San Cristobal*.

All too soon the galleass was left behind in the darkness. Distantly, she could hear someone shouting but was unable to make out the words. It might have been Khalif, but she couldn't be sure.

Throughout the long night she and Meylissah hung from the prow as, urged ever onwards by the sweating oarsmen, the galley headed through the lightening gloom towards some unknown destination.

Landfall, as dawn rose over the grey-green waters of the Gulf, was a long range of russet cliffs and, behind those, a distant snow-capped mountain with twin peaks. Charlotte, hanging in a kind of limbo-like state where time had all but ceased to exist, was roused by the releasing of the ropes around her ankles so that she now hung straight down, her feet just brushing the surface of the ice-cold water that raced past the bow. She turned her head in a slow, painful movement to look around as best she could, her whole weight now taken by the ropes cutting so cruelly into her wrists. She was unable to suppress a hopeless sob. The horizon was empty; the *San Cristobal* nowhere in sight.

Rough hands released her wrists and pulled her inboard where, unable to control her limbs, she slumped limply to the deck. 'Come, slave,' growled Jahwar, hauling her callously along the planking by her golden-blonde hair. 'I have a mind to take pleasure with you.'

A Girl Learns Obedience

Despite Charlotte's desperate pleas for mercy, Jahwar dragged her inside the little aft cabin, where he threw her to the floor at his feet. 'Kneel up,' he ordered, hands already fumbling at his robe.

Charlotte's face was white with fear and revulsion, even as she tried to gain control over her shaking limbs. 'No, please!' she begged.

Jahwar glowered at her. 'Kneel up,' he repeated in a humourless tone.

Charlotte could not help herself. 'No,' she whispered.

The Berber smiled grimly. 'So, slave,' he snapped, 'it seems you must learn what it means to disobey.'

The whipping he gave her was terrible; twelve full-blooded blows, shattering her resistance completely. A cacophony of screams issued from her contorted mouth at every stroke until, after the sixth, she was begging him to stop. Even so, the lesson continued until every promised lash had been laid across the flesh of her back, buttocks and thighs, marking her fearfully.

She was utterly defeated.

As soon as she was able she struggled desperately to her knees, sobbing hysterically and abjectly begged his forgiveness. Broken by the lash, she promised to do anything just as long as he did not whip her again, and meant every word.

Jahwar thrust a dusty foot in front of her face. 'Very well, slave. Beg to be forgiven like the slut you really are.'

Charlotte took a deep breath. The Berber's meaning was perfectly obvious. Her humiliation was to be complete.

'Lick!' he commanded. 'Show me how penitent you are.'

She closed her eyes in despair. No one could help her now. Jahwar meant to demonstrate his power over her; and desperately – oh, how desperately – did she not wish to be whipped again. Hesitantly she bent to her task, her soft tongue licking out gently over the calloused skin.

'Harder, slut. In between the toes,' he directed her. 'Lick carefully now. As you can see, my feet are in dire need of a wash.'

Reluctantly, Charlotte licked the salty sweat and dust from her captor's feet. First one and then the other, licking and licking until her tormentor finally ordered her to cease her labours.

'Now, slave, you may beg my forgiveness properly,' he said, loosening his robe to expose his already erecting shaft.

Tears in her eyes, dust in her throat, Charlotte looked up at the giant, her misery compounded. She was totally defeated, her back, buttocks and the backs of her thighs on fire from the terrible whipping. To refuse him would be to invite further punishment, and that was unthinkable. She would never survive it. She must obey. 'Forgive me,' she groaned, at last.

'What?'

'Forgive me – master,' she whispered, then hesitantly took his length into her mouth.

A short time later Jahwar pulled her head away with a muffled groan. He forced her hands behind her back and, submissively, Charlotte allowed her wrists to be re-secured. Then he gagged her with a sour-tasting piece of cloth.

For a moment she wondered why. Surely he could see she would offer no resistance? Then she pushed the thought from her mind. Jahwar was her master now; he had broken her and whatever he wished, she must bear. She moaned into the gag as the big hands roved unchecked over her squirming nakedness.

'Truly you were made to please men, *nasrani*!' growled the Berber, pushing her to her back on the dusty floor, his knee forcing its way between hers to roughly part her thighs. She moaned again as his weight pressed on her, the solid length of him already nudging at her entrance. He was large – not as large as Khalif, but still very big – and she was not yet ready for him. Suddenly panic-stricken she writhed and twisted beneath him, trying desperately to dislodge him, but it was useless. He was far too strong and far too heavy.

Tiring of her struggles he cuffed her viciously round the head. 'Be still, slut,' he snarled. 'This will not take long.'

Charlotte stared up at him as if in a daze. Slowly, deliberately not waiting for his victim's natural lubrication to ease his path, Jahwar forced his length into her as yet unprepared sexual passage. She screamed into the sour-tasting gag, begging him to stop, to give her time. But her captor would not listen; he wished her to know that she was powerless to prevent him doing as he wished.

With a satisfied grunt Jahwar slid into her right up to the hilt. Charlotte felt as if she had been split in two. He drove powerfully into her, ignoring her muffled protests as he sought and found his revenge.

At first, as Jahwar had planned, there was no pleasure in the act for the pinioned girl – only pain and humiliation. On and on he thrust, revelling in her discomfiture. The human body, however, is a marvellous instrument and after a time even Charlotte's sense of desecration could not stop her natural juices beginning to flow, thus aiding his penetrations. Slowly, the pain eased and the pleasure pangs began.

She was helpless to stop it. Her body was, even now, betraying her. Despite the loathing she felt for Jahwar, the ramrod battering at her lower belly was beginning to elicit an instinctive response as she was possessed sexually by a dominant male. Unconsciously, she relaxed and widened her legs further, allowing him even easier access.

Eyes glazed she no longer resisted – and in truth, no longer wished to. Sweat running freely on her pale skin, breasts heaving, she matched Jahwar thrust for thrust, building slowly yet inexorably towards climax.

'Now, slut,' gasped Jahwar, his pistoning action growing faster and faster as he neared his own climax, 'now you know what it is to truly serve a master.'

Even in her extremity, Charlotte divined his approaching climax and raised her hips to facilitate her own. With a muffled scream she arched her back, rising to her finish and, at the same time, bringing Jahwar to his.

When it was all over Charlotte lay still under the harsh-breathing body of the man who had ravished her. Now the moment had passed a deep sense of guilt filled her being as she remembered the illicit pleasure she had felt during a coupling she had tried so hard to resist. Dimly she became aware of Jahwar's diminishing member slipping stickily from her, and she shuddered.

Some time later he left her. She now stood on tiptoe, arms stretched up tautly, wrists tied to slave rings set wide apart in the beam above her head, spread legs attached to similar rings set in the cabin floor. She tried to come to terms with the hideous truth of what had happened to her. As he promised, the evil Jahwar had taken his pleasure with her, fully and completely, and she had also – God help her – found her own satisfaction in the act.

Straining to maintain her balance, Charlotte moaned softly as the pain from her ravaged buttocks and thighs made itself evident. It was unbearably shocking to realise that, despite the whipping and the trauma of what followed, she had actually climaxed during the brutal possession of her body.

She remembered how easily Khalif had aroused her in his cabin. How easy it had been to make her address him as 'master'. How right he had been. She was truly a slave, as much to her own passions as she would be to those who would own and use her in the future. Her shoulders shook and a sob gathered at the back of her throat as she thought of how Jahwar had used her – and of the pleasure she had experienced. There was no denying it, she was a slut, no more worthy than the lowest whore in the slums of Valletta. She had become a helpless slave to her own base desires. She felt the wet stickiness between her thighs and tears filled her eyes. Would she ever see Khalif again and, after what had happened, would he now even want her? Desperately she wanted to believe the former – yet feared the latter.

Shouts came from outside and the galley heeled over sharply. Charlotte gasped as, for a moment or two, she was forced to take her entire weight on her wrists. Desperately she scrabbled with her toes to regain her footing, suppressing a shiver of fear as she listened to the shouts and cheers coming from the shore and felt the galley bump along the quayside. From the noise there was obviously a large crowd on shore waiting for the ship to berth. She cringed inwardly, seeing in her mind's eye her own soiled and whipped nakedness paraded through the town for all to see.

Jeers and the rattle of chains heralded the departure of the captured Spanish sailors who had been forced to man the oars of the *Persephone*. Trembling, she listened to the taunts of those reviling the naked wretches as they were herded ashore, a sudden memory of the captured Moslem girls being similarly treated on the dockside back in Malta springing to mind.

She remembered what Meylissah had told her about the Barbary Coast. The Arabs had long memories and remembered only too well the atrocities committed by crusading Christian armies in the name of their crucified God. Life for a captured sailor was neither pleasant nor overlong. By and large there were only two alternatives: tortured servitude in the galleys or forced labour in the mines and salt flats of the Sahara. In both, life expectancy was short; two or three years at the outside in the galleys, maybe eighteen months in the mines.

Of course, if the captive was young and good-looking, he might be purchased by one of the rich men whose sexual preference lay in that direction. Even so, this was usually but a postponement of the inevitable. Sooner or later the man would become bored – after all, there was no shortage of young and handsome slaves – and send his plaything back to one or other of the living hells.

The door swung open and the huge figure of the Berber filled the opening. In one hand he held a cloth bundle, in the other a leash and some chain. With a grunt he dropped the items to the floor and knelt to release her ankles.

With a sigh of relief Charlotte drew her legs together to relieve the strain on her wrists.

'It is time, infidel,' grunted Jahwar, reaching up to unchain her wrists. 'Quickly now, hands behind your back.'

No thought of argument even entered Charlotte's head as she lowered her aching arms, so awed was she by the ease with which Jahwar had achieved mastery of her. Trembling, she pressed her wrists together behind her back, standing meekly as he fastened the slave bracelets together.

Becoming desperate, Charlotte dropped to her knees and thrust her face against his thigh. 'Please,' she whispered, 'do not take me like this, master. Allow me some clothing, I beg.'

Jahwar grunted, kneeling to lock one length of chain between her ankle bracelets. He could not fail to be aware of how compliant she was becoming. The word 'master' had slipped almost naturally from her lips.

'Do not worry, infidel.' He grinned. 'It would not be prudent to walk either you or your companion through the streets without clothing. There are many here who would gladly fight to possess such.' He slipped a hand between her thighs and smiled with satisfaction when she widened them accommodatingly. Swiftly, he fastened the chain between her ankles, then a shorter one from this to her wrists, lifting the first so it did not drag on the floor. He stood up and surveyed his handiwork. 'Good. Now stand while I put this on you.'

'This' proved to be a hooded, shapeless, sack-like garment which, when drawn over her head, covered her from top to toe. All that could be seen now were her chained feet. She breathed a little more easily. At least she was not to be paraded naked in front of the town's inhabitants. She stood quietly while the corsair slipped a leash around her neck before pinning a fold of the coarse material over her face. Tears scalded her eyes as she pictured how she must look now: totally anonymous; just another female slave to be disposed of as her captor wished.

'Come!' ordered the Berber, jerking on the leash. Shaking, Charlotte followed him from the cabin and out on to the deck to the leering looks and ribald comments of Jahwar's crew. There, dressed in a similar garment, Meylissah stood meekly, leash hanging down the front of her body.

Jahwar paid no attention to the jeers and coarse shouts of his men as he led both prisoners down the gangway and on to the shore, where a noisy crowd waited to greet them. For Charlotte, pride already shattered by her twin ordeals, this was the final blow to her self-esteem. Even as her bare feet touched the shore the crowd rushed at them – but Jahwar was ready. Brandishing his great axe in one hand he strode forward, pushing and shoving mightily to make a path through the jeering throng.

Charlotte was terrified. Forced to follow awkwardly, shuffling along as quickly as the chains on their ankles allowed, both girls flinched and twisted wildly as dozens of marauding hands grabbed at the soft contours under their loose coverings. Chained as they were, they were completely unable to protect themselves.

Then, suddenly, they were clear of the crowd and moving away down the dock. Jahwar looked back and grinned. 'Do not fret, slaves,' he said, 'I shall not let anyone hurt you. You are much too valuable for that.'

The Berber now slowed his pace somewhat and she found it a little easier to keep up. The hobbles on her ankles still threatened to trip her but, with a little practice, she found that by taking quick short steps she could actually keep pace with their captor and at least partially avoid the threat of the leash choking her.

She even found time to look around and was astonished at what she saw. The harbour was big, and so crowded with ships it seemed impossible that any more might find shelter there. Dozens of galleys, Arab dhows, graceful feluccas, even a big Ottoman war galleass, all jostled for space in the crowded water. A strange alien cacophony of sounds filled her ears: wood on wood; canvas billowing in the stiff breeze; the shouts of men; the cries of slaves, children and animals. The smell of strange spices, of cooking food filled her nostrils.

Helplessly, urged on by the insistent tugging on their leashes, Charlotte and Meylissah followed as Jahwar made his way confidently along the quay to the huge metal-studded gate which led into the city. The gate was guarded by a squad of blue-cloaked soldiers in strangely shaped felt headpieces. The English girl looked closer at the beardless, strangely European faces, and remembered what her uncle had told her about them. These were the dreaded Janissaries, sons of conquered Christian vassals, converted to Islam and instructed from boyhood in the arts of war. The Sultan's fearless and dedicated soldiers, they were the mainstay of the all-conquering Ottoman army, armed with crossbow, matchlock and sword. Even the Sultan treated these terrible men with the utmost respect, knowing he could not govern without their support.

The little party passed through the gate into the city proper. The streets and alleyways were crowded with people, dark faces looking curiously at the huge corsair and his charges as they passed. Charlotte, too, stared around in wonder as she trotted along. The shops and multitudinous stalls seemed full of the most incredible treasures. There were exquisitely sewn custom-made garments both for men and women, Tibetan coral, brilliant hand-dyed textiles, flowered fabrics, ornate silver jewellery, long filigree earrings, chokers, finely etched bracelets, smoky amber beads and many intricately carved items in ivory and bone.

And, of course, slaves.

A strange little procession approached and, at Jahwar's bidding, they stood aside to let it pass. Escorted by six black slaves and driving a small chariot-like vehicle was a richly robed man brandishing a long wicked-looking whip. Chained between the shafts of the chariot, hands pulled up tightly between her shoulder-blades and strapped to the heavy iron collar padlocked around her neck, trotted a young black girl, controlled by reins running from thick iron rings set in the flesh of her swollen nipples. Charlotte shuddered at the sight. Unlike most of the slaves she had seen thus far in the city, this girl was completely naked, livid crimson stripes from the carriage whip crisscrossing the tender flesh of her back and buttocks.

Charlotte was horrified. The girl looked to be younger than herself. Whatever might she have done to merit such treatment? Her heart thumped painfully in her chest and, beneath the all-enveloping garment, she began to sweat freely. Did a similar fate – or worse – await her?

Jahwar strode on through the maze of little streets and alleyways that led through the heart of the city. The two girls followed helplessly, from time to time stumbling painfully on the cobbled, often completely unpaved road.

Eventually they turned off the crowded streets into narrower passageways. There were no shops here, just shadowy, recessed doorways and the odd barred window through which the occasional dark face might be seen looking out. Both Meylissah and Charlotte were sweating freely now, forced into an ungainly trot in an effort to keep up with their long-striding captor.

Jahwar led the way until, eventually, they stopped in front of the rampart walls of a large and imposing building, guarded by half-a-dozen blue-cloaked soldiers like those at the dockyard.

In sharp contrast to the semi-darkness of the alleyway, the square in front of the building was open to the sunlight, the stone flags under Charlotte's bare feet warm to the touch. She glanced at the high walls and the massive metal-studded gate, and shivered with a sudden dread. What was this place?

'I have slaves for sale,' said the big corsair gruffly to the guard who met them. The Janissary glanced briefly at the two leashed figures then, tersely, waved them through the gateway.

Inside the confines of the building one of the guards led them into an antechamber where a robed man sat at a large table covered with papers. The man looked up as they entered the cool, shaded room and Charlotte shivered again. Tall and barrel-chested, running a little to fat and beard beginning to streak with grey, there was yet something about him that instilled dread in her breast.

'*Salaam aleyk*!' intoned Jahwar, touching his forehead, lips and breast with his fingers in the age-old gesture of respect and peace.

'*Aleykom es-salaam*!' replied the older man, repeating the motion.

'I am Jahwar, of the corsair galley *Persephone*. I wish to sell two slaves.'

The robed man rose and, filled with apprehension, Charlotte almost took a step backwards. He too, was a giant. Now he was standing she could see he was as tall and nearly as broad in the shoulder as Jahwar. A long curved sword hung at his belt, as a warrior might have worn it. 'I am Ali bin Hussein, of the house of slaves, steward to Lord Mulay Aruj, Bey of Tunis,' he replied, bowing politely.

Jahwar bowed in return, then turned to swiftly strip the two girls of their shapeless coverings. 'Kneel!' he grunted.

The older man's face showed some surprise as both girls dropped to their knees. 'Well now, what have we here?' he said softly, reaching out to touch Charlotte's mane of blonde hair. 'What is she? Circassian?'

Jahwar grinned proudly and shook his head. 'An English milady. Her uncle, it seems, is a lord in her own country. She is untrained, of course, but good slave-flesh even so. The other was her body slave. She is Circassian.'

'There was a need to punish her?' The steward was examining Charlotte's back and buttocks, fingers tracing the raised weals left by the slave whip.

Jahwar frowned. 'She was but recently captured. A lesson in obedience was needed.'

'Hmm,' mused the man, his hands on her abused nakedness provoking little gasps of pain from the humiliated English girl. 'And the collar... it is yours?'

'No, it belongs to he from whom I took them.' Jahwar paused for a moment, almost as if for effect. 'The sluts belonged to the corsair Rais, Khalif Barbar!'

Ali bin Hussein's eyes widened a little and he bent down to study Charlotte's face. 'So,' he mused, speaking slowly so that she might understand, 'you were the slave of Khalif the barbarian.'

Charlotte caught her breath in a sob and nodded weakly. 'Yes,' she managed, in a whisper.

'Your uncle?' queried the slaver softly. 'He really is an English lord? What is his name?'

Charlotte fought to keep her voice from shaking as the man's fingers swept, feather-light, over her body. 'Yes, it is true. My uncle is Sir James Brandon. He will pay much for my release. Please, I beg of you, send a message to him.'

'The English envoy?' The slaver was silent for a moment. 'Then I am afraid I have bad news for you. Your uncle is dead, killed a month past when his ship was taken by my lord Mulay's corsairs in the Gulf.'

'Uncle James... *dead*?' whispered Charlotte. 'Oh no, it cannot be true!'

'It is true,' he said. 'I am sorry – for both of us. I am sure he would have paid a large ransom for you. If it comforts you, I can tell you he died well with a sword in his hand, refusing to surrender despite the odds. He killed five men and wounded a dozen others before he died.'

Charlotte's eyes filled with tears and she choked back a broken sob.

'Is there anyone else who would pay for your release?' he asked.

Charlotte shook her head hopelessly. 'No, there is no one.'

The older man turned back to Jahwar. 'I think perhaps my lord Mulay will wish to speak to you on the subject of the barbarian.'

Jahwar nodded. 'Of course. I will tell what I know.'

Ali bin Hussein smiled. 'Well then, to business. Do you wish to sell outright, or risk them on the block? You understand that, if this is your choice, no guarantee can be given on how much they might make. Also, of course, the house takes one third of the final amount.'

Jahwar nodded agreeably. 'How much will you pay?'

Ali glanced at the cowering girls. 'Unchain them and have them stand up, and perhaps we shall see.'

Wearily, at Jahwar's gesture, Charlotte struggled to her feet, standing meekly as he unlocked and removed her chains.

'Legs apart!' snapped Jahwar.

She jumped to obey, blushing a little as Ali walked slowly around as if to study her from every angle while Jahwar unchained Meylissah. The slave dealer gestured at

Charlotte's collar. 'This will have to come off, of course.'
He chuckled. 'And I take it neither is virgin?'

Jahwar laughed shortly. 'No.'

The steward smiled. 'No matter; virgins are not greatly
prized here… and the blacksmith will have the means to
remove the collar.' The man moved around, both hands
cupping and weighing Charlotte's breasts, then reaching out
to probe boldly with his fingers between her thighs. Her legs
shook violently at the invasion of her private place, yet she
made no move to close them, the sudden slickness of her
passage as it clutched at his fingers telling its own story.

Ali removed his fingers and held them up in front of
Charlotte's face. His meaning was obvious and, trembling,
she took the shiny digits into her mouth to lick them clean.
Having tasted Meylissah intimately so many times in the
past months, tasting her own juices held no revulsion for
her, though there was a certain amount of embarrassment at
doing so in front of the two men.

'As you see, I have already impressed upon this one the
need for obedience,' snapped Jahwar.

Without comment, Ali turned his attention to Meylissah,
running his hands all over her body and even inspecting her
teeth to make sure all was well. She, too, was subjected to
the same intimate examination as Charlotte and, like her
companion, made no demur at licking clean the penetrative
fingers. 'I will not haggle and waste your time,' said the
slaver briskly. 'I offer fifteen pieces of gold for each. What
do you say?'

The corsair thought for a moment, then shook his head.
'To be honest, I expected more,' he admitted. 'Perhaps it
would be better to risk them on the block. My men, of
course, will expect to share in the price.'

Ali bin Hussein nodded and smiled. 'You may be right.'
He glanced at Charlotte. 'Young white-skinned slaves are
always in demand and this one looks to be of better than
average quality. He grinned at the Berber. 'You would know

this already, of course. So is this your wish? To risk them on the block?'

Jahwar nodded.

'It is agreed, then. Both will need training, of course, especially the English milady. The charge for this will be one gold piece each, deducted from the final price. Is this agreeable?'

Again Jahwar nodded.

'Very well then,' said the slaver. 'Wait here while I see them confined. Then I will write you a receipt and make arrangements for an audience with the Bey.'

Charlotte shook violently as the slave dealer took up her own and Meylissah's leashes. As brutal as Jahwar had been, he was the last link to the world she had known. Now, with Uncle James dead, she was quite alone in a strange and savage land with little or no possibility of rescue – even if anyone bothered to try.

'Goodbye, slave,' said the Berber gruffly, taking her by the hair to turn her face up to his. He had a strange, almost regretful look on his face. 'I wish you well.'

Tears blinded her suddenly. 'G-goodbye, master,' she muttered, choking on the words.

A jerk on the leash brought her back to reality and she followed Ali bin Hussein through a door at the rear of the room into a windowless and badly lit corridor. At the end of the corridor a dark and winding staircase led them downward into malodorous gloom, lit infrequently by smoking torches jammed into recesses in the damp stone walls. The steps descended to a large stone-flagged octagonal chamber, empty except for a heavy wooden table standing in the centre, at the side of which lounged a pot-bellied man dressed in dirty robes. From the eight sides of the chamber, like the spokes of a wheel, ran dark and forbidding corridors. Charlotte's stomach lurched as the acrid smell of sweat on unwashed bodies combined with that of human waste filled her nostrils.

Here the tall slaver handed over the leashes to the other with a casual, 'Slave rights are granted on these.'

The pot-bellied man looked the naked girls up and down and grinned lecherously. Then, without a word, he led them into one of the corridors. Shaking with fear and cold, Charlotte struggled to keep up as they passed row upon row of heavy wooden cell doors, each set with a barred metal grille. Occasionally a face could be seen at one of these, but whether the occupants were male or female it was impossible to tell.

Eventually they came to where one of the doors stood open. The gaoler indicated that Meylissah should enter, Charlotte standing quietly as the man first chained her friend to the wall before slamming and bolting the heavy door behind her.

Further down the corridor, her own small dark cell proved to be similar to Meylissah's, floored with straw stinking of human excrement and urine. Charlotte, trying to breathe shallowly, struggled to keep the contents of her stomach down as the man forced her against the wall. Her large breasts seemed to take his fancy and he put out his hands to caress them. Charlotte took a sharp intake of breath, yet made no effort to pull away from his touch. Desperately, she wanted to avoid further punishment. Soon the man's hands were between her thighs, fingers jabbing roughly up inside her. She squirmed, as much from the feel of the man's dirty, uncut fingernails as from any sexual sensation.

The man was sweating now and grinned at her with evil intent. He pointed at the floor and grunted unintelligibly, obviously meaning her to lie down. Shaking with fear, she obeyed. Roughly kicking her legs apart he fumbled with his robe to expose a stubby penis before kneeling between her splayed thighs. She offered no resistance and he thrust into her without preamble, though his shaft was so small she hardly felt it enter her. The coupling was over in moments, the man so intent on his own pleasure that he spilled his seed into the unresisting body beneath him very quickly. Then, breathing hard, he climbed to his feet and, readjusting his robe, left the cell without another glance at the sprawled Charlotte.

Twice more, in the next hours, the cell door opened to admit men. The first, a Janissary, was much like the gaoler, plunging into her for but a few moments before climbing to his feet and leaving the cell. The second took longer with her and, ignoring her piteous moans, seemed to gain much pleasure from suckling and biting fiercely at her breasts and nipples. Despite an initial feeling of loathing, the savage treatment only served to arouse her and soon she was shuddering in the first of several orgasms. From first to last neither man spoke even one word to her.

Later, two more soldiers entered. This time she was taken slowly and carefully by one as the other watched and waited his turn and, to her horror, she felt herself once more becoming aroused. Twice, as the first man took his pleasure with her increasingly willing body, she found herself surrendering to her rising passions.

The second man, observing her reaction, was even more thorough, as though enjoying the inescapable fact that the girl was actually welcoming his attentions. He took his time, arousing her with yet more attention to her sensitive breasts, causing her to cry out time and time again before, caught up in his own passion, he finally emptied himself into the wet softness of her sex as she writhed beneath him.

Marked as a Slave

Charlotte awoke with a start. For a moment she wondered what dread sound had so frightened her from sleep. Then it came again. A scream, female, terrified, ringing down the corridor beyond her tiny cell.

She heard the sound of heavy boots on the stone flags outside the cell and shrank back against the wall as the heavy door was thrown open. Two of the soldiers who had so recently taken her entered quickly and, without speaking, unchained her.

Charlotte had no thought of resisting as they took her firmly by the elbows to march her from the cell. She was numb with terror. Where were they taking her? Who had screamed just now? Unbidden, her thoughts went back to Khalif. Was he looking for her? Would he – could he – rescue her from this waking nightmare?

Arms held firmly by the guards, she was marched along the corridor towards the central chamber of the slave-holding complex. Here a new sickly-sweet smell among the many unpleasant odours of the place began to make itself apparent. It was familiar, yet she was unable to place it.

She was shaking uncontrollably. What was happening? What were they about to do to her? In the large central chamber one of the guards forced her to her knees while the other padlocked her neck chain to a slave ring set deep into the wall. She looked around the chamber, and had to fight hard to stop herself screaming. There, spread-eagled face down on the heavy table in the centre was the naked figure of Meylissah. Heavy straps had been fastened around her wrists and ankles to hold them in place while another, wider strap, buckled tightly across the small of her olive-skinned back, held the slave girl immovable.

Charlotte's mind whirled and she stared, horrified, as the pot-bellied gaoler put aside a shining needle before rubbing some kind of red powder into the wound on the girl's left buttock cheek. He stood up and beckoned, and the two soldiers hurried to unstrap the unconscious girl. Charlotte felt her stomach heave as she saw the clear design of the Moorish red crescent the man had obviously been incising into Meylissah's soft flesh. She also now recognised the sickly smell for what it was: the odour of vomit. Her stomach heaved again and then her water was running down her legs, wetting the filthy straw beneath her.

From the table the gaoler grinned, picked up the needle and swirled it about in a pot of dirty-looking liquid. Senses whirling, Charlotte thought for one moment that she might faint. It took little imagination to know who the next victim was to be.

The two soldiers lifted the unconscious Meylissah from the table and bore her away, the girl's long matted hair hanging down to obscure her face.

Within a short time they were back for Charlotte, swiftly unlocking the neck chain and, each taking an elbow and a leg, carrying her to the table. They threw her face down on the wooden boards, cutting the bonds at her wrists so as to spread her arms to each corner. Almost breathless with terror, she heard herself begging for mercy as her legs were spread and the broad leather strap was tightened across the small of her back.

The gaoler spoke to her roughly in a barely understandable dialect. 'Be quiet and lay still. First I must cut the collar from your neck and I do not wish to mark you there. Also, if the needle is not applied properly, I will be forced to do it again and the pain will be twice-fold.'

Charlotte's pleas lapsed into snorting breaths expended through flaring nostrils as the gaoler inserted the jaws of a cutting tool around the metal of her collar. The jaws closed, the man wrenched and suddenly her neck was free of the collar that had identified her as belonging to Khalif. She gave a silent sob. It had been the last physical link to the man she loved.

'That is better. Now, keep quiet until I have finished your mark. Then you may scream.'

Seconds later she felt the first jab of the needle in her bottom flesh. For long minutes she bore the increasing pain in silence, just the odd soft moan escaping her mouth as, slowly and progressively, the needle began its work. All too soon the discomfort began to approach a level Charlotte knew she'd be unable to bear, and her arms and legs flexed desperately yet uselessly in the straps holding her so tightly on the bench.

Ignoring his victim's increasing disquiet and voluble groans of pain and protest, the gaoler continued with his laborious work. Clouds of darkness began to close in on Charlotte from all sides and, as the pepper-like red powder was rubbed into the bleeding flesh of her bottom, she began to slide down into the black nothingness which rescues us all from that which we are unable to bear.

A vision of her mother came to her out of the darkness, voice soothing, chasing away all pain. 'Fear not, little one,' she whispered. 'I am with you always…'

Hours – or perhaps it was days – later, Charlotte opened her eyes to the rattle of keys in a lock and found herself lying prostrate on the straw-covered floor of her cell. The wound on her bottom felt as if it were on fire, though the pain had now diminished to the point where she thought she might be able to bear it without actually screaming aloud. Even so, a groan escaped her lips as she moved to sit up and found she was now denied the use of her hands. She twisted around painfully and groaned again as she realised her wrists had been chained to the heavy metal collar padlocked around her throat, the collar in turn padlocked to a slave ring set in the wall.

The keys rattled once again and the cell door opened. She cringed in her bonds, not daring to think what they might do to her now. Remembering the pierced teats and whipped flesh of the black girl drawing her master's chariot through the town, Charlotte sobbed and drew her knees up defensively to her chest.

It was the pot-bellied gaoler who had first made use of her body. 'Has no one instructed you on what to do when a master enters, girl?' he asked. He pointed to the floor at his feet. 'Come now, kneel here in front of me.' His tone, though brusque, was not unkind.

Though she could only make out the odd word, Charlotte nevertheless grasped the gesture and struggled awkwardly to obey, unable to stay a small cry of pain as her wounded flesh brushed against the prickly straw.

The gaoler was carrying two pans, one of steaming broth and another of water. Setting them on the floor at her side, he quickly released her wrists from the heavy collar and, clucking as if she were a naughty child, positioned her as he wanted.

Charlotte knelt as directed. It was not an unfamiliar position: knees widespread; painfully throbbing bottom resting back on her heels; hands clasped tightly at the back of her neck. However, it was one that allowed her no scrap of modesty. In this posture every part of her was perfectly revealed.

Still the gaoler was not satisfied. 'Come now, straighten your back a little more. Do not slump, girl. You have fine large breasts, so thrust them out. Do not be ashamed of your body; you must be proud of it. Make the most of it. It is the only thing of value about you. Even that you do not own. Now it is you who are owned.' He saw the look of despair on her face and smiled, almost gently. 'Do not worry, infidel,' he said quietly. 'I and others will teach you what you must know before you are sold. You are very beautiful. Be obedient and you need not fear.'

Understanding only a fraction of what the man was saying, blushing furiously at the enforced display of her intimate flesh, Charlotte blinked back tears of shame and pain.

'Now then,' continued the gaoler, taking a small pot of something from a pouch on his belt, 'bend forward and press your nose to the floor. I wish to inspect your tattoo.' He snapped his fingers and pointed again. 'Quickly now!'

Frightened, Charlotte obeyed the sharp gesture. Head

down in the straw, she felt his fingers gently applying some kind of salve to the mark that had been placed there so ruthlessly. Almost immediately the pain began to ease.

'A good mark,' commented the gaoler, as if to himself. 'It will not be necessary to tattoo you again.'

This time Charlotte understood the words clearly and her buttocks contracted involuntarily at the thought. The gaoler smiled and allowed his hand to stray between her legs. She shuddered at his touch, yet managed to remain as she was, even when he parted the sensitive lips to delve deeply and intimately inside. The tip of a finger brushed against Leila's wadded little sponge and he nodded understandingly. 'How long has this been in?' he asked.

'Since – since the ship. Three, no, four days.'

The finger pried at the sponge, pulling it from her body. 'Well, it must be removed now,' he said. 'Put back later. Understand?'

Nose pressed to the straw, hips writhing uncontrollably at the impersonal invasion of her sexual passage, Charlotte mumbled a barely coherent, 'Yes.'

'Good. Now kneel up as before,' he ordered.

Without argument Charlotte resumed her original kneeling position. Face red with embarrassment, she avoided his eyes.

'Hungry, *nasrani*?' He smiled at her reassuringly as he asked the question.

Charlotte nodded. She couldn't remember when she had last eaten. Days ago, she thought. And despite her pain, the hot broth in the pan smelt delicious.

'No, no, no!' he snapped, reverting to his native tongue. 'You must answer properly. For the present all men are your masters and you must address them as such. If and when you are eventually sold, and it is your misfortune to be purchased by a woman, you will address her as "mistress". All men, from now on, you will address as "master". If you do not you will be whipped. Is this understood?'

Charlotte's hesitation was but momentary. She clearly understood the words 'master' and 'whip' and intuitively divined the meaning of the rest of the gaoler's speech. The whipping administered by Jahwar had been a salutary lesson regarding the consequences of any disobedience to these terrible men. 'Yes... yes, master,' she murmured.

'Good. There is much to learn and time is short. The house will have its profit or much punishment will be yours to bear. Do you understand this also?'

Her answer came as a mere whisper. 'Yes, master.'

Satisfied, he indicated the broth and the pan of water. 'Remain as you are until I leave. Then you may eat and drink. And the next time someone enters, remember to place yourself as I have shown you. Also, keep your eyes downcast. While you are here it is forbidden to look on the face of a master or mistress unless you are so ordered. You must learn humility and respect and, most of all, you must learn absolute obedience. This is for your own good. A disobedient slave brings down much pain and anguish on her own head, so I advise you to learn quickly all that is demanded of you.'

With this advice, he left the cell.

Charlotte grabbed for the broth. Suddenly she realised she was starving. Everything else was forgotten as she spooned the delicious liquid into her mouth.

The Hammam

Charlotte remained in her cell for three days while the wound in her bottom flesh scabbed over and healed. During this time, though the pot-bellied gaoler visited her regularly to check on her mark and give her advice on how a slave should behave, she was not used sexually by him. Why, she never knew. Perhaps, for some reason, permission for him to do so had been withdrawn by his superiors. The blue-cloaked guards, however, continued to use her as they wished. They had evidently been given carte blanche to do so and, every day, she was forced to submit to a succession of lustful men – sometimes one, sometimes two at once.

To facilitate this, the guards' habit would be to secure her face down over a solid whipping bench, legs spread wide and fastened to the bench's feet. In this way two might use her at the same time, one in her vagina or anus as the fancy took him, while the other slaked his lust in her mouth.

Mostly the men were quite gentle with her, even one whose fancy was to insert a large carved wooden effigy of an erect penis into her vagina while he thrust his own, smaller, fleshy version into her tight anus.

Despite her initial disgust and revulsion at some of the things they did to her, like ordering her to impale herself on a wooden phallus and make her masturbate to orgasm, time and time again she found herself taking pleasure in the act. So much so that, eventually, just the act of tying her down was enough to set her juices running.

Each day the gaoler replaced the little sponge in her sexual passageway with a fresh one; an act for which she was profoundly grateful, especially when, some four days into her captivity, the fact that she was not pregnant was confirmed by a dull stomach ache and the appearance of menstrual blood on her thighs.

On that morning she was awakened early by another young soldier. Remembering her instructions, she quickly adopted the slavish and humiliating display posture: thighs spread wide; shoulders back; hands clasped firmly at the back of her neck. Inured by now to the guards' casual disregard of her, she was quite certain her bleeding would make little or no difference to the young soldier's usage of her. Already she could feel her treacherous body oiling itself in preparation for whatever he might choose to do.

'Stand, slave,' he ordered gruffly, unlocking the chain

from its ring on the wall and jerking her roughly to her feet. 'You are to come with me.'

'Please, master,' she whispered in halting Arabic as he corded her wrists together behind her back, 'where do we go?'

The young guard scowled at her. 'By all that is holy, you stink, slave,' he growled. 'You must be washed and cleansed before you go for training. Now be quiet and ask no more questions.'

Down the corridor to the terrible place where they had tattooed her they went, past the great table with its frightening straps, Charlotte forced almost to trot as the guard strode onwards to she knew not where. Stumbling along, trying desperately to keep her feet, she followed helplessly on her chain, up the stone steps, along the corridor and back to the room where Jahwar had first offered her for sale.

There, above ground level for the first time in days, she saw it was daylight. The tall steward, Ali bin Hussein, was there, seated at his desk.

'Kneel, slave!' snapped the soldier and immediately she dropped to her knees, bowing her head respectfully towards the seated man.

'So, infidel,' he said, rising from the desk and circling behind her, 'has your tattoo healed?'

At the question, the soldier reached down, pushing her forward so her nose was forced to the floor. Almost without thinking she automatically widened her knees and pushed her bottom back and upwards, feeling the slave dealer's hands on her flesh. The steward smiled, acknowledging that she was learning fast. 'Very good,' he said. 'Now stand up and go with the guard. It is time you were cleaned up.' He wrinkled his nose in disgust, indicating that he found her body odour offensive.

The young soldier jerked the chain and, ashamed, Charlotte struggled to her feet.

Outside she was led across a tiny courtyard, the sunlight dazzling after the torch-lit gloom to which she'd become accustomed. Then it was back inside and through another maze of corridors until they came at last to another heavily barred door at which they stopped. Again Charlotte stood submissively as the young soldier knocked peremptorily. Long seconds passed before the door was opened; not by another guard this time, but by a middle-aged woman, stripped to the waist, who bowed respectfully to the soldier before taking the proffered chain and leading Charlotte inside.

The door closed firmly between herself and the guard and Charlotte looked at the woman nervously. To be able to bathe and clean herself – could it possibly be true? She looked down at her dirt-streaked body and her nose curled in disgust. In truth, she really did smell. After everything that had happened in the last three days, a bath – or even just the chance to wash – would be absolute heaven.

'Mistress? Mistress Charlotte?' The whisper came from behind her and she turned to see the drawn face of Meylissah, who knelt chained to the wall, naked and almost as dirty as she.

Charlotte could hardly speak, so overwhelmed was she at seeing her erstwhile companion again. 'Oh, Meylissah... Meylissah,' she whispered. The attendant released her wrists and spoke to her harshly in a strange, guttural dialect which Charlotte didn't understand. She looked at Meylissah questioningly. Some of the words seemed familiar but the meaning was unclear.

'She say kneel down, mistress,' said Meylissah. 'She will come back soon.'

Charlotte dropped to her knees. She shot a sideways glance at Meylissah as her neck chain was padlocked to a convenient slave ring. Though her friend was dirty and unwashed, dark hair matted and uncombed, her beauty was still evident. She was certain the slave girl had been through a similar ordeal to herself. Charlotte remembered the painful tattooing with a shudder.

'You have heard about my uncle?' she whispered.

'Yes, my lady,' replied Meylissah sadly. 'My lord was a great warrior. Those who attacked his ship are the vassals of he who rules here, a Turkish Bey called Mulay Aruj. We are now his slaves.' She shook her head worriedly. 'I fear for us, mistress. The other slaves tell of this Bey, who travels not outside his own fortress except after dark. He wears a leather mask and no one knows what he looks like, but they say he is very cruel and truly evil; maybe a Djinn come from the dark regions to rule on earth.'

'What will happen to us?' Charlotte's voice quavered, her eyes brimming with tears.

'Maybe go to Bey's harem. Maybe sold to others. The guards not say.' She managed a tremulous smile. 'Meantime, maybe we stay together.'

Charlotte wiped her eyes, cheered a little by the fact that once again, if only for a little while, she had the companionship of Meylissah.

A short time later the attendant reappeared. She unchained the two girls and led them next door to a beautifully tiled little room, full of cloudy steam, where they were left to sweat for a while. Charlotte had heard of the practice, but this was her first experience of the steam bath. The heat was overpowering and conversation practically impossible. After a few seconds she sat down on one of the wooden benches, panting for breath as the perspiration began to run in streams on her body. Meylissah propped herself in one corner and closed her eyes, obviously much more at home in an atmosphere that Charlotte herself found almost completely unendurable.

Closing her eyes, Charlotte stretched out on her side as best she could on the planked bench, determined to endure the discomfort at least as well as her companion. Meylissah, seeing the movement, slithered along the bench and gently nudged her with one knee, making a pillow with her lap. Charlotte smiled and gratefully took advantage of the gesture, though she still felt much too hot to engage in any conversation.

At the end of half an hour, the attendant reappeared and led them into another, cooler room where she and another woman of about the same age released their wrists and helped them into a large tiled pool. Soap for washing was provided and both girls spent the next ten minutes or so washing each other and generally splashing happily about in the pleasantly warm water as they got rid of the accumulated filth of the past few days.

Eventually they were ordered from the pool and made to lie face down, side by side on padded stone slabs. Meylissah smiled reassuringly at a slightly apprehensive Charlotte as the two attendants, both stripped to the waist in the clammy heat, began to rub the two prone bodies with beautifully scented oil. After the steam room and bath the massage proved to be a most relaxing experience, and Charlotte soon abandoned herself to the knowing hands with real pleasure, her gloomy thoughts gradually subsiding in tune with her body's tensions. The masseuse's touch was incredibly soothing; each muscle was searched out individually and manipulated, and when the woman slapped her buttocks to indicate she should turn over, she took no umbrage but did so with alacrity, allowing the gentle hands to continue their work.

She jerked as one oily hand slipped briefly between her thighs, then relaxed as the hand was removed and the attendant turned her attention to her charge's long legs. Meylissah smiled at her again, indicating all was as it should be, and once more the English girl gave herself over to the more than pleasant sensations. Over the next thirty minutes or so the clever fingers worked their way up her body. At last, feeling incredibly full of well-being, both she and Meylissah were urged off the slab and back into the pool, where the next ten minutes were spent almost as pleasantly being repeatedly soaped and sponged until all traces of the body oil had disappeared.

Next it was back once more to the stone slabs, where Charlotte's hair was washed and rinsed repeatedly before being finally rubbed with a sweet, jasmine-like essence.

Then, after being urged to lay back on the stone slab, Charlotte's attendant grunted something and gently eased her charge's legs apart. Puzzled, she looked to Meylissah for a translation.

'She say take off hair now,' explained Meylissah, indicating the blonde bush at the juncture of the other girl's thighs. Charlotte trembled a little in anticipation, yet made no protest as the woman bent over her. How would the task be accomplished? she wondered. Would it hurt?

She needn't have worried. In the event it was all fairly simple and did not hurt at all. The woman worked fast, using some kind of yellow paste which she smeared liberally all over Charlotte's pubic mound. Then, pushing Charlotte's arms up over her head, she attended to her armpits in the same way. After a few minutes she removed the paste, together with the unwanted hair, by gently wiping the affected areas with a wet cloth.

Charlotte looked down at herself and was unable to prevent a slight shiver at what she saw. The sleek look of her pubic mound made a beautifully erotic display of her cleft and she suddenly had a clear vision of what the men who held her in thrall would demand of her body in future; a vision which left her abruptly breathless and quite moist with unbidden desire. How could this be happening? She was no uneducated slave girl. She was Lady Charlotte Brandon, English aristocrat and heir to a large fortune, used to giving orders and being obeyed. Yet her body was even now betraying her just at the thought of serving men sexually, with no thought to her own desires or wishes. Why was the thought so fascinating, so thrilling, so – arousing?

The answer was elusive. Had it been Khalif who had planted this powerful emotion in her breast? She had to admit that, even in the short time she'd been his prisoner, he had truly been, in every sense of the word, her master – both sexually and psychologically. She thought back to earlier times, to various unsatisfactory encounters with the other young men she'd known. Might these have been more pleasing to her had the men been more masterful and less concerned with her feelings? Had this powerful sexual submissiveness always been there, buried so deep inside her psyche it had taken the trauma of true enslavement to bring it out?

The attendant finished cleaning away the unwanted hair and, with a gruff order, signalled both girls to get back into the warm pool. There they were quickly bathed again, then rubbed down one last time with the aromatic oil. Then they were conducted to another tiny anteroom where, wrapped in huge towels, they were instructed to lie down on a pile of soft cushions. This time their hands were left free, though their neck chains were padlocked as usual to the ever-present slave rings.

Strangely, Charlotte was not at all resentful. Chains were part of her life now, to be accepted without question. Totally relaxed, warm and comfortable in the towel, it was not long before she closed her eyes and slept.

She was awakened an hour later by Meylissah who was sitting at her side and holding a small jar. Charlotte looked up and smiled. 'I feel splendid,' she said, marvelling at how refreshed and alive she felt. 'I don't think I've ever felt so clean.'

Meylissah smiled and held up the little jar, then moved closer to pull open Charlotte's towel. 'Mistress like?' she queried, pouring a small quantity of the fragrant oil on to one hand before rubbing it gently into the smooth skin of her companion's shoulders. 'A massage – like before, maybe?' she asked huskily.

Charlotte looked at her in surprise. 'Can we? Are you sure

it will be all right?'

Meylissah smiled happily. 'Oh, yes. We wait now until soldiers fetch us. Plenty of time. You like, remember?'

Charlotte lay back and took a deep breath as Meylissah's skilful fingers began to work the oil into her soft flesh. She looked down at the smooth, fig-shaped cleft at the juncture of her thighs, so naked and defenceless now. Somehow it only seemed to emphasise her new status. She had become exactly what those who owned her wanted her to be and, though she hardly dared admit it, perhaps even what she herself wanted to be. A slave, whose only reason for existence was to please her owner. A fearful fate for some, to be sure. And yet, now Meylissah was with her, perhaps a little less fearful than it might have been. Meantime, why should she not enjoy some of the wonderful pleasure Meylissah could give her?

'Yes,' she murmured, 'I like, God help me. I like!'

The Dance

The sounds of flute and drum were loud in the chamber where Ali bin Hussein was studying the parchments detailing the various attributes of slaves who were to be disposed of in the coming weeks. A lover of the fleshly delights, Ali was finding it particularly difficult to concentrate on the writings, his gaze drawn almost irresistibly to the other side of the chamber, where a slave was practising her dance.

She was naked. This, of course, was not in itself unusual. Most slave dances could not be properly performed when clothed. What was unusual was the girl herself. Much more generously curved than was common here, the golden-haired beauty had the milky-white skin of the infidel and beautifully shaped breasts which swayed seductively to the

135

primitive rhythm of the drum.

Another slave, dark-haired and about the same age, though not so tall and with far less generous curves, watched the dancer's efforts. Under her tutelage the bigger girl had laboured long and hard, learning the many complicated and varied movements of this particular dance. The tutor, though clearly also a slave, was not entirely naked. As taskmistress to the dancer, she had been permitted a scrap of red silk, tied to one side and worn low on the hips to display the erotic curve of her belly. Her breasts, of course, were bare, as befitted any girl in the house of slaves.

Interestingly, the dancer's nipples, outer labia and clitoris were all pierced and set with heavy gold rings. The rings also supported small golden bells, which tinkled softly with her movements.

Ali wiped his brow. It was hot in the chamber and the large-breasted female's performance was doing nothing to detract from the heat. Privately, he thought the rings added greatly to her erotic image.

Arms held wide, pelvis and hips swaying sensuously, the former Lady Charlotte Brandon moved in time to the music, her body gleaming with oil and sweat. She was tired, yet her efforts continued unabated. Meylissah – for it was she who was the teacher – had proved to be a harsh taskmistress and very definitely Charlotte did not want to feel the sting of her whip again.

For some weeks now the girls had been undergoing training. Ali himself had overseen Charlotte's piercings and they were now almost completely healed. The second trip to the dreaded octagonal room where she had received her tattoo had been as terrifying as the first. This time, however, she had not lost her senses, even when the red-hot needle had been thrust through her tender flesh. She had screamed, though, long and hard, continuing hoarsely even after the rings had all been set in place until Ali, tiring of the noise, quietened her by the simple expedient of stuffing a wadded cloth into her mouth.

Charlotte was aware of a strange excitement churning in the pit of her belly even as she danced. Who would buy her? Who would be her new master? For weeks she had prayed that Khalif would come for her, perhaps offering gold – or maybe even coming with soldiers to claim what was his. Despite all her prayers, though, he had not come. And now, in her heart of hearts, she could no longer cling to the hope that he would. She had to face the truth. Had Khalif been pursuing her, even the slower pace of the *San Cristobal* would have brought him long before this. Now she must reconcile herself to the fact that, very shortly, she would belong to a stranger: perhaps, as Jahwar had suggested, to a brothel owner, or perhaps to one of the half-dozen or so rich older men to whom she had already been displayed in private showing.

For the purpose of one such, Ali had dressed her in the European manner. The long red heavily brocaded dress had no doubt been looted from some Christian ship and was cut fashionably low at the front to display the swell of her magnificent breasts. Her hair had been carefully dressed by Meylissah as it might have been for a ball. There had been no underclothes or shoes, of course. Indeed, Charlotte had not expected any. She was now a mere sexual plaything, to be dressed or undressed at the whim of her masters. Underclothes were a thing of the past.

Ali himself had set the scene exactly. Chained standing in a large alcove lit by soft lamps, Charlotte had looked every inch the freshly enslaved Christian lady: a haughty, arrogant infidel waiting for a master to teach her the true meaning of humility and obedience.

For the benefit of his visitor, a richly dressed merchant, the steward had stripped her slowly. Charlotte, as instructed by him, writhed and twisted in her chains as might a free woman, pleading loudly and desperately not to be so displayed and humiliated.

Then had come the intimate inspection, a process which had taken the longest time. Each and every part of the captive's naked body had been closely examined by the merchant, who could not have failed to note the involuntary sexual responses of the chained girl as his fingers probed and investigated her secret places with gentle caresses which inflamed her almost, but not quite, to orgasm.

Then, and only then, had Ali and the visitor withdrawn, leaving Charlotte trembling and very much aroused.

Each morning she was made to insert one of the little uterine sponges and, every other day, in the company of Meylissah, she visited the Hammam, where both girls went through the same routine they had experienced on their first visit, except for the removal of pubic hair. This was done just once every eight days.

Then it was back to the slave compound where, under the watchful eyes of several black trainers armed with canes, both girls were put through a training programme of callisthenics designed to keep them fit and show them off to prospective buyers.

Also, to Charlotte's initial shame and eventual delight, there were lessons in lovemaking. She was not alone in this. Meylissah, though already fully trained in the erotic arts, was also made to complete the programme to Ali's satisfaction.

Here Charlotte's hitherto bridled sexuality was finally given free rein. Not only were there exercises in the hundred or so different positions of lovemaking which Ali painstakingly detailed to her, there were also very lengthy lessons in licking and sucking, as well as the more difficult flexing of the vaginal and anal muscles up and down a penetrating shaft. This was done sometimes with the aid of various artificial phalluses of different lengths and thicknesses, and sometimes with the throbbing shaft of a young black slave named Khigali who was only too willing

138

to have his erect flesh cozened by the warm wetness of the two girls.

At one point Ali decreed that Charlotte watch as Meylissah was forced to service three or four guards at the same time. Despite the men's obvious disregard for the beautiful girl at their command, the erotic exhibition had excited Charlotte almost to the point of orgasm as she'd watched her friend writhing so helplessly under the thrusting bodies of those who were using her. So much so that when, shortly afterwards, she'd been ordered to practice her own lessons in the flexing of the vaginal and anal muscles with the aid of Khigali's youthful shaft, she had been more than happy to comply.

Once Charlotte had been judged more or less proficient in all the programmes, Ali decreed that she learn the closely guarded secrets of the slave dances, one of the most difficult and exciting of which was the dance she was performing now; a dance which, what seemed like aeons ago, she had first seen performed by the Egyptian slave girl, Leila.

Perhaps sensing Ali's excitement as the climax of the dance approached, Charlotte turned her body towards the steward, as if parading her sexuality just for his benefit. With a flourish the music ceased and she fell to her knees, head to the floor, chain wrapped tight around her nakedness, hoping that she had impressed Ali with her dancing.

Meylissah's opinion on her performance was clear, however. 'No, no, no!' she cried in exasperation. 'You did not listen. The chain must be tighter when you go to your knees. Remember also, your eyes must be downcast and thighs well apart. Nothing must be hidden, except by the chain.' She spoke in Arabic, raising the short silver-handled whip she held in her right hand and shaking it at the gasping Charlotte. 'Again, slave. Do the last part again!'

This shaking of the little whip was clearly no idle threat, to which the fresh marks on the taller girl's sweat-streaked breasts clearly testified. And so, as the two hired musicians began to play again, Charlotte gave a muffled groan and went straight back into her routine for the final part of the dance.

Meylissah had been quite right. This time the improvement was quite marked. So much so that, as Charlotte's head touched the floor at the finish, even Ali could not help but give a little clap of appreciation. Flushed with effort, Charlotte lifted her head and smiled shyly.

Even the hard to please Meylissah was a little more impressed. 'Better, slave. Now start again at the beginning. See if you remember everything I have taught you.'

Charlotte was exhausted. 'Oh please, Meylissah – er, mistress,' she pleaded. 'Let me rest for a little while.'

Meylissah just smiled sweetly and flicked the whip at Charlotte's splendid breasts.

Charlotte flinched and the gold rings in her nipples trembled. She had learned to her cost that the little breast whip, especially in the hands of someone who really knew how to use it, was a great persuader towards more effort.

Meylissah frowned. 'Be silent, slave,' she said sternly. 'Our lord has commanded me to teach you the dances and, by Allah, teach you is what I shall do. Much practice will be needed, though, before you perform properly for masters. Now – again!'

Charlotte breathed deeply. She wanted desperately to rest. Even more desperately, she wanted to avoid the bite of Meylissah's whip. With a sigh of resignation she placed the chain on the floor once more and knelt beside it as she had been taught. What had Meylissah said? Perform for masters? Was this why she was being trained in the dance? Of course, to a brothel owner, a girl who could perform the slave dances would be a much more valuable acquisition than one who couldn't. Once more the musicians began to play and, this time, motivated by thoughts of the pain she must bear if she failed to get it right, her interpretation of the dance could not be faulted.

'That was much better, slave,' pronounced Meylissah with a triumphant smile. 'You have good rhythm and your body is well suited to the slave dances.' She cracked the little whip again and Charlotte jumped. Meylissah smiled slyly. 'Now, if our lord permits, you may serve his pleasure.'

Slowly Charlotte raised her head to look at the steward, who nodded casually. Her heart beat a little faster and, taking a deep breath, she moved forward on hands and knees. Ali opened his robe, and without hesitation Charlotte bent her head to lick gently at the tip of his staff. He was already erect, she noted with some satisfaction. So her dance had had the desired effect – even on a slaver of his experience.

Ali took a deep breath. 'You learn quickly and well, slave,' he said gruffly. 'Now, you may begin.'

'Thank you, master,' she breathed, just before she gathered him deep into the wet softness of her mouth.

Displayed

Charlotte stiffened with apprehension as Ali bin Hussein entered the little cell she shared with Meylissah. Both were dressed, if one could call it that, in scraps of scarlet silk tied loosely at one hip so the entire length of leg and thigh might be clearly seen and admired.

The big man held two braided leather leashes carelessly in one hand. 'Come, little ones,' he said. 'It is time to put you on display. Remember, you are valuable merchandise now, to be bought and sold. No one will hurt you so long as you obey, but our intention is to have a profit from your sale.' He looked at them sternly for a moment. 'This we will have regardless. Do you understand?'

'Yes, master,' the two girls answered in unison. In the past weeks Charlotte had learned much of the language and now had little difficulty understanding the sibilant Tunisian dialect. It was strange, she thought, but now the responsibility for her actions lay with others, it had become so much easier to accept these things. Now she had no say in anything her very helplessness seemed to fill her belly with a perverse kind of excitement. She shivered at the direction of her thoughts.

'Turn and give me your wrists, both of you,' ordered the slaver. Obediently both girls turned and allowed him to fasten their wrists behind their backs with the usual slave bracelets. Then he slipped the leashes over both proffered necks, Meylissah giving a little sigh as the Arab's other hand strayed under the silk at her waist to investigate the moistness between her thighs.

Then it was Charlotte's turn, the slaver's inquisitive fingers seeking and parting the ringed lips of her smooth cleft to confirm that she, too, was no less accommodating to his touch. A throaty moan was drawn from her as the fingers probed and then were withdrawn. Without expression, he offered them to her mouth, grunting with satisfaction as her lips quickly and obediently parted to allow them entry and she carefully and assiduously licked them clean of both her own and Meylissah's juices.

'Good,' Ali said. 'Now, do not forget what I have taught you.' He tugged on the leashes. 'Come!' he ordered and, humming happily, led them from the cell to the smaller courtyard which adjoined the auditorium. There, against one wall, was a small wooden stage-like structure, shielded by a canopy. The little stage was not particularly high, only some two feet or so off the ground, yet it was ideal for the purpose to which it was about to be put.

'Up you get, my beauties,' Ali urged, pushing them forward and up the steps. 'Stand there both of you and raise your arms,' he ordered, releasing their wrists and pointing to the front of the stage.

Both girls obeyed instantly, raising their arms and

standing quietly as the slave master efficiently roped them to rings set in the canopy support. When both were secured to his satisfaction, he turned his attention downwards, pulling both pairs of ankles well apart and fastening them, in turn, to more rings set in the floor. Then he left the stage and, as would a spectator, stood in front of the two spread-eagled girls, noting with satisfaction how they now stood straining on tiptoe, helplessly fastened in place.

Charlotte could not but be aware of how she and Meylissah would appear to the watching Ali. In that position very little was hidden from a prospective buyer. Meylissah's upper torso was already shiny with sweat as she twisted a little, trying to ease the strain. Charlotte, too, was beginning to perspire, both from the heat of the day and with the fear of the auction to come.

For over an hour they were exhibited on the little stage. Charlotte lost count of the number of men, and some women, who came to stare. As instructed, both girls begged each prospective customer, 'Buy me, master!' or 'Buy me, mistress!' as the case might be. One or two prospective customers, bolder than the rest, even reached up to touch the helpless bodies dangling so temptingly in front of them. One such, a pimply-faced youth of no more than seventeen, even reached boldly under Charlotte's silk to fondle the smooth ringed cleft at the juncture of her thighs.

Ashamed, she nevertheless intoned the mandatory, 'Buy me, master!'

'If I do, slave,' he said arrogantly, standing on tiptoe to slip two fingers easily inside the slick passage, 'you may be sure this will be padlocked shut when it is not serving my purpose.'

Charlotte's thoughts went immediately back to the padlocked labia of Leila, whom she had last seen on the *San Cristobal*, and she was suddenly even more aroused. 'Yes, master,' she breathed throatily, as the boy's fingers moved intimately between her spread thighs.

The boy removed his hand and walked on, leaving Charlotte distraught, tears running down her cheeks. To be so handled by a callow boy, yet still become aroused. Truly, she was soiled goods. She had been used and penetrated by so many men and objects in the past weeks that even she could not remember them all. She glanced at Meylissah through tear-filled eyes and received a sympathetic look in return.

Customers came and went; there seemed to be no end to them, and the time passed slowly. Still the two girls hung from their bonds, as Ali bin Hussein had intended, displayed to best advantage. By the time he came to release them Charlotte had managed to compose herself a little, the tearstains on her flushed cheeks small evidence that anything untoward had happened. If the slave master noticed, he said nothing, merely busying himself with releasing the two suspended beauties.

'Come,' he ordered. He did not fasten the slave bracelets, though he did leave the leashes in place. Gratefully, the girls followed him back to the little cell. 'You have done well,' he said gruffly. 'Make sure you do as well when you stand on the block.'

Meylissah bobbed her head in fatalistic acknowledgement.

Turning to Charlotte, Ali spoke sternly. 'Meylissah has been sold at auction before and knows what is expected of her. She will help you prepare.' He tangled his fingers in Charlotte's hair to turn her face towards him. 'This will not happen for a little while, however. For the moment, the Bey has requested that you be placed in his household to serve him.' He looked at her seriously. 'This is a great honour for me. Do not let me down. Fail in what I have taught you and I promise you will scream for many days before death releases you from torment. Do you understand?'

'Yes, master,' whispered Charlotte.

Ali smiled. 'All right, then. I will come for you when it is time. For the moment, both of you remove your silks and

144

rest for a while.'

'Thank you, master.'

He left without another word, bolting the heavy door from the outside.

Frightened, Charlotte looked at her companion as the door clanged shut behind the overseer and Meylissah put an arm around her shoulders reassuringly. 'Do not worry, Charlotte,' she whispered. 'You are very, very beautiful, and you will make a good slave. The Bey will be pleased and have no complaint, I am sure.'

'Slave,' repeated Charlotte wonderingly.

Gently, Meylissah pulled her close. 'Shhhh,' she soothed, a little catch in her voice. 'We must accept our destinies. For this one last time, lay close to me.'

Charlotte raised her head to look the other full in the face. A tear ran down her cheek. 'For the last time?' she repeated brokenly. 'Oh, Meylissah, how am I to bear it?'

They were still asleep, cuddled together, when Ali returned an hour or so later. He carried a comb and cosmetics.

'Come,' he crooned, shaking Charlotte awake. 'Comb your hair and apply perfume and cosmetics as I have taught you. The Bey's guards await and you must look your best. Quickly now. Time is short.'

In the Palace of the Bey

In the great hall of the Bey's palace, Charlotte knelt back on her heels to one side of the cushioned dais on which sat the obese figure of the leather-masked Mulay Aruj and the dark-bearded English privateer, Jack Fletcher, known as 'Mad Jack', come from Bizerte to trade and talk alliance.

Charlotte studied the two men from under discreetly lowered eyelashes. As usual, the Bey was robed entirely in black while the Englishman, in contrast, looked almost regal in a blue coat with gold epaulettes and silken breeches, probably stolen from some captured nobleman whose ship had been seized. Remembering her uncle, killed so brutally in similar circumstances, Charlotte suppressed a sob.

For once Charlotte was free of the padlocked iron belt with the tightly fitting chain-mesh crotch covering between her legs she'd worn from the time she'd entered the Bey's palace. The key to the device hung on a chain around her master's neck. To her added shame and humiliation, the device played host to two other intimate items; a pair of sewn-leather, sand-filled, penis-shaped protrusions, one large as a man, the other marginally smaller, inserted into her front and rear openings. Twice each day, morning and evening, these had been removed by Hamid, the Bey's chief eunuch, to allow her to complete her toilet and to replace the mandatory liquid-soaked uterine sponge with another. Why, she could not fathom. With the iron belt in place there was simply no way intercourse of any kind might take place.

For Charlotte, her young body trained and drilled to a daily diet of regular sexual usage and pleasure, this was perhaps the most distressing part of her new captivity; the constant movements of the phalluses within their fleshy sheaths driving her almost frantic with desire as she went about her domestic duties.

These duties had varied little since her arrival. During the daylight hours she was forced to labour long and hard at the most menial and filthy tasks her overseers could find in the kitchens, stables and dungeons. She would then have an hour or so in which to clean herself and apply perfume and cosmetics before Hamid arrived to conduct her to her master's bedchamber, where she would be chained to the side of his sleeping couch. Here, her suffering and misery increased day by day as not once did her fat, leather-masked master deign to use her in the way a man normally uses a woman. Instead, from time to time, her chain being long enough for the purpose, he might casually command her to use her lips, tongue and mouth on his cudgel-shaped penis to bring him to climax.

Sometimes, at Mulay Aruj's whim, two beautiful perfumed slave boys would attend him while she, encouraged by the repeated use of his whip, continued to lick and nibble as he directed until her mouth ached. This was the worst time for her. While he made free with the smooth bodies of the young men, seemingly taking great delight in bringing them to rapturous orgasm, his blonde slave girl was left to writhe painfully at his side.

She had been desolate. Terrified of this man who held the power of life and death over her, the verity of her slavery, both to him and the unbridled erotic feelings running riot through her body, had become an established *fait accompli* in her mind. The two leather phalluses continued to torment and excite her yet, as he decreed, she remained totally and miserably unfulfilled. And so for long days and nights she remained exactly as he wished, driven by an increasingly desperate desire.

Then came the day when she was ordered to attend her master in the torture chamber. To her utter astonishment the man who lay awaiting the torturer's attentions had been none other than her erstwhile master, the man who had stolen her from her beloved Khalif, Jahwar of the Berbers. Gradually information had been extracted from him as to how he and Khalif had executed the raid on the *San Cristobal*, and how Khalif was to take their booty to his fortress on the island of Djerba, before meeting up with Jahwar in Algiers. Charlotte was offered the chance to exert her own bloody revenge on Jahwar by excising his genitals, but brutally as she had been treated by the man, she had been unable to use the proffered knife on him. As her master tried to coax more information from Jahwar the man's tormented body had shaken violently from side to side. Then he drew his last breath, his tortured features relaxed and his head fell lifelessly on to his chest...

Coming back to the present, she shifted her stance, conscious of the weals Mulay Aruj had so recently inflicted on her back and bottom.

She was no longer naked. Hamid had himself dressed her for this important occasion. The costume, of course, covered little. Set low on her hips and secured by a single catch, she wore an ankle length, semi-transparent, saffron-coloured silk skirt, split to the waist at both sides to reveal tantalising glimpses of hip and thigh every time she moved. Above the waist a tiny unbuttoned bolero jacket framed and revealed her full breasts. Belled bracelets on wrists and ankles completed the ensemble.

Around the large chamber were many other tables at which sat a hundred or so guests: a dozen or so of the Englishman's crew; a sprinkling of the Bey's most favoured corsair captains; a few important personages invited from within the city; the remainder officers and guards serving in the Bey's personal entourage.

Twenty or more scantily-clad girls served the assembly with food and drink. Charlotte, however, was required to serve only Mulay Aruj and the fashionably-dressed English pirate.

Having been deprived of clothing for so long she no longer felt awkward at being naked, or nearly so, in front of men. Tonight, though, was different, especially since Mulay Aruj had already informed Fletcher about her lineage. The two men had gone on to candidly discuss her physical attributes, a crude discourse which had her blushing with shame before the banquet even started. As if this had not been enough the Bey then, to her utter shame, casually commanded she remove her skirt and posture herself so he and Fletcher might more closely examine the tattooed red crescent on her bottom and, finally, the heavy gold rings piercing the intimate flesh beneath her depilated mound.

Fully aware that she had no choice but to obey, Charlotte

obediently knelt with her back to the two men, nose pressed firmly to the floor, thighs widely parted as directed, and crimson-faced at the knowledge that, once again, every intimate part of her was perfectly displayed – and this time to a man of her own race.

Her embarrassment was increased a hundredfold when, at Mulay's urging, Fletcher actually accompanied him from the dais to look more closely.

'She was disobedient?' asked the Englishman, noting the fading purplish weals on Charlotte's belly and breasts.

'No, not really.' Mulay chuckled cruelly, reaching forward to delve deeply within her open sex. 'But it pleased me to impress on her what will happen if she is.'

Charlotte squirmed uncontrollably at the Bey's intimate touch, immediately aroused despite her embarrassment at what was being done to her. Kneeling as she must, she fought to hold herself steady as the cunning fingers delved deeply. Her thoughts were chaotic. Two nights ago, after Jahwar's dreadful demise in the torture chamber, the masked Bey had at last unlocked and removed the iron belt with its phallic protrusions and tossed it carelessly to one side. 'Tonight your body brings me much pleasure – and you much pain, slave,' he'd said softly, shedding his robes to reveal the misshapen and gross body beneath. To say that Mulay Aruj was fat would have been an understatement. The man was huge, with a pendulous belly that made him look, ridiculously it seemed to Charlotte, as if he might be pregnant. Yet his huge shoulders were still massively muscled under the fat, as were his arms and legs.

Charlotte's heart thumped painfully in her chest at his words. Then, as the leather mask was finally discarded, her fear increased at her first sight of his ruined face. From his left eye right down and across his cheek a deep scar ran to the corner of his mouth, twisting the whole visage to give him a quite fearsome aspect, like a gargoyle. His fingers had closed on one tender gold-ringed nipple and she shivered with sudden dread. 'Yes, master,' she'd whispered as the fingers of his other hand thrust roughly between her slippery, pierced lower lips.

Determined to play her part, Charlotte had moved her hand down over the grossly distended belly to the already erect penis, catching her breath at the sheer size of the thing. Fat he might be, but Mulay Aruj's erection was as large and as virile as any she had known.

Running her fingertips lightly up and down the length of the shaft and around the hairless testicles as she'd been taught, she had trembled and taken a deep breath as the man's fat hands closed on her breasts, kneading, squeezing and pinching the swollen nipples. Then she was seized in an iron grip and forced to kneel on the divan, face crushed into the cushions with knees spread and bottom raised obscenely.

Lying there, face pressed into the divan, Charlotte had been suddenly panic-stricken at the thought that the man was about to force himself into her back passage, and tried vainly to pull away. She had been too late. Mercilessly, Mulay Aruj inserted the tip of his rod into her unprepared rear opening and, with a grunt, embedded himself in her wriggling body. The pain had been incredible. Charlotte felt her senses slipping away as the tight passageway was stretched almost beyond endurance.

Mulay Aruj wriggled his naked hips more dextrously than she would have thought possible and his great buttocks swayed as he continued to force his huge manhood mercilessly into her defenceless body, ignoring her protests and pushing in to the hilt, his fleshy belly resting on her buttocks as, with deliberate intent, he spread her vagina wide and thrust three fingers deep inside. To her astonishment he massaged his shaft through the thin wall separating the two passages.

He had drawn back, relieving the pressure on her stretched flesh, then surged right back into her once more, delving as deeply as he could.

Charlotte's eyes rolled back in her head, her breath coming in short gasps. Pinioned by the man's vast bulk, she had been unable to move even a little to facilitate his entry.

'Now slave, now!' he gasped at last, and then grunting and groaning he at last emptied himself into Charlotte's helpless body.

Charlotte had breathed a sigh as she felt the great shaft inside her at last softening and growing smaller. The pain lessened and she became aware of her shameful position on her hands and knees, loins raised and skewered by the Bey's fleshy staff.

At last Mulay Aruj had rolled off her, flopping on his back on the divan, great paunch heaving, a dribble of semen escaping from his shrinking penis.

Charlotte, shaking uncontrollably as if from an attack of ague and desperately hoping he would demand no more of her, had remained as she was, face pressed into the material of the divan.

Her hopes, however, were doomed to disappointment. Within five minutes he had been ready for her again. Grasping her long hair he forced her up until she was kneeling astride his massive thighs, then grasped her by the waist to pull her slowly on to his invigorated shaft. For a moment he paused, no doubt savouring the warmth of her channel before, with a swift movement, thrusting deep inside her.

Charlotte attempted to welcome the invasion as best she could, lifting her loins and widening her thighs to make it as easy as she could for him as he slid slowly and methodically in and out of her soft wetness, her breasts bobbing enticingly above his heaving chest. As she had known it inevitably would, her vagina stretched and was now oiling itself in order to accommodate him. Already she could feel the faint stirrings in her belly heralding the advent of at least some pleasure to be taken and savoured from the Bey's rough treatment.

For long moments Mulay Aruj continued to thrust, she matching him with desperate movements of her own as she began to move inexorably towards her own long-denied release. But it was not to be. As she approached climax the Bey's hot seed spilled deep into her, and he had withdrawn before she could reach her own satisfaction.

She hoped he would leave her, his gratification complete. Instead, for his own twisted pleasure, Mulay Aruj chained her spread-eagled against the wall for the rest of the night. Then, while he watched from the comfort of his couch, his two catamites were admitted to the chamber and told they could torment her as they wished.

Jealous of their master's attention to the blonde slave, the young men had proved just how cruel and inventive they could be when presented with a helpless victim of the opposite sex.

First they whipped her front, slowly and methodically, before continuing with a thin cane on her thighs, belly and breasts until she was twisting and shrieking in her bonds. Then they turned their attentions to her breasts. Coarse cord was wound around the base of each perfect sphere until they were forced into bulging caricatures of their previous loveliness. Only when the two slaves threatened to heat the golden rings in her flesh with a lit taper had Mulay Aruj stopped her torment.

It had taken three days for Charlotte to recover from her terrible ordeal and even now, kneeling as she must in front of the Bey's dais at the banquet, the marks on her body were plain to see. Fighting to stay still as Mulay Aruj continued to plunder her sex with his fingers, Charlotte breathed heavily, plaintive gasps of rising passion escaping her mouth as, once again, her body betrayed her. She was torn by guilt, knowing she had betrayed Khalif. Although her torment had been, as Mulay Aruj promised, painful to the extreme and final orgasm had been denied, she nevertheless at one point began to find a certain pleasure in what had been done to

152

her. The fact that, in truth, she had been offered no choice was of little comfort. A man who disgusted her and of whom she was terrified had possessed and used her in the most brutal and disgusting way – and, once again, she found some perverse excitement in the act. And even now, if she was honest with herself, a similar thing was happening. His fingers within her body were arousing her even as they were humiliating her. Jahwar and Dragut Bey had been absolutely correct when they called her a slut. It was exactly what she was!

Mulay Aruj stepped back from his examinations and Charlotte allowed herself to relax a little, yet still she could feel her juices running.

'I wonder, your excellency,' Fletcher enquired casually, 'would you consider selling her to me?'

Heart thumping wildly as she heard the question, Charlotte dared not risk the Bey's displeasure by looking round. Yet she awaited the answer with some trepidation. To be sold as a slave to an English pirate? Surely that would be the ultimate debasement?

'I am sorry,' replied Mulay Aruj. 'For reasons which need not concern you she must stand on the block in a few days. However,' he continued smoothly, 'you are welcome to attend at the house of slaves and bid for her. Be warned, however, such sluts as these are not cheap. There are many who will have a strong desire to own an infidel slave such as this one.' He shrugged carelessly. 'She may even fetch fifty gold pieces or more.'

Fletcher's eyes widened. 'Fifty?' he echoed.

Mulay grinned. 'But worth every *piastre*, I think. Do you not agree?'

Somewhat reluctantly, the Englishman nodded. 'Hmm,' he murmured, 'I will admit she is – interesting. And to have such a lady as my slave would be, to say the least, quite a coup. Still, it is a very high price to pay. For such a sum I might buy three or four octoroons in Bizerte.'

'But would your octoroons bring you as much pleasure as an English milady, obedient to your every wish?' Mulay asked slyly.

Fletcher frowned. 'And the gold in her flesh?' he asked hastily, changing the subject. 'Why was this done?'

Mulay Aruj smiled. 'Do you not like it? For my pleasure, Ali, my steward, had her ringed so. The fitting was easily done by means of a heated saddler's needle.' He reached down with one hand to caress Charlotte's breasts and, though she trembled, she immediately squared her shoulders to thrust them out for his touch. 'They suit her well, don't you think?'

Fletcher seemed impressed. He obviously realised that her nipples were still very tender, yet she steeled herself and made no move to draw away, even when the masked Bey took one of the swollen nubs between finger and thumb to stretch it out painfully from its base.

'Fascinating,' commented the privateer. 'My compliments to you, excellency. Obviously, you know well how to train a slave.'

'I have trained many such,' said Mulay Aruj, self-deprecatingly. 'It is a skill born of practice.'

Mad Jack Fletcher made a face. 'Fifty gold pieces,' he repeated. 'I will have to look to my finances.' He looked down seriously at the kneeling Charlotte. 'I agree, though, that such a slave might serve me well.'

Mulay released his grip on Charlotte's nipple and she breathed a heartfelt sigh of relief. 'Perhaps so,' he chuckled. 'Perhaps so!'

Sold

Hands chained behind her back, shaking with apprehension, Charlotte stood at the bottom of the wooden steps at the rear of the auction platform and listened to the baying of the crowd as Meylissah was sold.

The day before, Hamid the eunuch had returned her to the house of slaves, where she was briefly reunited with her friend. Ali bin Hussein, perhaps cognisant of Charlotte's ordeal at the hands of the Bey, had proved to be compassionate and allowed the two girls to spend the night together.

Charlotte was dressed in the fashionable, heavily brocaded European red velvet dress in which Ali had so successfully displayed her to the rich merchant at the private showing weeks before. As well as the starched petticoats, she had this time also been allowed camisole, underdrawers and, wonder of wonders, a pair of shiny buckled shoes a size too small but into which, at Ali's urging, she finally managed to squeeze her feet. She felt hot and uncomfortable in the cumbersome garments. So long had it been since she was allowed European clothes that she now felt positively awkward and unattractive in them.

As she listened from the foot of the steps her heart was racing. A roar from the crowd signalled that the final bid had been accepted. Meylissah had been sold; the jeers of free Arab women and the clank of chain indicated that the Circassian slave girl was being led away by her purchaser. Charlotte knew what would happen now. At the entrance to the auction house the slave's chains would be struck off, to be replaced by those of the purchaser. The house sold the slave, not the chains. Her new owner might have brought clothing for his purchase – or not, as it pleased him.

Charlotte's thoughts turned bitterly to Khalif. Despite her many ordeals she had always cherished the belief that sometime, somehow, he would rescue her from this pain and degradation. She remembered the times she had lain in his arms, her only thought to serve him. First he had captured her body and then, in making her his slave, had also made captive her heart. He was her true master, the only one to whom she gave herself willingly.

Yet he had not come!

How foolish she had been to imagine that such a man could ever have any real feelings for her. He was a corsair chief; a pirate and a brigand. There would be no shortage of beautiful and willing concubines to fill his bed and his arms.

Her hands, secured by the slave bracelets behind her back, curled tightly into fists and, suddenly angry, she resolved to give the mob a lesson in how an English aristocrat behaves. She would be aloof and reserved, she decided. She would not co-operate with Ali's commands as she had been ordered.

Then her determination faltered as she thought about the graphic stories of disobedient slaves being crucified or impaled on the city walls, or even sometimes sewn into weighted leather sacks and cast alive into the sea.

She shook her head. It was no use. She would have to obey; she had no choice. Her captors would have absolute obedience, no matter what. They would tolerate nothing less. She moaned under her breath, trying her pitiful strength against the obdurate steel of the bracelets. Nothing happened except that her muscles cracked. Her hands remained fixed behind her back, just as her masters intended.

The curtain at the top of the steps swished and Ali appeared. His eyes glinted and he no longer seemed quite as affable as before. 'Come then, *nasrani*!' he growled. 'It is time. Remember what I have taught you.' Reaching down to take hold of her leash he led her up the steps and through the curtain. She stepped out on to the stage, and for a moment there was complete silence.

Suddenly Charlotte felt faint.

The large auditorium was packed with people: desert dwellers seated alongside city folk; men and women from all walks of life sitting or lounging on the tiered benches arranged in a semi-circle in front of the stage. With great effort, remembering what would happen if she disobeyed, she managed to compose herself enough to stop her legs from buckling under her.

The slave master led her to the centre of the stage where, casually, he allowed the leash to fall, hanging down between the full mounds of her silk-clad breasts as he bowed slightly to the audience.

Charlotte shifted uneasily, a frightened captive awaiting his command, while Ali touched his forehead in a salute to acknowledge the sprinkling of applause that greeted them.

Then he began his opening palaver. 'Masters,' he said, almost diffidently. 'I am afraid I must apologise to you in advance for the clumsiness and ignorance of the slave you now see before you.' There were a few groans from the mob, though most remained silent, preferring to wait and see what the slaver had to say. 'Of course,' he continued, 'she is quite attractive in her foreign way, and does have one or two – how shall I say? – reasonably good features.' With powerful hands he ripped open the front of both the red velvet dress and the camisole beneath, thrusting the ruined garments from her shoulders to bare her splendid breasts with their ringed nipples.

As if the shame was more than she could bear, Charlotte hung her head and half turned away. Ali, an angry look on his face, caught her roughly by the hair and, bringing her head up, held her still so all could look their fill.

An appreciative murmur came from the crowd.

'Unfortunately, my friends,' continued Ali sadly, 'she was but recently captured and remains virtually untrained in slave duties.'

There was a displeased murmur from the mob. This was the last lot to be sold. The *pièce de résistance*, as it were. They expected better fare than this richly-dressed, admittedly beautiful, yet untrained *nasrani*. There were shouts from the front benches. 'What can she do then? She is useless. No good, no good!'

'Gentlemen. Gentlemen, please!' Ali protested. 'I beg

you, have patience. It is not the house's fault that the girl is new and untrained. Just look at this marvellous body and imagine the pleasure you will have in training her yourself. In addition, she is quite intelligent and already responds well to simple commands.'

'Show us! Show us!' chanted the crowd, while Charlotte flushed once more at the disparaging way the slaver had discussed her shortcomings.

'All right, my lords, all right,' cried Ali hurriedly. 'We will see what she can do. I beg you, however, to make allowance for her ignorance.' He released Charlotte's hair and moved to stand behind her. He snapped the catches on her bracelets so the top part of her dress and the ruined camisole might slide free. Though they were no longer confined, Charlotte kept her hands behind her back as the slaver's hands moved to her waist and, with another powerful wrench, allowed the remainder of the dress to slide down her legs to lie in a scarlet puddle around her daintily shod feet.

There was a trickle of applause as the girl, clad now only in her underdrawers and shoes, hung her head in shame once more. Ali snapped his fingers and slowly, hesitantly, she went to her knees. He snapped his fingers a second time, and bringing her hands round, she went gracefully into the deep traditional obeisance position, placing her head to the floor at his feet.

Ali looked around at the audience expectantly.

This time there was a little more applause, and a young man dressed in the robes of a desert tribesman shouted, 'One gold piece. I bid one gold piece!'

The crowd laughed and Ali smiled at the young Bedouin. Deliberately the auctioneer thrust out a foot, and slavishly Charlotte began to kiss and lick delicately at his toes.

Suddenly the mob became a little more attentive.

'Three gold pieces!' called the young Bedouin again.

'Five!' This from a fat brothel owner, seated in the third

row.

Charlotte knew the man. Only a few weeks ago she had been exhibited to him privately. The fat man was Achmed, owner and operator of a well-known brothel in the harbour area known as 'the house of chains'. This time the slaver acknowledged the bid. Then, stepping back from the girl, he snapped his fingers a third time and she went straight to her belly on the boards. Another snap and she turned to her back. Gracefully she kicked off her shoes and, bringing up both knees, swiftly slipped off her underdrawers. She was completely naked now, the perfectly depilated mound and puffy gold-ringed lips adding beautifully to the effect.

The applause that followed was genuine as the mob finally began to realise Ali had been less than honest regarding the girl's capabilities. His fingers snapped again and she reached back, stretching her arms and arching her spine as if to lift her breasts for the crowd's attention. Then, with a flourish, he brought her back to her knees where she remained, thighs wide apart, shoulders back, hands clasped tightly at the back of her neck.

Reaching down, the slaver parted her lower lips to clearly expose the final gold ring transfixing her swollen clitoris. Then, taking his hand away, he snapped his fingers once more and Charlotte went straight into the series of callisthenics she had practised so hard. They were complicated manoeuvres, taking long minutes to complete and designed to show her magnificent body off to perfection. When she had finished she was breathing hard, her body shiny with sweat, the weals inflicted by Mulay Aruj showing crimson on her pallid flesh. With another flourish Ali brought her back to her knees before dismissing her to the deep, traditional bow of the slave girl to her lord.

There was absolute silence for a moment, then as men realised how perfect had been the exhibition, thunderous applause. Gracefully Charlotte knelt once more at the slaver's side, gasping for breath as she recovered from the punishing exercise. Ali, reaching down, fastened her hands behind her back.

A man seated in the centre of the front row caught her eye and smiled approvingly. Charlotte recognised him. He was a merchant to whom she had once been exhibited privately.

'Forgive me, gentlemen,' called Ali smoothly. 'I forgot to mention that although the slave has not been properly trained in a slave's general duties such as pulling a plough or even a cart, the house has managed to school her reasonably well in the movements of the seven slave dances. In fact, I can assure you I have never seen them performed better.'

Charlotte flushed with pride. This was high praise indeed from such an experienced trainer of slaves.

'Ten pieces,' called the merchant.

'Twelve!' called fat Achmed.

'Fifteen!' called the Bedouin.

'Twenty,' came from the merchant.

'Twenty-five!' called Achmed again.

On and on went the bidding, men vying with each other to see who would own this lovely slut of a slave, and one whose body promised so much delight for her owner. At last a beaming Ali gestured to the two guards and they stepped forward to lift the trembling girl to her feet and hold her firmly between them.

Abruptly the crowd was silent. It was time for the handling.

Charlotte was taken completely by surprise. This she had not practised and no one had forewarned her. Held tightly by the two guards, she writhed helplessly as the slave master subjected her to a series of traditional caresses designed to show the watchers the involuntary sexual responses of the chained girl.

Now Charlotte's shame was no longer counterfeit but real. So cunning and clever was the slaver's touch that her first orgasm was upon her almost before she knew it. The second and third climaxes exploded in her belly shortly afterwards and soon, to the mob's delight, the helpless girl was writhing in the throes of a series of involuntary orgasmic convulsions that threatened to rob her of her senses.

Men in the front rows cried out with delight. Women hissed. Charlotte was beside herself with shame. The slaver's caresses had betrayed her innermost nature. All now knew how it was with her. She had no secrets, no defences left.

'Thirty-five!' From the middle of the auditorium the English privateer, Mad Jack Fletcher, lifted a hand to enter the bidding.

'Forty!' called a veiled woman in the middle row.

'Forty-five!' responded Achmed the brothel owner.

There was a short pause, then Fletcher called, 'Fifty!'

Near the front of the hall a robed figure raised a hand. 'Sixty!'

Charlotte trembled.

The English privateer nodded. 'Seventy!'

'Eighty!' The robed figure's bid was loud, authoritative.

Another long pause. Then faintly, Fletcher responded. 'Ninety!'

There was a breathless hush in the auditorium. Ninety gold pieces! No one could remember anyone, not even the Sultan's agent, paying so much for a slave – not even a white-skinned one as beautiful and responsive as this one.

The response was immediate. 'One hundred!'

There was a stunned silence; not a sound was to be heard for long, long moments. Then a woman laughed shrilly, before her husband bade her be quiet. Other mutterings and whispering began to be heard until there was a general hubbub from the gathered crowd. 'Who is it? Is he mad? Who would pay so much?'

Ali bin Hussein was beaming. This was better than anyone might have dreamed. 'One hundred gold pieces! My lord Gebhr offers one hundred gold pieces for the infidel.' He paused for a moment and looked at Fletcher. 'Are there any more bids?' he asked briskly, opening his hands preparatory to clapping them together.

Mad Jack, white-faced, nodded. 'One hundred and twenty-five.'

Again the response was loud and immediate, implying that no matter how much it cost, the robed man was determined to purchase this particular slave. 'One hundred and fifty!'

Fletcher hesitated, then very reluctantly shook his head.

'Are there any more bids?' asked Ali, his voice a little strained as he looked around the arena. 'Any more?'

There was a dead silence, as if the audience was stunned.

Briskly then, Ali clapped his hands. 'Sold, then!' he cried. 'The slave is sold to Lord Gebhr for one hundred and fifty gold pieces!' He turned hurriedly to Charlotte as the robed man left his seat and moved towards the stage. 'Quickly now, girl,' he whispered urgently. 'Bow to your master!'

The slaver's training had been thorough. Without even really thinking about it, yet shaking uncontrollably now the moment had come, Charlotte thrust her blonde head to the dusty floor of the stage.

The Hunt

In the centre of a little clearing by the spring known locally as the Oasis of Jamal, two days' journey from Tunis, the blonde slave known as Charlotte stood blindfolded in the centre of a roped circle. She was naked save for the heavy leather collar buckled around her throat. She was breathing heavily and the tiny bells fixed to her nipple and genital rings quivered slightly. As yet, however, they made no sound.

It had been several days previously that the slaver, Gebhr, had successfully bid for her at auction. Meylissah, too, had been purchased by him, together with the young black slave, Khigali, and a number of others, all members of Jahwar's crew who'd been enslaved by Mulay Aruj. The little column was now on its way by a circuitous route that was to take in a number of small villages, overland to a city called Sousse, where she was to be delivered to a certain Aga of Janissaries. She tried not to think about the future, concentrating her attention on the forbidding task in front of her.

The smell of burning pitch from the flaring torches, combined with the campfire smells and the spicy odours of cooking food, filled her nostrils as she listened to various ribald comments, from which it was abundantly clear that the new slave met with general approval.

The hunt was about to begin.

Seven men were in the circle with her. Six, stripped to breechclouts and blindfolded as was she, were the hunters. The seventh was Gebhr himself, not wearing a blindfold and bearing a long peeled willow switch. He was referee.

Lady Charlotte Brandon, former English aristocrat, now a mere slave, was quarry.

The six blindfolded mercenaries were standing quite still, straining their ears to hear anything that might betray the girl's whereabouts.

Gebhr smiled cruelly, striking the motionless girl a savage blow across her buttocks. With a cry of pain and a swirl of bells she darted away. Immediately the men moved towards the sound, but already the slave had changed direction and was now standing, trembling yet silent, to one side.

With a growl of triumph one man blundered into another and enveloped him in his outstretched arms, before cursing and pushing him violently away when his questing hands discovered the undoubted maleness of his capture.

Again the willow switch struck, painfully persuading the girl into movement. As before she ran and then stopped, changing direction several times before standing quite still to evade her pursuers. Over and over again the scenario was repeated, Charlotte each time somehow managing to avoid capture, though the men, now acting in unison to a prearranged plan, were beginning to close her down.

The end, of course, was inevitable, and a few minutes later, perhaps disorientated by a particularly cruel cut of the switch across her naked breasts, she ran straight into the arms of one of her pursuers. With a bellow of triumph the man tore the rag from his eyes and gleefully regarded his prize. She trembled, yet stood meekly as his hands roughly explored her body. Excited by the chase the pursuer was already massively erect, and throwing her roughly to her back, thrust her legs apart with an exultant cry.

Conscious of the instructions given to her at great length by the slaver, Charlotte attempted valiantly to welcome the man's member into her body, though due partly to her own fear and partly to the man's haste in penetrating her, she was as yet dry and unready for him. She remembered the savage whipping inflicted on her by Mulay Aruj's catamites, the fading marks of which could still be seen. The lesson had been salutary. Ready or not, Charlotte had made up her mind to do absolutely anything to avoid similar treatment by her new master. Gasping and crying, frantically attempting to match the initially uncomfortable thrusting movements of the man on top of her, she tried her best to bring him to a swift conclusion. In fact, the man's own excitement proved to be his undoing and, within a minute, he was jerking spasmodically, emptying himself uncontrollably into the warm tunnel of flesh cozening him so sweetly.

A little abashed at his poor showing, the mercenary still made the best of it. Red-faced and sweating he climbed from Charlotte's recumbent body, cheerfully accepting the ribald jeers of his fellows.

Charlotte continued to lie as she was, awaiting permission to move.

Roughly, Gebhr lifted her to her feet and pushed her once

more into the centre of the circle, spinning her round and round so she had no way of knowing in which direction she faced. Then, moving back amongst the men, he retied their blindfolds before spinning them also.

Tradition demanded that this should be done. The hunt had to be even-handed.

The man who had just coupled with her made his way out of the circle and sat by the campfire, grinning widely, to watch. His part in the hunt was finished.

Inside the circle Charlotte was once again standing rigid, attempting to control her breathing so no sound from the bells would betray her position. The slaver had been quite clear. She was to play the game out for as long as she possibly could. Any perceived slacking and her punishment would be most severe.

The switch flicked out again, catching her this time across the delightfully curved mound of her smooth and depilated pubis, and once more she jerked into motion. The game was shorter this time; she was caught quickly and taken swiftly while the others cheered. Despite herself, she was beginning to become aroused, and this, coupled with the first man's seed, aided the second's passage into her body. She lifted and spread her legs as he pounded rapidly into her quivering flesh. Then, almost as quickly as the first, it was over and this man, too, took his place by the campfire.

Theoretically, with fewer men in pursuit, it should have been easier for the girl to avoid capture, but each time she was taken her stamina became further sapped and the uncontrollable trembling of her body set the bells quivering to give her position away.

Two more seizures followed in quick succession, each followed by a forceful penetration; the last – to great applause from the watchers – in her tight back passage.

Finally just two men remained and Charlotte resorted to one final subterfuge in an effort to evade capture. Breath coming in short gasps, she knelt in the sand with head bowed as the two hunters blundered about with outstretched arms.

Gebhr frowned as he considered where to strike her again. Where the switch fell, of course, would have some bearing upon which direction she ran. He pondered for a while as the men searched blindly for their quarry, then the decision was taken from him as one of them tripped over the hunched figure and sent her spinning to her back. With a cry of triumph his groping hands instantly recognising the sweat-streaked nakedness beneath him. The mercenary fell on her, Charlotte's legs opening automatically to receive him as his fellows applauded wildly.

Hearing the applause the remaining man removed his blindfold and, scowling angrily, strode to the fire, to be teased unmercifully by his comrades. He was the loser and as such would be denied the use of the slave's body.

In the circle, despite this being her fifth capture, Charlotte was fast approaching her first orgasm, though the heavyset man was not exactly being gentle with her. Lifting her legs he placed them over his shoulders to allow him greater penetration. Charlotte made no protest, simply matching his thrusts with equally savage movements of her own. At the same time, as she had been taught, she milked him with the rippling walls of her vagina and undulated her whip-marked breasts against his chest.

Of course it was all too intense to go on for very long and, with a loud oath, the man began to spend inside his lovely prisoner, holding himself rigid and impaling her deeply. Charlotte also, quite unable to help herself, cried out as she exploded into a succession of rippling orgasms which left her gasping and exhausted.

Once he had withdrawn and regained his feet, this last man reached down to remove her blindfold. Charlotte, fighting to catch her breath as her last climax began to subside, looked up at him with a mixture of fear and curiosity. She knew him. The man was Chasim, commander of the mercenaries and a fierce warrior. Twice in the past days she had seen him use his fists to discipline the men under his command. He had not made use of her up until now, yet quite obviously it had been his intention to make sure of her pleasure as well as his own. Casually he gestured, and struggling to her knees she cleaned him with her mouth, licking and sucking gratefully until he reached down to lift her to her feet.

'That was well done, slave,' he said, still breathing deeply from his exertions. He looked at the faint bruises on her body and smiled. 'I think you will not be whipped tonight.'

'Thank you master,' gasped Charlotte, and greatly daring, added, 'and thank you for my pleasure.'

The man grinned and patted her on the head, much as one would stroke a pet dog or cat. 'Truly you were made to serve men, infidel. I wish I owned you myself.'

Gebhr waved the switch impatiently, and Charlotte excused herself. She ran back to the slave wagon. Now she must clean herself thoroughly and be back at her other duties within minutes, kneeling at the feet of her temporary master to please him with every ounce of her being or risk more punishment.

A Hazardous Mission

On a quiet beach a few miles south of Tunis, four men dressed in Arab robes watched silently as the darkened shape of the big galleass headed back out to sea in the gathering gloom of the North African night.

'Ready?' asked Khalif quietly, hefting a large waterproof leather bag on to one brawny shoulder and turning his face upwards towards the steep rocky ridge they would now have to climb.

From under one of the dark hoods that shaded and

167

partially hid the faces of the four men, white teeth flashed momentarily as Zamil voiced his acknowledgement. 'Ready!' he confirmed, shouldering his own, no less hefty burden.

'Ready!' echoed the English captain, Matthew Hawkins, regretfully turning his face away from the friendly ocean. Just behind his captain, master gunner John Frith hoisted his own pack with a barely audible grunt of resignation. Neither had any illusions about the difficulty of a night trek across territory patrolled by Janissaries, nor the dangers they must face by actually entering Tunis; 'stepping into the lion's den', as it were. On top of this, they first had to negotiate a difficult and dangerous climb in full darkness. Khalif had been very definite. Guarding the easy route along the coast was a small, stone-palisaded fort, probably garrisoned by Janissaries. The climb, though difficult, was necessary.

Weeks earlier, on the afterdeck of the *San Cristobal*, Khalif had looked on impotently as Jahwar and the *Persephone* – and Charlotte – disappeared into the darkness.

'Well, what do you think?' he'd asked savagely, turning to Zamil and Issa. 'Tunis?'

Zamil had nodded slowly. 'Tunis,' he'd agreed. 'Jahwar will join this Mulay Aruj's alliance with the rest of them. He thinks not of tomorrow – just what is important to him today. You shamed him when you took the girl and he wishes to take his revenge.' He paused for a moment. 'It is probably in his mind that you will not dare follow him into Mulay Aruj's city.'

Issa spat over the side. The Tunisian shipmaster's face was dark with suppressed fury. 'It is I who am to blame, lord,' he said bitterly. 'I should have placed a stronger guard. Achmed was no match for Jahwar and his cut-throats. It is only by Allah's mercy the boy is not dead.'

'What will you do?' asked Zamil.

Khalif thought hard. 'I cannot risk the gold or the cannon

168

and we would soon be separated from both – and from our heads – were we to sail openly into Tunis harbour.' He frowned. 'No, first we must deliver our cargo safely to the fortress. This I promised, and this I shall do. In the meantime, send someone after Dragut in the skiff. If I am to risk the *San Cristobal*, I would have him know what has happened.' He placed a hand on the hilt of his scimitar. 'Then it will be time to visit this Mulay Aruj,' his face had darkened, 'and perhaps make a reckoning with Jahwar. In the meantime, fetch the Englishman Hawkins and his gunner to my cabin. We have much to discuss.'

Twenty minutes later he was relating what had happened to the little group gathered in the stern cabin.

'Tunis, you say,' murmured Matthew Hawkins contemplatively. The privateer, now clothed in robes from Khalif's own trunk, already showed much improvement, though his ordeal at the oars of the *San Cristobal* had taken an obvious toll on him. The French girl, Fleur, knelt at his side with a tray of freshly cooked food, looking up with concern from time to time as her lover painfully shifted position to favour the wounds inflicted by the Spanish oarmaster's whip.

Across the cabin a happily grinning John Frith, similarly dressed to his captain, reclined on a mound of soft cushions while a *sifsari*-clad Leila tempted him with titbits from another tray. Behind the slave girl, glowering in a proprietorial fashion, lounged Zamil. Obviously the big Nubian now considered the beautiful Egyptian to be his own personal property.

'Well... I suppose it might be done,' Hawkins continued, 'but believe me, it will be difficult. I know the city well but we won't know where the girl is being held and, now that Janissaries garrison the city, it will be difficult to move around without being challenged. Still, it might be done. I have a few friends there.'

'Good,' replied Khalif savagely.

Hawkins looked reflectively at Leila. 'Tell me,' he said, 'why all this fuss about two slave girls? I am sure both are beautiful, but,' he indicated the kneeling Egyptian, 'surely you have other women just as lovely?'

Zamil scowled, clearly prepared to give him an argument about the ownership of the Egyptian.

As if totally unaware of the man's disapproval, Hawkins went on, 'Is this one so special that you would risk your life for her?'

Khalif hesitated, looking a little uncomfortable. 'One of them is English,' he said finally.

'English, you say! Who is she?'

'She is – was – Lady Charlotte Brandon, niece of Sir James, the English special envoy to Spain. She was a passenger on the *San Cristobal*.'

Hawkins let out a low whistle of surprise. 'I see. No wonder you want her back. She must be worth a king's ransom.'

Again Khalif looked uncomfortable. 'Yes,' he said. 'Jahwar took her for revenge, thinking himself slighted. Allah knows what tortures she has suffered because of me. If she is still alive, I must reclaim her if I can.'

Hawkins' eyes widened a little at the desperate note in the corsair's voice. Suddenly he understood. This was definitely not a matter of ransom. 'I am sorry, my friend,' he said quietly. Reaching down he traced the lovely line of the French girl's cheekbone. 'Now I understand. We owe you our lives. Of course we will help.'

The climb was every bit as dangerous as it looked. Twice disaster threatened: the first time when Zamil slipped and slid some fifty feet or so headfirst down the treacherous rocky slope; the second, further along the ridge, when the same thing happened to Frith. This time the straps holding the English gunner's pack had snapped during his headlong descent, causing the leather-wrapped bundle to finish up on a ledge a further fifty feet down. It had been Zamil who, climbing down somewhat precariously, retrieved the precious pack containing, amongst other things, the two longbows Matthew Hawkins had insisted they take with them on their mission.

Luck stayed with the little party, however, and a few hours later saw them none the worse for their adventure, save for a few bruises, and gingerly crossing a rickety rope bridge over the deep ravine at the far end of the ridge.

'Keep close together,' Khalif's whisper reached Hawkins' ears clearly. 'Soon we will be close to the village I told you about.'

Carefully and silently they moved down the rocky path until, at last, the ground levelled out and they were able to quicken their pace. At last, a hundred yards or so ahead of them in the gloom, among groups of slender palms, pepper trees and plantations of mandarins, the white-painted shapes of houses could be made out in the semi-darkness. They had not gone more than a few yards or so towards these, however, when Zamil's hissed warning brought them to an abrupt halt.

'Someone follows!'

Khalif reacted swiftly, indicating with pointing gestures that they should spread out in a semi-circle and take cover. Then, drawing his sword, he too crouched down in the shadow of a small outcrop of rock. They did not have long to wait. Small noises, as of the scrape of a foot on gravel and faintly whispered words heralded the cautious approach of two hooded shapes, obviously following them. Silently, as the shapes passed by, Khalif moved out from cover, as did Zamil and Hawkins. Khalif and Zamil pounced at the same time, pulling the hooded forms to the ground to a chorus of feminine shrieks.

'Fleur!' exclaimed Hawkins as the hoods were pulled back to reveal a pair of very wet, frightened girls.

'Leila,' murmured Zamil.

'What do you think you're doing?' growled an exasperated Khalif. 'Don't you know you might have been killed? How did you come ashore? Why are you following us?'

Leila, winded by her fall, merely threw her arms around Zamil's neck as she gasped for breath. Fleur looked up entreatingly at Hawkins as Khalif released her. 'Please, oh please, *mon amour*,' she pleaded. 'I have almost lost you once already. Do not send me away!'

Hawkins looked at Khalif with a somewhat bemused expression on his face. Obviously he was only now coming to terms with the depth of the French girl's feelings for him. 'So what do we do with them now?' he asked. He glanced at the wet robes of the girls. 'I don't know how they got away, but they have – and swum ashore to boot, by the look of them.'

'Allah help us,' groaned Zamil, his arms full of wet and deliciously wriggling girl – a girl, furthermore, who it could now be seen was quite naked under the loose and flapping robe.

Khalif swore softly. 'I know... I know! But we can't just leave them here. Mulay's patrols will pick them up as soon as it's daylight. We have no choice. We will have to take them with us.'

'*Mishallah*,' said Zamil. 'I think I whip you good, Leila.'

'Yes, lord,' agreed the Egyptian, pressing even closer and entwining her arms around his neck. Delicately, she nibbled at his cheek. 'Whatever my lord wishes.'

Hawkins couldn't prevent a smile forming on his lips. 'Watch out, Zamil.' He chuckled. 'That little bint has her eye on you, that's for sure.' He reached down to part Fleur's robe, clucking in feigned disapproval as a second naked, shivering girl was revealed. 'What – you too, Fleur? Where are your clothes?'

'It was our keeper, the boy Achmed, *mon amour*. Hearing us planning to follow you ashore he commanded us to

172

remove our clothes, then locked us in the cabin. There were cloaks in one of the chests, so we made bundles of these, then climbed out through the port and jumped into the sea. The ship was at that time only just under way, so we were able to swim ashore.'

'And what about currents, or cramps – or perhaps sharks?' growled Zamil. 'Did you not think about these things?'

Leila buried her head in the big Nubian's shoulder. She was still trembling with cold. 'I had to be with my lord.' She paused for a moment, then went on, 'Even had these thoughts come to me, still would I have followed.'

Loosening the clutching arms around his neck, Zamil set the shivering Egyptian on her feet. 'Disrobe,' he commanded gruffly. Leila shrugged off the soaking garment with alacrity, standing proudly as he first dried her, then covered her nakedness with his own heavy woollen cloak. 'Maybe we can find you clothes in the next village,' he muttered. 'Meantime, keep yourself covered.'

Hawkins, not to be outdone, removed his own cloak and wrapped it around the tremulously smiling Fleur. 'Dunno what you're smiling about, girl,' he said seriously. 'Zamil is quite right; you both deserve a good whipping.'

'*Oui, mon amour*,' whispered Fleur, drawing close and pressing against him, 'and if this is your wish, gladly will I bear it. But I could not bear to be parted from you again.'

'Have you two quite finished?' Khalif's irritated voice interrupted them. 'If you can control your women for a moment or so, perhaps we can get on with the business in hand?'

Zamil squared his huge shoulders defiantly. 'Yes, Khalif, of course. We can leave them here while we reconnoitre.' Turning to Leila he ordered, 'Stay here and make no noise.'

Khalif spoke quietly to Hawkins and John Frith. 'Matthew, it would be best if you and your gunner stay with the two girls while Zamil and I take a look at the village I spoke about.'

Hawkins nodded. Still not over his tribulations on the rowing bench, the climb had tired him more than he cared admit.

As Khalif and Zamil made their way off into the gloom, Hawkins and Frith settled down with the girls; Fleur beside her lover, nestling contentedly under his shoulder and pressing up tight as if to draw warmth from his body. Leila, still shivering, moved so she could sit at Frith's side and, with a little sigh, the gunner put his other arm around the bundle of feminine pulchritude. And so they stayed, drawing warmth from each other as the minutes passed.

It was an hour or more before Khalif and Zamil returned, leading four horses. Hawkins, who had been dozing, woke with a start as they approached. 'Khalif? Zamil?' he whispered into the darkness, leaping to his feet and drawing his sword. 'Is that you?'

'Quickly,' came Khalif's urgent whisper. 'Let us be away from here. Several of the villagers were most curious about us.'

'What about clothes for Fleur and Leila? Did you get anything?'

'Yes, but there is no time now. They can change later. Quickly now. The girls can ride double with you and Zamil.'

The little group mounted their horses, and with Khalif leading moved off into the night. They took a wide swing around the small village before coming back on their original course, which would take them into the city itself. It was cold, and the girls hunched deep into the woollen robes as the little party made its way across the valley and into the flatlands.

Daylight brought welcome warmth from the sun and found them well on their way, riding alongside a swirling river. They managed to cross at a shallow point and here, as dawn broke over the land, Khalif called a halt in a small grove of palms and acacias. The early spring smell of jasmine was in the air and Hawkins breathed deeply and pleasurably as he dismounted and lifted Fleur from the saddle.

'This is where we stay for the time being, so I suggest everyone make themselves comfortable,' said Khalif, as Zamil tethered the animals in the shade of the trees.

'How far to Tunis from here?' asked Hawkins.

'About an hour's riding.'

'Do you have a plan?'

Khalif shook his head. 'Nothing specific,' he said slowly. 'From here we can enter the city and make enquiries. Zamil and I will go in once it is dark. If we learn nothing today we will go in again tomorrow. Someone somewhere will know what has happened to her.'

'I will go with you,' said Hawkins firmly. 'I, too, have friends in the city.'

Khalif smiled gratefully. 'Thank you, my friend.'

Soon the blankets were laid out in the shade of the trees, preparatory to sleep. The girls collected grasses, small sticks and wood to make a small fire. Once this was going, Khalif set them to collecting dates and water which he distributed to the others before they all settled down to rest and sleep. Fleur, without being told, stripped off the shapeless Arab *ha'ik* which Khalif had managed to obtain in the village and crawled naked under Hawkins' blanket. Not to be outdone, Leila also disrobed and crept under Zamil's.

Khalif sat down comfortably on the opposite side of the fire. 'I will take the first watch,' he volunteered. 'Zamil, I'll wake you in two hours. Matthew, you take the third, then Frith.'

Zamil nodded and curled up with the Egyptian nestled in his arms.

Hawkins grinned happily as he lay down with his own naked armful of girl. Fleur wriggled closer against him and he felt himself hardening immediately. He sighed and allowed her to nibble gently at his neck as his gaze met

Khalif's. The French girl's wiles were becoming harder and harder to resist, but he was damned if he'd take her publicly like this. Then his breath quickened as her soft nakedness pressed against him. He knew now how Khalif felt about Charlotte, and why the corsair had embarked on this apparently suicidal course. This was *his* woman. It felt right, so right, to have her cradled in his arms.

Zamil woke Hawkins four hours later. For a moment the Englishman was totally disorientated, then Fleur moved fitfully in his arms and everything came back to him. He looked down fondly at the sleeping girl and then, carefully, so as not to wake her, climbed from the blankets and donned his robe. The sun was high in the sky and it was incredibly hot. Even so, it was very pleasant in the shade and he was content to sit with his back to one of the palms to keep watch.

A few yards away Leila was awake, watching with huge eyes as Zamil removed his clothing prior to ducking back under the blankets with her. Hawkins looked at her and grinned. The expression on the girl's face said it all. Whatever Zamil wanted was all right with her.

Three days passed before Zamil spotted the slave caravan approaching the little oasis. The day before Khalif had come back from the city with the news that both Charlotte and Meylissah had been sold and would definitely be on a slave caravan journeying southwards to Sousse. By the time the canvas-covered wagon had drawn up at the little clump of trees the others were already on their feet and fully dressed. Fleur and Leila, swathed and veiled anonymously, were tending the cooking fire.

'*Salaam aleyk*!' said the wagon driver, a Sudanese by the look of his clothing and the tribal scars on his cheeks. Khalif judged him to be in his forties, just beginning to run to fat. The man turned lazily on the wagon seat, dark eyes flitting quickly around the campsite as if to assess any possible threat.

'*Aleykom es-salaam*!' Khalif gave the return salutation at once, his hand nevertheless resting unobtrusively on the hilt of his slung scimitar. Zamil, Frith and Hawkins likewise turned to face the newcomers. The group of six villainous looking horsemen accompanying the wagon were obviously hired mercenaries.

'This is all of you – your whole party?' asked the hooded man innocently.

Khalif nodded casually.

The man relaxed, and looping the reins around the wagon brake, dismounted and made a deep bow in Khalif's direction. 'Well then,' he said slowly, 'with your permission we shall join you in the shade for a while.' He jerked a finger at the wagon and the dozen or so nearly naked, sun-blackened and exhausted figures chained in coffle behind it. 'I have live cargo which must be fed and watered if it is to arrive at our destination in good condition.' He advanced towards Khalif, making the traditional Eastern gesture of goodwill by touching fingers to forehead, lips and breast. 'I am called Gebhr.' He indicated the six horsemen. 'These others are my retainers.' He grinned suddenly, teeth very white against his dark skin. 'I am a slaver.'

'I had already supposed it,' replied Khalif in the same easy manner he had displayed from the start, 'and of course we bid you welcome.' His casual gaze passed over the line of slaves without comment. 'My name is Salim bin Rahdi,' he continued smoothly. He indicated Zamil and the others. 'These are *my* retainers. Please, take salt with us; share our fire and our food.' He glanced across at the wagon. 'May I ask your destination? We journey to Tunis and, from your route, it would seem that you come from there.'

The slaver grunted. 'Yes.' Again he indicated the chained wretches. 'I purchased these few poor slaves and some others in the market there some days ago. Now I journey first to Wadi Hussein and then to Sousse, where a certain rich Janissary Aga is waiting to take delivery of a trained white-skinned pleasure slave. From there we take ship to Alexandria where I hope to sell the others at a small profit.' He spat delicately into the fire. 'The white-skinned slave is very beautiful and has remarkable responses. She has cost the Aga much gold. Allah knows, they are increasingly rare these days!'

Khalif's face remained expressionless. 'A white-skinned slave, eh?' he said casually. 'Then we are indeed well met. Perhaps I might view her? I, too, have a liking for such.'

Gebhr grunted again. 'I am sorry... she belongs to the Aga, who entrusted me with the gold to purchase her. I cannot sell her to you.'

Khalif forced a smile. 'Of course.' He lowered his voice confidentially. 'Yet might not this Aga – as rich and as honourable as he surely is – understand if, before she came properly into his ownership, some generous person such as myself were to be granted an hour or so's slave rights over her?'

Gebhr's eyes gleamed and he smiled. 'Ah well; that would be a different matter, of course. What kind of generosity did you have in mind?'

Khalif reached into his robe to bring out a weighty leather bag. He untied the drawstring and reached inside to bring out a coin. 'What shall we say? A gold piece, perhaps?'

Gebhr smiled again. 'The slave is very beautiful, friend Ali,' he said smoothly, 'and fully trained. She cost the Aga a small fortune, yet brings me small profit. Perhaps two gold pieces would be nearer her worth.'

Khalif nodded. 'Very well, two gold pieces. But first I would like to see her and if she proves suitable, as I am sure she will, I will need the shelter of one of your tents for my purpose.'

The slaver grinned again. 'But of course. A man must have privacy to properly enjoy the gifts a girl as accomplished and as beautiful as this can bring. Two hours then and my tent for your comfort. Agreed?'

'Agreed.'

'Just one thing.' Gebhr's tone was casual. 'Her previous master felt there was a need to punish her. There are still some marks on her body, which you may find unpleasing.'

Khalif's eyes narrowed, though he managed another smile. 'No matter. I care not about such things as long as she serves as well as you say.'

'Very well.' Gebhr gestured to two of his men. 'Behzad, Achmed,' he ordered, 'see that the horses are cared for and the slaves properly secured. Chasim, have Touati and the others set up my tent. We rest here for a few hours.'

The slaver was as good as his word. No sooner was the black tent set up and furnished, its divans, cushions and thick carpets all in position, than he personally conducted Khalif to the slave wagon where the white-skinned pleasure slave, in company with another young female, were secured. Both were hooded, but Khalif's heart lifted as he recognised both Charlotte and Meylissah.

To one side of the wagon a young black male was secured. He too was hooded; the usual precaution in a slave caravan. Khalif had seen such slave hoods before. These, as others, almost certainly contained a thick wad of leather forced into the wearer's mouth to preclude speech. All three slaves were naked, of course, as was usual in such a caravan. The accomplished slaver did not waste money by clothing his charges, a naked slave being far easier to keep clean, and far better suited to serve a master or masters sexually as and when required.

Khalif cast his eyes over the spread-eagled young slave. He had been fastened, standing upright, with broad leather straps to the wagon's framework side. His skin was covered in a fine sheen of sweat, and on his left thigh he bore a fresh deep brand.

The two girls were secured on a low wooden bench

directly in front of the male, each chained by the ankle to a metal ring on a central pole running from front to back. The glint of gold on Charlotte's body caught his eye and he saw how she had been pierced and ringed; very recently, by the look of her swollen nipples and sex lips. As Gebhr had mentioned, Charlotte's body still bore the marks of a recent fearsome whipping; faint, blue-black welts barely evident on the soft flesh of her breasts and belly. Whatever her offence had been, it must have been grave, Khalif thought. Only rarely were female slaves so severely lashed on the front, most slavers preferring to target the more fleshy buttocks and backs of thighs so as not to risk permanent injury to so valuable a property.

Khalif bent as if to examine the damage more closely, his nose wrinkling slightly as he did so. Obviously both girls had been very recently used – probably, from the all-pervading scent of sex on their bodies, by more than one of the villainous mercenaries. This also would be normal routine for such a small caravan; allowing the guards free and unlimited use of female captives would be a normal part of the terms of hire.

'Do you wish to see her unhooded?' asked Gebhr.

'No need,' said Khalif enthusiastically. 'Her body promises all that I wish.'

A muffled groan came from the young black man and Khalif gave him a second look, noticing how his body had been completely depilated: his chest, genital area and even the armpits were plucked or shaven quite clean. Something about the prisoner's genitals took his attention, and as he looked closer everything suddenly became clear. A noose of thin waxed string had been drawn excruciatingly tight around the victim's testicles; a small stick passing between string and flesh serving as the method of slowly increasing the tightness. Already the testicle bag was very swollen and an unhealthy blue colour. Khalif had heard of this before. It was the classic Turkish method of castration: restricting the blood flow and tightening the string a little each day until the testicles became partially atrophied, at which time they could then be cut off with a lesser risk that the victim might die from loss of blood.

Gebhr saw the look of distaste on Khalif's face. 'There is a merchant in Sousse who, the last time I saw him, begged me to bring him a young black eunuch for his household,' he said. 'If this one lives when we finally neuter him, he will show a nice profit. If not,' he shrugged, 'I had him cheap, so it is but a modest gamble.'

The youth must have heard and at least partially understood the words, for his head snapped up, the sweat-streaked body shaking violently as a muffled shout emerged from beneath the leather hood.

Gebhr grunted, and reaching down to the noosed testicles, slowly turned the stick another quarter, bringing an anguished though muffled scream from the spread-eagled victim.

Khalif fought down an urge to fold his hands defensively over his own groin. 'How long?' he asked slowly. 'How long does this – this operation take?'

Thoughtfully, Gebhr weighed the swollen ball sac in his hand. 'Oh, it will be a few days more before we make the final cut. And then he will be a man no longer!'

Sickened, Khalif reached inside his robe for the money pouch. 'Thank you, Gebhr,' he said, forcing another smile. He took out two gold coins and handed them over. 'Please allow the pleasure slave to bathe, and then have her brought to me.'

It was some twenty minutes later, as Khalif lounged on the silk cushions in Gebhr's tent, that one of the guards entered with a freshly washed and combed Charlotte. Carefully, so she should not see his face, the corsair kept his back to her as she went automatically to her knees.

'Remember, just two hours, warrior,' said the guard with a chuckle.

As soon as the man had left the tent Khalif turned and lifted her to her feet, crushing her to him and placing a hand over her mouth so she could not speak. Silently, he pointed to the entrance and held a warning finger to his lips. Then he removed his hand from her mouth and released her from his grasp. 'Are you thirsty, slave... hungry, perhaps?' he asked loudly.

'Yes... er, yes... lord,' she croaked, astonishment and a dawning understanding showing on her face as she recognised him.

'Drink then, and eat,' he said in the same loud tone, indicating the tray of dates and pastries which Leila had earlier brought to the tent. There was a jug of water next to it. 'Then I wish you to please me.'

Shaking with suppressed excitement, Charlotte noisily took a long swallow from the jug. Obviously it had been some time since she'd been fed and watered.

As the naked girl ate and drank Khalif's dark gaze flickered over the marks on her body, noting in particular the red crescent tattooed on the flesh of her bottom. He made no comment, however, waiting patiently for her to drink and fill her belly. Then he shed his robes and lay back on the cushions. 'Come, slave,' he ordered loudly again. 'You may pleasure me now.'

Her response was automatic, as if she had been a slave all her life. 'Yes, master,' she replied, dropping to her knees and crawling obediently to his side.

Soberly, as Charlotte laid beside him on the cushions, Khalif drew a silken robe over them both. He put an arm around her gently and pulled her close, she in turn pressing tightly against him and casting her arms around his neck. She was shaking uncontrollably, tears running unchecked down her face.

'Is it true? Is it really you?' she sobbed.

'Shh! Make no noise that others might hear,' whispered Khalif in English.

Charlotte nodded and pressed even closer. 'You came... you *came*.' Her voice was hoarse. 'I thought never to see you again.' Then, suddenly frightened, she looked up at him. 'But you are too late,' she said tearfully. 'I am already sold to a Janissary Aga. The slaver, Gebhr, is but his agent.'

Khalif's expression darkened. 'Not too late, slave. Never too late. You are alive, and you are mine. Whatever else has happened, only Allah can alter this.'

Charlotte could not hold back her tears. 'But how? Lord Gebhr will not let me go,' she sobbed hopelessly. 'I am the property of the Janissary Aga.'

Khalif shook his head stubbornly. 'I have told you, I *will* have you back, Aga or no. Neither Gebhr nor anyone else can prevent this. Now tell me what has transpired since Jahwar took you from me.'

'Jahwar? Jahwar is dead, killed by Mulay Aruj. I was there. It was horrible!'

'Why? What happened? I thought Jahwar would join the Bey's alliance.'

'I don't know. Mulay Aruj tortured him for information about the *San Cristobal*'s treasure, and about you and Lord Dragut.' Quickly then, and in more detail, Charlotte related events as she remembered them: the house of slaves; Jahwar's torture; her time as slave to the huge, scarred Bey; the way in which she and Meylissah had been sold and, lastly, the news of her uncle's death.

'Your uncle... dead?'

Charlotte suppressed a sob. 'His ship was taken by corsairs out from Tunis. They tried to take Uncle James prisoner, but he would not surrender.'

Khalif's mind was racing. Jahwar dead – tortured for information. A big fat man with a scarred face, and he'd held Charlotte for only a short time before selling her. Could it be... could it possibly be the man he sought? After all these years?

'They say the Aga tires quickly of his slaves,' whispered

Charlotte, interrupting his thoughts. 'Very rarely does he keep a girl for more than a few months, then sends her back to Gebhr to be sold. If this should happen, perhaps then I can be purchased.'

Khalif ignored the suggestion. 'Tell me,' he asked curiously, toying with the rings in her nipples, 'why were you so grievously whipped?' He rolled her on to her back and moved to lie on top of her.

Charlotte reverted immediately to slave status, spreading her legs and lifting her hips slightly to allow him easy access. 'It was the Bey, Mulay Aruj. It pleased him to have me whipped and caned by the young men who serve him after he had himself used me for his pleasure.'

Khalif's expression was hard. 'I see,' he said thickly, his erect maleness sliding easily into her already lubricated channel. 'Very well then, listen closely. This is what I have decided to do if friend Gebhr cannot be persuaded with gold...'

At the end of the promised two hours Gebhr returned. 'Well, warrior,' he grinned, as a red-faced Charlotte scrambled from Khalif's side to kneel at the slaver's feet, 'was she as good as I promised?'

Khalif nodded soberly. 'Yes, truly remarkable. Your Janissary friend will be very pleased with her.'

'As I told you... as I told you,' chuckled Gebhr, taking hold of Charlotte's leash and tugging her to her feet. 'And as many of my guards can testify.'

'Wait a moment, friend,' said Khalif softly as the man turned to leave. 'Are you sure she is not for sale? I would be willing to pay a good price – perhaps double what your Janissary paid for her.'

Gebhr frowned. 'You know I cannot do this, warrior. A slaver's word is his bond, and as I told you earlier, the Aga has already paid for her. Were I to do as you suggest I would be no better than a thief.'

Khalif shook his head regretfully. 'Still, I would purchase her if I could. Perhaps three times the amount might make your decision a little easier.'

Gebhr looked angry. 'You impugn my honour, warrior. Had we not taken salt together this insult would warrant bloodletting.' He turned and tugged sharply at Charlotte's leash. 'Come, slave,' he growled. 'It is time we were on our way.'

Khalif was disappointed. Quite obviously Gebhr was genuinely insulted. Even as he pulled on his robes to go back to his campfire, Khalif could hear the slaver giving harsh orders to his men to secure the slaves and strike camp.

Ambush

Gebhr's slave caravan moved slowly into the rocky defile at dusk, the slaver's keen eyes darting keenly around at the surrounding rocks. In front of them the floor of the pass was dotted with bushes and small trees twice the height of a man. The Sudanese was nervous. He had travelled this ground many times before and, although he had faith in his mercenaries, he knew from experience that this was an ideal place for an ambush. Also, the tall warrior had been very persistent regarding the white-skinned slave. Briefly, Gebhr wondered if it would not have been more prudent to have negotiated for her back at the campsite.

And he was right!

From behind the slow-moving wagon came the rumble of falling rocks and he jerked round to see an avalanche of boulders and earth sliding down the almost perpendicular cliff face, totally blocking the pass behind them. He cursed volubly. The narrow rocky ravine ahead, cluttered with debris on either side, now looked incredibly uninviting.

The sudden hiss of an arrow passing close to his head to

stick, quivering, in the wood of the wagon seat heralded his worst fears. Gebhr reined in the horses and sat stock still, dark eyes darting as he tried desperately to spot the attacker. Behind the wagon the six mercenaries quickly urged their horses apart. The arrow had merely been a warning. Had he wanted, the archer might just as easily have killed; but even so it made good sense not to present him with an easy target where one arrow might well do the work of two.

Up in the rocks, with Leila and Fleur safely out of sight, Hawkins fitted another arrow to his bow. 'Get ready!' he whispered to John Frith. 'The guards are behind the wagon.'

Frith nodded and moved to where he could see Zamil and Khalif on the other side of the ravine. Zamil was armed with a crossbow. Waving to attract their attention, Frith held up six fingers and pointed to the rear of the wagon.

The message was clear, and down below Zamil nodded, moving carefully to where he could command a better view of the defile.

Gebhr's shout was hoarse with tension and suppressed anger. 'Well, thieves? What do you want?'

For a moment there was no reply, then Khalif walked out into view, hands empty and held out to emphasise he had not drawn his sword. The corsair's face was grave. 'I want the pleasure slave, Gebhr,' he said quietly. 'She was stolen from me and I have sworn to have her back. There is no need for bloodshed. I will pay treble what the Janissary Aga paid you for her.'

The Sudanese scowled. 'I have already told you. The slave now belongs to him. I but deliver her.'

Khalif sighed. 'I understand, friend,' he tried persuasively. 'But surely your Janissary can have no knowledge that you have actually managed to secure a white-skinned slave for him? I offer you the chance to make a fair profit here and now. Treble what he paid. The Aga need never know.'

Gebhr's eyes flashed angrily. 'I would know!' he growled. 'I, too, was once a warrior. Would you have me break my word?'

Zamil's shout was clear – as clear as the warning made by the arrow in the wooden seat. 'Better that and keep your life, slaver!'

The Sudanese shook his head sadly. 'I took salt with you, and honoured your request for a sojourn with the girl. Is this how you repay me?'

'I am sorry it has come to this, Gebhr,' said Khalif gravely. 'But our salt taking was honoured, as you well know. While you were at my fire you were treated as any honoured guest should be, and I paid good gold for my sojourn. Now, I ask you to be reasonable. My claim is just. Sell her to me so that we may all be on our way and no one the worse.'

It was Frith who spotted the danger first; three riders charging in a dead run down the ravine, long swords flashing in the dying light while at the same time the three others broke out from behind the wagon on the other side.

Frith met the immediate threat on his side of the pass, his arrow taking the leading attacker in the centre of the chest and knocking him out of the saddle. Hawkins, meantime, had loosed an arrow at the other assailant, his shaft taking the man in the throat and passing almost right through before the fletchings stopped further passage. The guard gave a strangled scream and pitched from his steed's back.

Meanwhile, on the far side of the ravine, Zamil had already brought down the first of the three other attackers with a well-placed bolt from his crossbow while Frith, turning back once he saw Hawkins was in no further danger, had already loosed a shaft at a second. The English gunner's hurried bowshot missed the man, but managed to bring down his horse, sending the unfortunate mercenary tumbling head over heels to the hard ground, where he lay with blood pouring from a deep wound on his forehead. Frith grunted with satisfaction, certain that the man would take no further part in the proceedings.

All this left Khalif and the remaining two mercenaries facing each other in the narrow defile. The two Arabs reined in their horses and looked around warily. With bowmen on either side they would have little chance if they continued the attack.

Khalif recognised one of the men as the commander of the mercenaries and spoke to him reasonably. 'The choice is yours, Chasim. Stay and be killed, or leave this place with your comrade,' he said softly. 'Think about it. Would you lose your lives for a mere slave, even a white-skinned one?'

Gebhr's order to his escort echoed clearly around the ravine as, drawing his sword, the Sudanese dismounted from the halted wagon. 'Chasim, Touati!' he shouted. 'Withdraw now! This is now between the thief and myself.'

Chasim hesitated for a long moment, then as his employer began to walk forward purposefully, slowly turned his horse and, gesturing for his remaining man to follow, rode back the way he had come.

'There is no need for this, Gebhr,' shouted Khalif reasonably to the advancing Sudanese. 'Why not sell me the slave? Surely she is not worth dying for?'

Gebhr laughed grimly and hefted his sword. 'Perhaps you also should think about this, thief! Perhaps it will be you who goes to paradise this day!'

Khalif smiled easily. 'Perhaps, if Allah wills; but I have sworn to recover my property and I *will* fight for her if I have to.'

'What about your bowmen?' queried Gebhr. 'Are you warrior enough to do battle honourably, or will you have me shot down without a chance to defend myself?'

Khalif shrugged. 'Hawkins, Frith, Zamil,' he shouted, 'this is between the slaver and myself. You will not interfere... understand?'

The Nubian's reluctant shout of assent could be clearly heard. 'I understand, Khalif, but why not let me kill him where he stands? I can spit him easily from here.'

The Sudanese looked sharply at his antagonist. 'Zamil? Khalif…? Khalif Barbar? You are he?'

Khalif nodded. 'You know me?'

'I have heard of you.' The admission came reluctantly.

Khalif again spoke reasonably. 'I have no quarrel with you, Gebhr. I but seek to reclaim my property. I ask again… will you not let me purchase her?'

Pale-faced but stubborn, Gebhr shook his head. 'I am sorry, Khalif. I cannot – will not – break my word to the Aga.' He lifted his sword. 'Defend yourself, warrior!'

Khalif, too, shook his head regretfully as he lifted his own weapon.

A cold wind stirred the dust and the shadows lengthened a little in the defile as, for a long moment neither man moved. Then, suddenly, Gebhr rushed forward, the heavy blade in his hand striking down savagely at the corsair's head.

But Khalif was not there.

Three times Gebhr charged, and each time the corsair moved easily aside from the killing blows. The fourth time Khalif slipped inside the other man's guard, the point of his sword just nudging at Gebhr's throat. The Sudanese stood very still. Then Khalif stepped back, his sword falling to his side.

'It has been a long time since you were a warrior, Gebhr. Clearly I am your master with a sword. Yet I do not wish to kill you. Give up now. Just sell me the slave and we can all be on our way.'

Warily, the two men faced each other for long moments, Gebhr white-faced and angry, Khalif calm and self-possessed.

Then the Sudanese charged in one violent final effort. This time Khalif met the charge head on, striking the other's blade to one side and, with the speed of a striking snake, countered with a vicious thrust of his own. Gebhr wheeled back with a grunt of pain, the sword dropping from his suddenly nerveless fingers as he fell to his knees, hands scrabbling vainly at the blood welling from the deep wound in his chest.

For a moment there was silence, then the clatter of hoofs heralded the reappearance of the two mercenaries. The Arabs approached warily to where their employer lay in the bloodstained sand.

Khalif lifted his sword once more and Chasim held up empty hands to show his peaceful intention. 'You have won, barbarian,' he said slowly. 'It was a fair fight and the slaves are yours.' He looked to where Gebhr lay ominously still. 'Is he…?'

Grimly, Khalif nodded. 'He gave me no choice. Yet truthfully, I did not wish to kill him. He was a brave man.'

The mercenary agreed. 'He had the warrior's code. Yet he was a fool. He knew the pleasure slave truly belonged to you, of this I am sure.' He hesitated for a moment, then continued. 'I do not blame you for fighting for her, Khalif. Truly, she is excellent slave meat. Were she mine I would never part with her.'

Khalif lifted an eyebrow. 'I hope she served you well, Chasim. I shall whip her myself if she did not.'

Chasim looked a little uncomfortable, but answered boldly nevertheless. 'Gebhr judged her to be, in his words, unpleasing. This was a lie, told merely as an excuse to whip her. Last night she was belled and hunted in the circle. I was last to have her.' He smiled. 'She was, as I say, excellent.' He began to dismount. 'Do we have your permission to bury Gebhr and the others?'

'Will you give me your word that you will depart from this place and say nothing of what has happened?'

'I will,' said the mercenary, slowly, 'but only until we reach Sousse. There Gebhr's Janissary friend will demand a true accounting and I have my own code to honour.'

'Fair enough,' replied Khalif. 'You may do your burying and I give you my word that you and your comrades may depart in peace. There has been enough killing today.'

Slowly and carefully, he wiped the bloody blade of his sword on a corner of his robe before sheathing the weapon. 'The ground is hard,' he said quietly as the Arab dismounted. 'Do you wish my men to help you?'

'No. He was my employer, the others my friends. It will be our task to see to them.'

'Very well then,' Khalif said. 'Bury them deep so the wolves do not disturb their bodies. They too had honour. Such men should not be defiled in death.' He looked across to where the mercenary whose horse Zamil had brought down was struggling to his feet. The man's right arm hung limply at his side, obviously broken, and blood ran freely from a gash on his temple.

Hawkins and Frith came slithering down through the rocks closely followed by the dusty figures of Leila and Fleur. 'Dead?' enquired the English captain, indicating the prone body of the Sudanese.

Khalif nodded and shouted to the approaching Zamil. 'See to that one,' he ordered, indicating the man with the broken arm. 'Dress his wounds.'

Zamil scowled and glanced darkly at the shovel-wielding Achmed. 'Better to cut their throats and be done with it,' he muttered.

Khalif smiled to himself. The man was full of contradictions. On the one hand he was a savage and ruthless warrior, yet was capable also of great gentleness, as his growing relationship with the Egyptian dancer clearly demonstrated.

Clearly Zamil was besotted with her, and woe betide anyone who tried to take the girl from him now. 'Catch up the horses and release the male slaves,' he said quietly to Hawkins and Frith.

Inside the wagon Charlotte had heard the sounds of conflict, but was unaware of the outcome. Chained and hooded once more by Gebhr before they had set off, she'd had no chance to warn Meylissah of Khalif's plan. Obviously there had been an ambush, but who had triumphed? Was the Sudanese still master, or had Khalif been victorious?

The wagon tipped suddenly as someone climbed aboard. Fingers fumbled at the cords of her hood and she gasped with relief as it was removed and she saw Khalif's face.

Knife in hand, the corsair moved to where the black slave stood strapped against the frame of the wagon. He looked closely at the young man's noosed genitalia and muttered an oath, then reached round swiftly to cut the lacing at the back of the hood. Gently he pulled the sweat-sodden leather away from its wearer's head. The slave's eyes were glazed with pain, with no sign of recognition in them.

'What is his name?' he snapped to Charlotte.

'Khigali. He was with us at the house of slaves.'

Khalif spoke slowly and carefully. 'Khigali!' he said urgently. 'I know you are in pain, but you must listen to me carefully.'

The youth groaned and swung his head from side to side.

'Khigali! Can you hear me? Do you understand what I am saying?'

'Yes... I hear you.' Khigali's voice was no more than a pain-filled croak.

'Listen. I am going to cut the cord around your balls, but it has sunk very deep into the flesh. So if you want to keep them stay absolutely still. Do you understand?'

The boy's eyes widened with sudden hope. 'Yes... I understand. I will not move... but do it quickly, please!'

Khalif's voice was hardly more than a whisper as he eased the point of the knife as gently as possible under the waxed cord. 'No movement then – unless you wish me to finish the job Gebhr began.'

Khigali groaned pitifully as the sharp blade sawed momentarily at the deeply-embedded cord, yet with great effort of will managed to stand perfectly still until the noose finally released its agonising grip on his genitals. Then, with a great sigh he went limp in his bonds. He had fainted.

Swiftly Khalif unbuckled the holding straps, and very carefully laid him on the floor of the wagon. Then he turned his attention to Meylissah. 'Gebhr is dead, Meylissah,' he said quietly to the wide-eyed girl as he removed her hood and unshackled her. 'I am taking Charlotte with me. Do you wish to come?'

She nodded eagerly. 'Oh yes, lord. Of course.'

Khalif turned his attention to a large chest in one corner of the wagon. Opening it, he discovered to his satisfaction that it contained a large quantity of clothing. 'Clothe yourselves,' he ordered.

'What about Khigali?' asked a much relieved but still shaken Charlotte as she pulled a robe about her.

Khalif looked at her sternly.

'Master!' she added hastily.

He shrugged. 'I think the cord was released in time, but he will be in pain for a while yet.'

'Will you leave him here, master?'

'We must be on our way before Gebhr's men, or perhaps the Janissaries, get on our trail,' said Khalif tersely. 'I for one have no wish to be seated on a sharpened stake or hung on a cross.' He frowned. 'We have a choice. Leave him – in which case he will probably be quickly caught and impaled as a runaway – or we take him with us.' He looked down at her seriously. 'Charlotte, I leave the choice to you. He will slow us down, but I would rather not leave him here. What do you say?'

Charlotte hesitated only for a moment; she could not bear to think of the young slave suffering any more than he already had. 'No, do not leave him,' she replied firmly. 'Let him come with us, at least until we are safely away from this place.'

Meylissah, well acquainted with the cruelties practised on runaway slaves by the blue-cloaked soldiers of the Sultan, also nodded.

Khalif turned to leave the wagon. 'So be it,' he said gruffly. 'Make ready to leave as soon as possible.'

A Reckoning

Full dark saw the little column cautiously skirting the darkened village where Khalif and Zamil had bartered for the horses. There was no sign of life, except for a couple of mangy dogs that skulked snarling into the pepper groves as they moved past. The little group now numbered twenty-one, all the freed slaves having elected to join them though the shortage of horses meant that some had been forced to ride double.

There were twelve male slaves, all former corsairs. All had suffered at the hands of Gebhr and his men, but were looking much happier now they were clothed and had swords in their hands.

Khalif rode with Charlotte seated in front of him while Meylissah rode with Khigali, supporting his weak, swaying figure. Quite obviously the young lad was still in a quantity of pain. Leila and Fleur rode with them, while Zamil, Hawkins and Frith ranged ahead, scouting for possible danger.

Khalif had already decided to return to the little bay by the same route, thus avoiding the possibility of running into the Janissaries stationed at the fort. The climb down to the beach in darkness would be rugged, but at least they could lay up safely during the day.

The wind from the sea was very cold as they approached the rope bridge spanning the ravine, and Charlotte was shivering. 'Are we there?' she asked, pressing tightly against Khalif as he lifted her from the saddle.

Khalif nodded tersely. 'Once we cross the ravine.' He gave her the roll of blankets from his horse. 'Then we can rest.'

'Will the ship come today?' Charlotte eyed the rickety planks of the bridge nervously.

'Not until after dark. Then we will climb down to the beach and Issa will send a boat to pick us up.'

The bulky figure of Zamil loomed out of the darkness. 'What shall we do with the horses?' he asked.

'Picket them back in the orange grove out of sight for now. We can turn them loose when the ship comes.' He indicated the bridge. 'Tell the men to cross no more than two at a time. Oh, and leave three men on this side to watch our back trail, just in case. Everyone else can bivouac on the ridge. No fires until daylight, though, and even then only small cooking fires. No smoke. I don't want the Janissaries looking up here.' He turned to Charlotte with a reassuring smile. 'Come, hold on to me as we go across, then go find a place to lay out our blankets while I see to the men.' He bent his head and kissed her lightly. 'Tonight we can keep each other warm.'

Holding tightly to Khalif's waist, Charlotte allowed herself to be led across the swaying construction to the other side of the ravine where she selected a spot sheltered by a pile of rocks to unroll and lay out the blankets.

Zamil and Leila joined them a moment later, closely followed by Hawkins and Fleur. Charlotte, without a moment's hesitation, stripped off her clothes and, quite unashamed, crawled beneath the covers. As the others began to lay out their blankets she looked up at Khalif with huge eyes and held out her arms. 'I am cold, master,' she whispered.

Zamil grinned broadly as a slightly embarrassed Khalif joined her under the blankets. Charlotte, smiling happily, wriggled as close as she could to him, placing her arms around his neck to pull him down on top of her. Her soft nakedness enveloped him from chest to groin and, immediately, he began to harden. For a moment he tried to pull away, conscious of the others not an arm's length away. Charlotte was not to be denied, however, reaching between them to guide his shaft purposefully between her welcoming thighs. Khalif was lost, and ignoring the amused gaze of both Zamil and Hawkins, he rolled his blonde slave on to her back and, imprisoning her arms above her head with one hand, thrust vigorously within her sweetly captive body.

Hawkins looked at Zamil and frowned. 'A shameless slave,' he observed.

Zamil grinned back. 'A shameless master, also,' he said dryly.

Full daylight found the lovers asleep in each other's arms. Charlotte woke first, rising to prop herself on one elbow to first look at the sleeping Khalif, then around at the others. Despite the obvious danger of their situation she was blissfully happy. Khalif had come to rescue her and had claimed her for his own. She took no thought of the future. Only the moment was important.

Around the little ridge the freed slaves were rising and already Leila and Fleur were tending a little smokeless campfire from which the appetising smell of food was drifting through the rocks. A short way off, in the shelter of another pile of rocks, she saw Meylissah's cloud of dark hair spread out on the young Khigali's shoulder. The two were still asleep. Sliding gently from Khalif's grasp, the English girl donned her robe and moved stiffly to the fire.

'You sleep well?' grinned Leila.

Remembering the passion she and Khalif had shared, Charlotte had the grace to blush. Sleep had been the last thing on either of their minds, and once aroused Khalif had demonstrated an insatiable need for her, taking her to climax after dizzying climax until, finally exhausted, they both drifted into contented slumber. She rubbed a painful spot at the base of her spine and managed a rueful smile. Neither of them had taken any account of the uneven rockiness of their boudoir.

There was a commotion down by the bridge and a corsair came scrambling hurriedly towards them. 'Khalif?' he gasped. 'Where is Khalif?'

Zamil lifted his head. 'Here,' he rumbled. 'Over here. What has happened? What is the matter?'

'They're gone. The three men watching the trail – they are gone!'

'Gone?' Khalif slipped from his blankets and hurriedly pulled on his robe. He recognised the man as Chasim, one of Jahwar's men. 'Are you sure?'

'Yes, Khalif. I ventured back along to within sight of the village. They are gone.'

'Any sign of anyone else? Soldiers, Janissaries, anyone?'

Chasim shook his head. 'Something strange about the village, though. At this hour there ought to be someone up and about, but it looks completely deserted. No people, animals… nothing.'

Zamil and Hawkins were already donning clothes and weapons, and Khalif picked up his sword and a crossbow. 'Charlotte, you and the girls stay here,' he ordered. 'Zamil, Matthew, we'll go with Chasim and have a look at the village. Bring Frith and the longbows.'

Cautiously, the little group made their way back over the bridge, Hawkins and Frith with nocked arrows and Zamil hefting a loaded crossbow. The motley collection of white-painted houses came into view and they stopped, taking cover in the palms.

'You see. As I told you,' whispered their guide. 'The place is deserted.'

'Not quite,' replied Matthew Hawkins quietly, pointing to where the sprawled body of a woman lay in the shadow of one of the houses. As they got closer they could see her throat had been cut.

Slowly and carefully they moved in amongst the

buildings. Apart from the body of the woman they could find no one; every house was deserted. The stench hit them first and then, in the village square, they found the reason. There, lying in a tangled mass of limbs, were the bodies of the villagers. Men, women and children lay where they had fallen, some bristling with arrows, others with wounds inflicted by sword or spear, and still others with their throats cut or heads chopped off. In the centre of the square five stakes had been erected. On two of these were impaled the bodies of a middle-aged man and a woman. Khalif did not recognise either of them, though they could have been the headman and his wife. On the other three stakes were the men Zamil had set to watch the trail.

Matthew Hawkins spat. 'What d'you think?' he asked, eyes scanning the village for immediate danger. 'Janissaries?'

Khalif nodded slowly. 'It looks like it.'

'Why kill all the villagers?'

'Who knows? Perhaps they found out they sold us horses.' He gestured towards the impaled bodies. 'Whatever, it doesn't much matter now. Quickly, let's get back to the others before we finish up like them.'

They were nearly at the bridge when there was the drumming of hoofs on the hard ground and Zamil, at the rear, growled, 'Janissaries!'

Glancing back Khalif saw a group of blue-cloaked horsemen closing in on them fast.

'Matthew! Frith!' he ordered. 'Get across the bridge as fast as you can. We'll cover you with the crossbows. Then you can give them something to think about with those big bows of yours while the rest of us get across.'

Zamil leaped straight into action and, down the trail, one of the pursuers pitched from his horse with a crossbow bolt transfixing his neck. The Nubian gave a satisfied grunt. Chasim, too, was loosing bolts as fast as he could and the leading Janissary, an officer by his uniform, threw up his arms to fall with a strangled scream. The rest of the pursuers faltered momentarily, then arrows from the English longbows began to drop amongst them.

More blue-clad figures began to fall from their horses. It was enough. Pursuit ceased as the Janissaries dismounted and took cover.

Hurriedly Khalif and the others crossed the swaying bridge, crossbow bolts hissing past like angry hornets. 'Zamil, give me a hand!' panted Khalif, crossing to the supporting ropes and drawing his sword. Swiftly the ropes were cut, and with a crash and a cloud of dust the entire structure of the bridge dropped into the ravine.

'Khalif!' The shout came from Chasim. He was pointing up the ridge.

Grimly, Khalif looked to where the corsair pointed. The area was suddenly swarming with soldiers, some already stripping the four girls while others with levelled crossbows surrounded the little group of corsairs.

'Treachery, Khalif,' growled Zamil. 'We are betrayed.'

'A trap, certainly,' replied Khalif. 'Somehow someone knew we would come this way. Maybe that was why the villagers were massacred, so we should not be warned.'

'But how could they know?' queried Zamil angrily. 'And if they did, why didn't they take us as we came up past the village last night? Why wait until now?'

A squad of helmeted Janissaries came down the hill towards them, crossbows at the ready and, warily, the five backed to the cliff edge. Khalif looked down. There in the bay, sails furled, a galleon and three corsair galleys lay at anchor while a dozen or more small boats ferried what looked to be a full company of soldiers ashore.

Khalif pointed. 'There's your answer. Those ships have just arrived with fresh troops. They wanted to make absolutely sure we didn't get away.'

'So what do we do?' asked Matthew Hawkins, nocking an arrow to his bow. Frith did the same and Zamil lifted his crossbow.

With a sigh Khalif lowered his sword. 'Nothing, yet,' he whispered. 'We have no choice. Put down your weapons.'

Chasim was still looking down at the beach. 'There!' he hissed, pointing to where a huge black-robed man in a sinister-looking leather mask sat astride a prancing white horse at the head of a troop of blue-cloaked horseman. 'Mulay Aruj, the devil Bey himself.' He lifted his crossbow with shaking hands. 'I say we fight! I saw what was done to Jahwar, whose head now sits on a spike on Tunis' gate. Better to die quickly now than inch by inch like that.'

'Courage, friend,' whispered Khalif. 'Trust me. All is not yet lost. Wait for my word.'

Chasim hesitated for a moment, then as the others discarded their weapons, slowly and reluctantly did the same.

Stripped and bound, Khalif was separated from the others before being taken down the treacherous cliff path to the beach. As he was led away he looked round to see Charlotte and the other girls being thrown to the ground by grinning Janissaries. It took little imagination to know what was about to happen to them.

The climb down was difficult to say the least, with his hands bound, and several times he nearly fell. When he finally reached the sand he was kicked to his knees and a noose dropped around his neck. Then a shadow fell over him and he looked up to see the massive figure of the Bey on the white horse. He squinted to look closer, but could not make out the man's face behind the leather mask.

'Here, my lord,' said one of the guards, tightening the noose around Khalif's neck with a powerful jerk which threatened to strangle him. 'This is the barbarian.' Silently, the masked man held out his hand for the rope, which he swiftly tied to the pommel of his saddle. Then, as Khalif climbed painfully back to his feet, he kicked the horse into motion and made for the fortress at a brisk trot, his captive forced into a desperate run to keep up or risk being dragged by his neck.

Inside the walls of the fortress the Bey handed his hard-breathing prisoner's leash to an officer. 'Take him,' he ordered gruffly. 'Chain him as I told you.'

Khalif heard the words and glanced up once again at the masked man. The officer gave him no time to look closer. Dragging on the rope until once again Khalif was struggling to breathe, he dragged him into the fortress proper and down to a dungeon carved deep in the rock. There, with the help of four other Janissaries, the struggling corsair was eventually chained spread-eagled between the two stone pillars supporting the ceiling.

'Comfortable, dog?' growled the officer, tightening the chains viciously until Khalif's spread feet only just touched the ground. Receiving no answer, he backhanded Khalif left and right across the face with a mailed fist. 'I said, are you comfortable, dog?'

'Your time will come, coward,' Khalif muttered, blood running from his split mouth. 'And perhaps sooner than you think.'

The Janissary laughed harshly. 'But not before yours, barbarian. Rest as you are and reflect. The Bey comes to visit you shortly and then we shall see who is the coward.' He paused and looked deep into Khalif's eyes. 'After he has visited your female slaves and made arrangements for their disposal.'

The Janissary sighed regretfully and, reaching down to Khalif's dangling genitals, began to squeeze slowly and carefully. Writhing in agony, sweat running unchecked on his naked body, Khalif was unable to stifle a series of deep groans as the pitiless torture continued.

'My lord wishes you to send a message to your patron, Dragut Bey,' the torturer went on smoothly. 'In return for your life – and the life of your slut – he asks that Redbeard now join his alliance and bring his ships to Tunis. What say you, barbarian? Will the old man take heed of your words?' Releasing his hold on Khalif's aching ball sac, he stepped back, regarding his prisoner with some satisfaction.

Khalif shook his head in a vain attempt to clear his vision. The agonising pain in his genitals was subsiding, but only slowly. 'Dragut responds badly to threats,' he croaked, 'and knows that I would never ask this of him. Your Bey made a bad mistake when he sent those demands. Dragut will not join him, either in this or in any other venture.'

The Janissary frowned. 'Let me warn you, dog! If you refuse, my lord has already promised the unlimited use of your slave to the palace guard, until he is ready to pass judgement on her treason.' He chuckled nastily. 'And for my part, I have promised the slut shall serve well and often. Believe me, she will not find her service pleasant. My men and I have little love for infidels. Now then, what do you say? Will you help and spare her much pain?'

Gathering as much phlegm as he could in his dry mouth, Khalif spat directly into the guard's face. 'Here, this is what I think of you and your Bey!'

'My lord anticipated that this might be your answer,' rasped the Janissary, wiping the spittle from his cheek. 'I am pleased, also. My men and I are looking forward to the use of your slave.' Coldly and efficiently he began backhanding his helpless prisoner once more, stopping only when Khalif was hanging limp and unconscious in his chains.

It was a long time before Khalif returned to pain-filled consciousness. He blinked his eyes to rid them of blood and tears and saw, as if through a mist, the sinister black-clad figure of the masked Bey standing in front of him.

'So, you are back with us, barbarian,' said Mulay Aruj. 'I am afraid the commander here has been unnecessarily rough with you. Still, here you are now. Tell me before further pain is yours to bear. Is your answer still the same?'

With some difficulty Khalif lifted his head to stare defiantly at the inquisitor. 'I thought it was you, filth, when first I heard you speak,' he whispered. 'Now I am sure.' His voice strengthened. 'Many years have I sought you, Mulay Aruj, or whatever your name really is.'

The fat man laughed harshly. 'And now you have found me.' He reached up to remove his mask, revealing the scarred and demonic features that had so frightened Charlotte. 'Though I think it will do you little good.' Slowly he rubbed his forefinger down the deep jagged scar on his ruined face. 'I expect you remember this – and how I came by it?' He spat deliberately.

'Now then, I would persuade you to help me bring Dragut to Tunis.' Stepping closer and reaching into his robe, Mulay Aruj brought out a handful of sharp slivers of pitch-soaked wood, each about two inches long. 'You know what these are, I think?'

Khalif made no reply, but was unable to suppress a groan as, carefully, Mulay began to insert the slivers under the skin of his chest and belly, leaving perhaps half an inch or so of each protruding from the sweat-soaked skin.

'What say you?' he asked again, slowly and deliberately pushing a sliver through each nipple, bringing a deep choking groan from his helpless victim. 'Persuade Dragut to come to Tunis to negotiate our alliance and both you and your slut go free. Refuse, and I promise you shall both have very slow and very painful ends.'

'Rot in hell, filth!' The defiant answer finished on another deep groan as yet more splinters were inserted under Khalif's skin.

'Very well. We will see.' Stepping back, Mulay signalled to the grinning Janissary. 'Light them!'

Casually, the Janissary lifted a blazing torch and, brushing it slowly over the front of the corsair's body, made sure that all the little pitch-soaked slivers were well alight.

'Come now, barbarian,' said Mulay Aruj softly, as the tiny

wooden spears flared briefly, then continued to burn slowly and agonisingly under Khalif's skin. 'Why continue to suffer?' He smiled lazily as Khalif's mouth contorted and he jerked wildly against the chains holding him aloft. Receiving no reply, he went on, 'Or would you rather watch your precious slut wriggling on a sharpened stake as did your mewling sister? I promise you, this can and will happen if you continue to refuse me.'

This time he got a vocal reaction as Khalif pulled even more violently against his bonds. 'Do what you will with me, but it will gain you nothing to hurt the girl. You know I cannot – nor will I ever – help you in this.'

'Well, no matter,' said Mulay Aruj. 'Sooner or later I shall have Redbeard, as I have you. Then there will be a full settlement.' With a scowl he put a hand up to his face, running his fingers down the length of the scar which disfigured him. 'It was your sister who did this to me, remember?' he hissed. 'She paid the full price of my discomfort. Now I have decided you will do the same – if only in the memory of my friend.'

For long moments the only sounds in the little cell were Khalif's harsh breathing and suppressed groans as he continued to writhe in agony, the smell of burning flesh from his spread-eagled body drifting up to fill the noses of the watching men. 'Filth,' he managed to gasp, beginning to drift towards unconsciousness again. 'It is time someone rid the world of you!'

With an evil smile, Mulay Aruj reached out to run his fingers over the sweat-sheened skin, feeling where the wood was still burning away. 'Maybe,' he chuckled. 'But I think it will not be you.' He grasped his victim's penis and squeezed hard. 'Perhaps I should have finished you then, as I did your sister. Certainly the friend to whom I sold you would now still be alive.' His hand moved to Khalif's defenceless ball sac and he squeezed again. 'Come now, he was not such a bad fellow, was he? All he wanted was the use of your body.

Did you have to kill him?'

Khalif just managed to suppress a scream, the renewed pain in his balls becoming almost unbearable. 'He was a pig and died like one,' he finally managed to croak, 'as you will one day, Mulay Aruj.'

Mulay chuckled. 'I think not, barbarian. It is you who hang in chains, not I. Perhaps I will send your balls to Dragut, as he returned my messenger's head to me. Would he appreciate such a gift, I wonder?'

'Dragut will separate your head from your body, pig,' gasped Khalif, black unconsciousness approaching once more.

Mulay Aruj grunted impatiently and stepped back, signalling the grinning guard commander with a wave of his hand. 'This is a waste of time. Sixty lashes to teach him manners,' he barked. 'Then hang him in the cage in the main hall.'

Mercifully, Khalif slipped into oblivion long before the terrible sentence was completed. Even so, every lash continued to be stroked across the bleeding flesh until the entire sixty had been properly laid on.

The blue-cloaked commander of Mulay Aruj's palace guard led Charlotte up from the dungeon where she had been imprisoned with the other girls. Unhampered by bonds, except for a leash fastened on her throat, she was led naked into the hall, her heart turning to ice as she saw the bleeding figure of Khalif imprisoned in an iron cage suspended from the vaulted ceiling over a burning brazier. The cage was bobbing and jerking crazily, Khalif taking his weight on his manacled wrists to keep his feet up as far as possible from the hot metal below. Trembling with fear, as much for Khalif as herself, she allowed herself to be led forward until she stood in front of the dais where sat an unmasked Mulay Aruj with the dandified English pirate, Mad Jack Fletcher.

'There hangs the traitor, Khalif Barbar,' growled the scar-faced Bey, pointing at the cage, 'who, with his English slut, is accused of treason against the Sultan and the empire!' He indicated the two rough-hewn wooden crosses lying on the ground in front of the dais. 'The verdict is guilty. The sentence, crucifixion.' He looked malevolently up at the caged Khalif. 'The *nasrani* slut first, then the traitor himself.'

'Leave her alone, you bastard!' shouted Khalif from the cage. 'Do what you want with me, but leave her alone. She has done nothing.'

Terrified, Charlotte looked up into the dark unyielding face of the guard commander. 'For pity's sake, no,' she whispered. 'Not that, please!'

'Come,' ordered the guard commander grimly, pushing her forward. 'Here, in Lord Mulay's hall of justice, you and the barbarian shall both live out your last hours in agony; a fitting example to all who contemplate treason against the empire.'

She was lifted easily by four Janissaries and laid roughly on her back on the cross, her pleas for clemency completely unheeded by the men. Her arms were seized and jerked outwards, the backs of her hands scraping painfully against the wood as she strained uselessly against the firm grip of the guards. Her pitiful struggles were unavailing and she twisted in pain as the rough thin cords were secured around her wrists, pinioning her outstretched arms firmly to the crosspiece.

Dimly, she became aware that Khalif was shouting her name, then her feet were brought together and tied tightly.

So great was Charlotte's terror that for a moment or two she couldn't even scream. Snorting gasps emerged from her mouth as the cross was lifted by four guards and dropped with a bone-shaking thump into its hole. Swiftly the guards piled the waiting rocks and earth into place, wedging the crucifix with its grim burden firmly into the upright position. Charlotte's entire weight now depended from her shoulders and outstretched arms, the thin cords holding her firmly in position.

Pain began to hit her in successive waves and little sparks of coloured light flashed before her eyes. Suddenly, shockingly, she screamed and screamed again, her muscles contorting in violent spasms of agony as the increased pain became an awful reality. The pressure in her chest grew greater with every second and she began to find it increasingly difficult to breathe. She shook her head in a desperate attempt to clear her vision and another wave of agony hit her. Her screams faded into gasping moans and blood from a bitten lip ran in a thin stream down on to her chest. She knew she was dying.

From below the hated voice of Mulay Aruj called out, then something cold and metallic pressed against the ringed opening to her sex passage. She waited for the pain that she knew would inevitably come, then there was a great crashing noise followed by yet more shouting and, moments later, the clash of steel on steel. It was then her tortured body gave up the unequal struggle and she finally retreated into the comforting blackness of insensibility.

Khalif went berserk as Mulay's guard commander lashed Charlotte's outstretched arms to the cross. Then the cross was set brutally upright and her desperate screams began to fade. Calling out her name, mindless of the pain in his burning feet, he kicked out again and again at the unmoving, obdurate bars of the cage.

Mulay Aruj looked up at the bobbing cage with a sneer. 'Worry not, barbarian,' he called, 'soon it will be your turn.' His lip curled contemptuously. 'You should thank me, Khalif Barbar. It is not everyone who has the chance to die with the one he loves.' He stood up and drew a jewelled dagger from its sheath, then moved casually to the foot of the cross. 'You *do* love her, do you not?' he called, reaching up to press the sharp blade against the fig-shaped cleft between her thighs. He laughed as the barely conscious girl jerked and flinched away. 'Myself and the corsair Jahwar, too, I think, gave her much pleasure by our use of this and other parts of her body. Truly, she is nothing but a *nasrani* slut.'

'Don't,' shouted Khalif, terrified of what Mulay might do to Charlotte with the knife. 'Leave her alone, you scum! Leave her alone!'

With a huge crash and bang part of the wall seemed to explode in front of his eyes and a great hole appeared, scattering large chunks of wood, masonry and plaster over those crowding around the dais.

In the confusion Mad Jack Fletcher leaped to his feet and, drawing his sword, strode across to kick over the brazier. 'Now!' he shouted to his men, slashing wildly at the rope holding the cage aloft. 'Now is the time. Engage the guards!'

Even as Khalif's cage dropped to the floor there was another loud explosion and more stone and plaster rained down. Panic-stricken Janissaries trying to leave the hall were thrown back as the twin doors suddenly burst in to admit the red-bearded figure of Dragut Bey followed by a mass of heavily-armed corsairs, cutting down all who challenged them.

Khalif crawled painfully from the cage, the door of which had been sprung open by the impact of hitting the floor. Moving forward to protect his ally, Mad Jack suddenly found himself with a fight on his hands as four Janissaries attacked him from different sides. A dozen or more of Fletcher's crew rushed the dais to aid their captain and a Janissary reeled back, blood frothing from his mouth as a sword pierced his throat. The fight was over quickly, the remaining three blue-cloaked soldiers swiftly overwhelmed by the English sailors. Steel crashed against steel all around the hall and, from the direction of the harbour, there came the distant but distinct rolling thunder of cannon-fire.

Meanwhile, Dragut's crossbowmen were loosing shafts as fast as they could aim and reload, and all across the hall Janissaries were falling. On the dais, Mulay Aruj and a few of his personal guard were backed against the wall, engaged in desperate close combat with the attacking sailors of Fletcher's crew.

'Dragut!' shouted Khalif to his approaching friend. 'A sword, quickly!'

Sparing a troubled glance at the still-twitching figure hanging on the cross, the old corsair threw him his sword. 'Settle with your enemy!' yelled Dragut Bey. 'I will help the girl!'

Khalif hesitated only a moment, then ignoring the pain in his burned and blackened feet, sprang into the fray, splitting one Janissary's skull with a mighty blow and running another cleanly through as he limped forward deliberately towards the scar-faced Bey of Tunis. 'Mulay Aruj,' he shouted. 'Your time has come. Stand and face me, you filth!'

Only two of the guards defending the Bey remained on their feet, and snarling, Mulay Aruj waved them forward. The attacking corsairs, well aware of Khalif's prowess with a sword, stood back to watch the spectacle.

The two Janissaries separated, going against their intended victim from both sides as they had been taught. Khalif, however, was no victim. Moving with a speed and power born of rage and hatred, his flashing sword easily evaded the first guard's defence, cleaving him deeply and mortally from armpit to belly.

The watching corsairs cheered mightily and the remaining Janissary backed off. Khalif smiled grimly. This was the guard commander, the one who had beaten and tortured him in the dungeon and so brutally tied Charlotte to the cross. Khalif moved straight at him, bringing his sword down at his adversary's head with absolutely no attempt at deception. The officer managed to block the crashing blow with his own blade, but still it staggered him. The contest was short and brutal, Khalif's sword cleaving through the Janissary's guard almost as if it did not exist. With an anguished scream the man fell, dead before he hit the floor.

Khalif stepped past the man's body and moved threateningly towards the large figure of Mulay Aruj.

The scarred Bey, obviously shaken at the ease with which the naked corsair had despatched his two guards, tried to bolster his own courage with defiant words. Menacingly, he hefted his double-edged sword. 'Come then, barbarian,' he spat. 'I will be only too glad to put you to your rest, as I did your feeble sister and the rest of your kin.'

The words were almost his last. Khalif sprang like a striking panther, limbs a blur. Sheer speed took him on top of the other man almost before he could raise his sword in defence. Even the watching Fletcher caught his breath at the tempo of Khalif's attack. Belatedly, Mulay Aruj's sword flashed up to catch the dreadful downward blow. There was a great clash of steel on steel and he staggered back, sword arm almost paralysed by the force of the attack. Another blow came and another, and each time he was compelled to move back a step. His arms seemed to be having trouble holding up the sword, until finally they could no longer do so. The blade fell from his nerveless fingers and he slid to his knees, courage finally deserting him. Screaming and gibbering, shaking with a sickness born of pure terror, Mulay Aruj cowered away. Then the blade crashed down, cleaving straight through his neck to separate his head from his body.

Mulay Aruj, late Bey of Tunis, fell lifeless to the floor at Khalif's feet.

The cheers of the watching corsairs shook the rafters and the few remaining Janissaries threw down their weapons. Khalif, without a further glance at the decapitated corpse, turned back to where Dragut and several other corsairs had finally managed to uproot Charlotte's cross. Gently, they laid it flat on the floor.

'She still lives, but her pulse is weak,' observed Dragut. 'Still, she is young and strong. I am certain she will recover.' He looked round the hall. 'What about Zamil and the others? Are they still in the dungeons?'

Khalif nodded. 'Yes. Mulay planned to impale them on the walls of the city as a warning to any who might contemplate rebellion.'

Dragut indicated the corpse of Mulay Aruj and spat contemptuously. 'We will take this cur's head back to Tunis and spike it over the city gate so that all may see the fate of tyrants!' Handing Khalif a bloodstained tunic to cover his nakedness, he strode off on his mission.

'Send Zamil and the girls to me as quickly as you can,' shouted Khalif after him. 'I shall need their help.'

'Is the girl all right, Khalif?' Mad Jack Fletcher wiped his sword on a torn piece of cloth as he arrived back at the dais. 'I am sorry we could not act sooner.' He shot a regretful glance at the limp figure of Charlotte. 'I would have spared her that had I known what was in the devil's mind. You knew, of course, that we planned a rescue?'

'Yes. I recognised your ship in the bay.'

Fletcher smiled grimly. 'Dragut sent me on ahead when your message reached Algiers. It was as we thought. Mulay Aruj, greedy for loot and allies, made us welcome. Even so, we were lucky Dragut spotted our ships in the bay. Had he been sailing further from shore the outcome might well have been different.'

Khalif, breathing easier now, looked suddenly as if a great weight had been lifted from his shoulders. 'Once again I owe him my life,' he said softly. 'And now my mother, father and sister are avenged at last.' There was a quality to the corsair's voice which clearly indicated the depth of his feelings. 'Until I heard his voice on the beach I had no idea, but this so-called Bey was the devil I have searched for all these years.'

211

Fletcher glanced at Mulay Aruj's body in surprise. 'So this was the man who murdered your family,' he said. He looked around the hall. The carnage was over, bodies littering the floor and all the surviving Janissaries disarmed and chained. 'Then Khalif Barbar's private Jihad would seem to be finished.'

It was at this moment that Dragut came back with Zamil and the three girls. 'Mistress… oh, mistress,' sobbed a distraught Meylissah. She turned a tearstained face to Khalif. 'What have they done to her? Will she live?'

Zamil looked from the weals, burns and other marks of torture on Khalif's body to the girl lying so still in his arms. 'What happened?' he queried.

Khalif gently shifted Charlotte so that she lay more comfortably and cast a glance filled with hatred at Mulay Aruj's corpse. 'That murdering devil had her crucified,' he growled. 'Thankfully Dragut arrived in time and Fletcher was on hand to help, but she has suffered terribly, Zamil. I fear for her life.'

'Leila has some knowledge of medicine; she can aid Charlotte. She will recover, Khalif. Do not worry.'

Khalif got up and swayed, unsteady for a moment, then turned for the door with his unconscious burden. 'I will take her aboard the *San Cristobal* then,' he said decisively. 'We can make her more comfortable there.'

Dragut Bey nodded. 'I will come to see you later. Right now the men are looking for spoils.' He grinned. 'Remember, also, Tunis now awaits us unguarded. Let us hope Mulay's treasury proves to be as rich as people say.'

Separation

'Curse Jahwar's soul for placing her in that devil's hands,' said Khalif savagely. They were in the large stern cabin of the *San Cristobal*, moored in the harbour at Tunis. Zamil, Dragut, Hawkins, Mad Jack Fletcher and John Frith at the table with Khalif, while Charlotte lay covered with furs on the large sleeping couch. Her wounds were superficial, but her ordeal had weakened her and she seemed feverish. Meylissah knelt at her side, gently wiping her perspiring brow with a damp cloth as the men conversed.

'You spent time with Mulay.' Khalif addressed Fletcher. 'How did he know where we would be?'

'I don't really know,' replied Fletcher, 'but I would suspect that someone from that village recognised you and told the Janissaries at the fort. It was common knowledge in the city that Jahwar had taken Charlotte from you and brought her to Tunis to sell.' He pondered for a moment. 'As I recall, Mulay refused to sell her to me at the palace, insisting she be sold on the block. I think maybe he concocted this whole business with Gebhr just to trap you.'

Charlotte struggled to sit up, the gold rings in her uncovered breasts glittering in the light of the oil lamps, her face pale and wan. 'Oh, Khalif. I thought I would die. The Bey had a knife. I thought he would cut me...'

'Shhh,' whispered Khalif, quickly covering her nakedness with the furs. 'It is all over, thanks to Jack and his men. Lie back and rest. As soon as you are well enough to travel, we sail for Djerba and the fortress. As Allah is my witness, no one will take you from me again.'

'I love you,' she whispered, 'and when you took me from Gebhr I was happy.' Her shoulders began to shake and she turned her face away to hide her tears. 'But Jahwar called me slut, and now I know this is what I am. Mulay Aruj and the slave trainers all knew it well, as did all the other men who took their pleasure with me. How can you still want me when at every turn my body betrayed both of us?'

Khalif stroked her neck gently. 'Hush now,' he said softly. 'It is you who were betrayed, little one. Did you choose to be at the mercy of Jahwar and Mulay Aruj? Did you ever have any choice about what was being done to you?' He answered for her when she made no reply. 'No, of course not.'

She continued to cry, great sobs shaking her shoulders. 'But they tattooed me... and other things.'

Khalif shrugged carelessly. 'Slaves are usually marked in some way or other. As for the rings in your flesh, they can be removed – if I decide they do not please me.' He smiled then, white teeth gleaming in his dark face. 'But I shall leave them where they are for the time being. I think I shall enjoy having you belled sometimes.'

Charlotte reddened and cast an embarrassed, sideways glance at the three Englishmen.

'Nothing that has happened has been your fault,' Khalif went on. He sighed. 'Much of the fault was mine. It was I who first enslaved you, and I who took your maidenhead.'

Charlotte looked up shyly. 'Not against my will,' she whispered. 'You gave me much, and all that you took from me, I gladly gave.'

Khalif went on as if he had not heard her. 'Had I not left you virtually unguarded, Jahwar would never have been able to take you.' He stroked her blonde hair gently. 'I know now that, even though I would have stood you on the block so that your value might be shared, I would have bought you myself, no matter what the cost.'

She looked up at him tearfully. 'Leila said this, but when you told me I was to be sold in Algiers, I thought you didn't want me. And yet all the time, with Jahwar and Mulay Aruj and in the house of slaves, I prayed and prayed you would come. Oh, Khalif... all I ever wanted was to be yours. I love you. I really do love you!'

'And I you, slave, though I did not truly know it until it was nearly too late,' he whispered back. He kissed her gently on the forehead. 'I have heard of this thing and thought it to be nothing more than a female fancy. Yet it is true. I cannot deny it. You are my love slave.' He looked down at her possessively and pulled her even closer to his chest. 'I will not give you up.'

Fletcher gave an embarrassed cough. 'Perhaps we should talk about this mysterious Spanish fleet,' he said.

Khalif looked up. 'Spanish fleet?' he asked. 'You said the Dey of Algiers was worried about it? But why? How does it concern us?'

Fletcher shrugged his shoulders. 'It seems the Spanish are assembling a large fleet for an invasion of England. The Dey's spies have told him there are well over a hundred ships already in the ports of Lisbon and Cadiz.' He chuckled grimly. 'My countryman, Drake, has been raiding the Spanish settlements in the New World. He completely destroyed their fortifications at Saint Augustine, taking much gold and many prisoners.' He paused for a moment to let what he was saying sink in. 'At first the Dey thought that we in the Mediterranean might be threatened. The corsairs have, after all, taken many Spanish ships since the disaster at Lepanto. But evidently it is not so. Though his emissaries are still bargaining at the English Court, it seems King Philip has now had enough of Drake and the other English privateers. The fact that Elizabeth has imprisoned Catholic Mary, the Scottish Queen, and now threatens to execute her has not endeared the English to him, either. From what we have been told, Philip seriously intends to try an invasion across the English Channel.'

Hawkins nodded. 'Philip is quite convinced that he is master of the world. And if he succeeds in such a venture, who can say what his next will be? Algiers, Bizerte and all our safe havens may well come under fire.'

Fletcher smacked a fist savagely into his palm. 'I sail for England now that this matter of Mulay Aruj is settled. I cannot stand by and watch my homeland threatened. Most of the other English privateers will do the same, I think.'

Both Hawkins and Frith nodded emphatically. 'With your permission, Khalif, we will sail with Fletcher,' Hawkins said. 'If and when an invasion comes, our place will be with Drake and Howard in the English Channel!'

Khalif nodded. 'I understand. But what if the Dey's spies are mistaken? Maybe Philip intends to deal a blow against us first.'

Charlotte looked up at him. 'Captain Fletcher speaks the truth, my love,' she said weakly. 'My uncle discovered the plan in Valletta. It was why he was hurrying back to England; why he had to leave me when I had the fever.' She broke off as a coughing spasm took hold of her and Meylissah took the opportunity to wipe her brow again. The spasm subsided and the English girl went on: 'What the Dey did not discover is that there is not to be one fleet, but two. One from Spain itself and one from the Netherlands full of soldiers; coming together in the English Channel.' She paused for a moment, collecting her thoughts. 'They have many large fighting galleons and galleys,' she whispered, 'as well as heavily-armed Indiamen and a whole flotilla of smaller vessels.' She shivered and pressed herself even closer to Khalif. 'And there are enough transports for the army sailing from Rotterdam. A famous general — my uncle called him Guzman, or some such name, I think – is to command.'

Hawkins whistled soundlessly. 'Alonzo Pérez de Guzman, Duke of Medina Sidonia.' His fingers drummed the table. 'He certainly is their best general. Philip must really mean business this time.'

'Yes, that was the name, I remember it now,' said Charlotte. 'And if they cross the Channel unopposed, England will certainly be vanquished. My uncle was on his way to warn the queen. Now it is up to us.' Her tone was filled with anxiety.

'Shhh, everything is going to be all right,' soothed Khalif, gently squeezing her shoulder. 'Fletcher and Hawkins will warn your queen, never fear.'

She rubbed her cheek against Khalif's broad chest, red-rimmed eyes enormous in her pale face. 'You and I both know Fletcher and Hawkins to be honourable men,' she whispered. 'But who in England will believe them? Most will see them as common pirates.' She looked apologetically at the little group. 'Please, I do not mean it unkindly. Uncle James told me what it was like. Traitors are everywhere – even among the Queen's closest advisers, and she knows not who to believe. It was why she sent my uncle to the Mediterranean, to find out exactly what was going on.'

Fletcher was quiet for a moment as he considered her words, then he nodded. 'It is true, Khalif,' he said quietly. 'Privateers like Hawkins and myself left England because we were being threatened with imprisonment. The queen was advised to have us arrested by powerful Spanish sympathisers at the court in order to placate Philip. Drake himself only escaped because he was the queen's favourite.' He snorted. 'Yet these are the men who must defend England if an invasion comes. Our army is small and mostly untrained. Without ships, Philip knows England will fall like a ripe plum.'

'So, what is to be done?' asked Khalif. 'How will you convince those who need to know that what you report is the truth?'

There was silence for a moment. Then Fletcher spoke. 'There seems to be only one way,' he said quietly. He hesitated for a moment. 'Lady Charlotte. If she were to come with us, there would be no problem.'

Both Hawkins and John Frith nodded eagerly. 'Of course,' said Hawkins. 'She is the niece of the queen's envoy. With Sir James dead, the queen would have to believe her.'

Khalif shook his head immediately. 'No,' he replied flatly, his tone of voice clearly denoting he would brook no argument.

Charlotte laid a bandaged hand on his and looked up at him pleadingly. 'Please, Khalif,' she whispered.

Khalif shook his head impatiently and pushed her hand

away. 'Be quiet, slave,' he said gruffly. 'I am master here, not you.'

Hawkins coughed apologetically. 'We understand how you feel, Khalif. We would not ask if there were any other way.' He looked down sadly at the pale-faced girl. 'Our queen placed great trust in Sir James and knows the Lady Charlotte – er, your slave – very well. Were she to confirm our report there would be no question, and the traitors would be thwarted.' He smacked a fist against the table. 'And do not forget; if England falls, the whole of the Mediterranean will almost certainly fall under Philip's sway.'

Khalif set his jaw defiantly. 'It is out of the question,' he growled. He looked angrily at the three Englishmen. 'For the love of Allah, think what you are saying. Just a few hours ago Mulay Aruj was trying to kill her. Do you wish to finish the job yourselves?'

'I can think of no other way,' said Fletcher, softly.

Hawkins nodded agreement. 'He speaks the truth, Khalif,' he said. 'The queen will not believe us alone. We need Lady Charlotte to go with us. I know how you feel and I wish it were not so, but it is the truth.'

There was absolute silence for a long moment as Khalif considered what had been said. His expression was dark as he made his reply. 'I grant that no one here is helped if England falls,' he admitted finally. 'But what is that to me? I am not English – and if Philip sends ships to Djerba, I can assure you they will have a very hot reception.'

Charlotte reached up to touch his face. 'Please, Khalif,' she whispered. 'These are men who risked their lives for us. Can you not help them in turn?' She gently traced the outline of the scar on his temple with one finger. 'I beg you, let me go with them. It is my duty.'

Khalif hesitated again, clearly undecided about what he should do. 'You wish to go with them?' he asked Charlotte gruffly. 'You do not wish to stay with me?'

Charlotte smiled up at him, her eyes brimming with tears.

'Oh, my love, it is my dearest wish to stay with you forever. But don't you see? I must do this. I would never forgive myself if by staying I caused my country's downfall.' She paused for a moment. 'I do love you and I always will. I will return as soon as I can.'

Khalif shook his head, defeated, and looked at the three Englishmen. 'Very well, then. As soon as Leila and Meylissah can assure me that she is recovered sufficiently to travel, I will allow her to go to England with you. You, in turn, shall guarantee to bring her back to me once your danger is over. Is this agreeable?'

Fletcher nodded. 'Of course. A few days will make little difference, and will give us a chance to find a ship and provisions. And as soon as I can, I will personally bring her back to you. You have my word.' He held out his hand. 'Agreed?'

Khalif took the outstretched hand in one of his own and shook it. 'Agreed,' he said quietly.

Satisfied, Charlotte pressed close to Khalif. Fletcher hid a smile. Whatever the merits of the master/slave relationship between Khalif and the lovely English girl, to the outsider it was perfectly clear who really had the upper hand.

Hawkins, also well aware of how much Charlotte meant to the big corsair, smiled as she reached up to throw her arms around his neck, uncaring that the furs no longer covered her upper body. 'All right, all right,' he admonished. 'There will be plenty of time for that later. Now we need to talk about a ship. These damned Mediterranean galleys will be no use in the Bay of Biscay. Wouldn't last more than five minutes in a half-decent blow.'

Fletcher coughed apologetically. 'I'm afraid my ship will be no good, either. We were badly holed in our last engagement with the Spanish. She would never last the journey.'

'There is a captured English ship in the harbour,' said Zamil. 'I saw her when we rowed out to the *Cristobal*. She

219

is still seaworthy by the look of her. Called the *Triumph*, I think.'

Charlotte's eyes brimmed with tears. 'Uncle James's ship,' she whispered.

Khalif held her close. 'Yes, your uncle's,' he agreed softly. 'And what better to take you to your queen?'

Finally, he disengaged himself from her clutching arms. 'Now it is time for you to rest,' he asserted. 'I leave you in Meylissah's care while we make plans for the coming journey. Try to get some sleep if you can.'

The men stood up to take their brief farewells of the English girl. As Khalif ushered them out through the cabin door, Meylissah leaned forward. 'You know he loves you very much,' she whispered. 'Lord Jack said he would have died for you had it been necessary.'

The door closed behind the others and Charlotte looked up questioningly at her friend. 'Lord Jack? You mean Captain Fletcher? Is this how you call him?'

'He is very nice, mistress.' Somewhat uncharacteristically, Meylissah was blushing a fine shade of red.

Charlotte smiled and tried to sit up, then groaned and sank back as the throbbing muscles and tendons in her neck and shoulders made themselves felt once more.

'It still hurts?' asked Meylissah anxiously.

Charlotte nodded breathlessly. 'My neck and shoulders where they hung me on the cross.' She shuddered. 'I remember them tying me to the thing and that was bad enough, but when they lifted it upright and I was just hanging there... Oh, Meylissah, it was agony. I couldn't even breathe properly. Never have I felt such pain.'

'Do you not remember Khalif bringing you to the ship?'

'I vaguely remember being carried, I don't know by who, but not very much more than that.'

'My lady means to journey to England?' asked Meylissah.

Charlotte nodded. 'Yes, in a day or so, when I am strong enough. I will come back soon, though.' A thought struck her and she looked pensively at the other girl. 'Would you like to come with me? I shall need a nurse for a while.'

Meylissah's face lit up. 'Oh yes, mistress.' She hesitated for a moment then continued, 'Perhaps my lady will not mind if maybe I also serve sometimes Lord Jack?'

'Fletcher?' A glint of understanding showed in Charlotte's eyes. 'I see,' she smiled. 'Well, I suppose he is quite handsome in a way. But what about Lord Jack? Does he feel the same way?'

Meylissah blushed and looked away. 'It seems so, mistress,' she said shyly.

Charlotte reached out a hand and laid it gently on the other's arm. 'I am pleased, Meylissah. Captain Fletcher has been a good friend, despite his occupation, and you I love as if you were my own sister.' She frowned. 'Although it was not always so. I can remember a time when you were mistress and I slave – and you taught me the slave dances.' She grimaced. 'That little whip of yours was awful.'

Meylissah had an innocent look on her face. 'My lady holds it not against me?' she asked. 'Of course, she will remember that I was but obeying our master's command when I kissed her flesh with it.'

'Kissed? Kissed?' Charlotte looked wrathfully at her companion. 'I don't remember it as being kissed.' She faked a glare. 'It hurt like the devil. I feel the sting still.'

For one tiny moment Meylissah looked apprehensive but then, as the English girl began to chuckle, she too began to smile. Charlotte held out her arms and the former slave girl fell readily into her embrace. 'Oh, Meylissah, we have been through so much together,' she whispered. 'Now we are as sisters.'

Epilogue
February, 1589
The island of Djerba, off the coast of Tunisia

Standing at the ship's rail, Lady Charlotte Brandon looked eagerly at the island lying off the starboard bow. The island of Djerba, legendary home of the ancient Lotus Eaters. The island fortress of Dragut Bey and Khalif, the island which had been in her thoughts and dreams for so many months; those long months which had seen the great Spanish Armada scattered and destroyed by the forewarned English fleet.

The February afternoon sun was low in the sky, and from the Gulf a cold breeze raised goosepimples on her bare shoulders. With a shiver, Charlotte pulled her cloak closer about her.

'It is time, mistress,' said Meylissah softly from behind her.

Charlotte nodded, and turning, made her way back along the deck to where the tiny companionway led below decks. In the tiny cabin she quickly undressed, handing the heavy European dress and layers of underclothes to Meylissah, who carefully packed them away.

'You are sure, mistress?' asked Meylissah softly, holding out the implements she had earlier been commanded to have ready.

Charlotte shivered, hesitating for the merest moment, then said breathlessly, 'I am sure. Chain me, quickly.'

Efficiently, Meylissah did as she was told, first locking the slave bracelets around her companion's wrists before fastening them together behind her back. Then she knelt between Charlotte's parted legs to fit the ankle bracelets and lock a length of chain between them. A shorter chain ran from this to Charlotte's wrists, lifting the chain between her ankles so that it did not drag on the floor. Charlotte trembled. She had been chained like this once before, in Tunis harbour, by Jahwar the Berber corsair. How long ago that seemed now.

With a conspiratorial smile, Meylissah planted a feather-like kiss on the other girl's smooth and hairless mound, then fastened a heavy little gold padlock through the rings in her labia. Rising to her feet, she then carefully attached a tiny golden bell to each nipple ring. She stood back as if to admire her work for a moment then whispered, 'You look beautiful, mistress!'

Charlotte smiled gratefully, standing submissively as Meylissah carefully drew the hooded, shapeless, sack-like *ha'ik* down over her friend's nakedness, pinning the loose part of the hood across her lower face to act as a veil.

Minutes later there was a knock on the door and Meylissah opened it to admit the immaculately dressed figure of Mad Jack Fletcher. The Englishman was carrying a braided slave leash in his hand. 'Your master awaits, slave,' he said gently. 'Are you ready?'

Beneath the *ha'ik*, Charlotte took a deep breath. 'Yes, master,' she whispered. 'I am ready!'

For a copy of our free catalogue please write to

Chimera Publishing Ltd
Readers' Services
PO Box 152
Waterlooville
Hants
PO8 9FS

or e-mail us at
info@chimera-online.co.uk

or purchase from our range of superbly erotic titles at
www.chimera-online.co.uk

The full range of our titles are also available as
downloadable e-books at our website

www.chimera-online.co.uk